Ravens in the Sky
A Dark Compass Novel

WILL BLY

ISBN: 1512074535
ISBN-13: 978-1512074536

Dedicated to my mom, Donna Blydenburgh, and her courageous spirit.

CONTENTS

ACKNOWLEDGMENTS

There are many people who I owe a great debt, these include (but are certainly not limited to!):

Michelle Blydenburgh, my wife, for walking with me through this new world, for her edits, formatting, and support.

My family for their never-ending enthusiasm and support.

Dani-Lyn Alexander for the editing of this book and for being such a generous mentor.

Shardel for the cover design.

The Fantastic Fantasy Writers Facebook group for providing advice, support, and inspiration. This group is always welcoming newcomers with open arms.

Anyone who has ever had a part in my education of life and academics.

CHAPTER 1: A LONG NIGHT

An icy chill caressed Irulen's face. His breath blew hot against the winter air. He pictured the moisture striking valiantly into the open cold only to freeze and fall to the ground absent sound. Often Irulen found solace in unforgiving weather, the kind that made most people barricade themselves indoors to wait for the cyclic signs of spring to come again. *Perhaps that's why I like the cold so much, it acts as people repellent.*

Be that as it may, Irulen's profession kept him busy year round, hot or cold, rain or shine, sun or snow. His travels, while offering moments of solitude and peace, meant he always had to make landfall among other people at one time or another. He didn't enjoy the actual working part of his existence, but he had felt a filial duty to send coin back to his aging parents and mentally deficient brother. Living off the wild might keep him happy for a while, a long while even, but the burden of responsibility always got the better of him, sooner or later.

Using the gift of foresight, his mind traveled the path ahead. The village drew near. For now, though, he enjoyed the sharp crunching of the snow underfoot and the quiet company of the raven on his shoulder. A blue streak illuminated a feathered throat, and golden glimmers pierced beady eyes. Max the raven was Irulen's only true companion.

The wizard would send the dark creature to local towns with a sign around his neck; "*Crimen? Mysterium? Leave note and offer in leg pouch.*" The raven would wait around, sometimes for days on end, for an unfortunate soul to invest a note and then bring the letter back to his master. Otherwise, if no note came, Max would move onto the next town with his master in tow.

Since they currently had a job waiting, Max sat comfortably on his shoulder-throne. Irulen sifted through his cloak pocket and pulled out a piece of smoked meat, holding it up to his feathered friend. Like a disappearing act, the morsel was gone in an instant. The bird's beak grinded gleefully. The sun had all but fallen, and dusk was fast claiming its domain. The traveler continued on, further enjoying the contrast of his crunching feet against the deafening silence of the snow.

After another hundred paces or so, the path veered slightly to the right, and a few strides more brought the village wall into view. The wall, made of towering wooden pylons, was shut up tight. The village might as well have been under siege.

For Irulen, this picture was a familiar one. *Humans are paranoid creatures; we love to lock things down, especially when something is awry.* The tendency of communities to be self-subjugated by fear had always baffled him. While the village walls appeared ominous, it seemed that security, in reality, was hard to find. The walls were vacant. He stood out in the cold for a heavy handful of minutes, pounding on the door. Finally, there was a sign of life as a chubby face peered over the top of the fortification. The plump head chattered its jaws quickly. "Who goes there?"

"Good morrow. I am Irulen, traveling wizard. I come to fulfill a contract sent to me by raven: 'One murder by unknown creature in exchange for 20 silver. Signed, William Steadfrost.'"

The wizard stood, increasingly annoyed as the fatty cylinder paused momentarily then retracted over the wall without a word. *What is this world coming to if people cannot exhibit common courtesy!* Fantasies of different ways to inflict pain on the little mole-man flashed through his mind. The gates screeched in protest, but reluctantly opened as men inside chipped at the ice that had frozen the portal shut. The doors eventually swung wide, and a tall, ominous figure stood some fifteen feet inside the village.

"I am William Steadfrost." The man boomed as he gazed at Irulen and then at the raven. "It is I who hired you, welcome to Frostbridge." Steadfrost towered over Irulen, most of his face obscured by a powerful beard. His black hair served as stark contrast to the whiteness of his surroundings, as if the falling snow refused to stick to it.

Irulen motioned toward the portly gatekeeper. "And what might the man who first greeted me be called?"

Indignation colored the mole-faced man's cheeks a shiny red. "I am Lew, head of the town watch."

Dismissing Lew, Irulen returned his gaze to Steadfrost. "So he has a title as well as a name. Pardon me, kind sir, but are you titled as well?"

The giant man stood stone-faced. "I am the chief of this village."

"Excellent. I am Irulen, mystery solver, and I believe you have a killing that needs my attention?" He allowed his gaze to wander the crowd. He kept Lew in the corner of his eye.

Lew piped up with his squirmy voice. "You aren't *just* a mystery solver, but one with *magic*...supposedly." He squinted at Irulen. Suspicion filled his black, beady eyes.

Irulen graced his statement with silence.

Lew began again, a little louder this time. "I don't suppose you could *demonstrate* for us—as a token of assurance—something magical?"

"My dear sir." Exasperation flooded through Irulen, touching his voice, though he tried to control it. "I'm sure you are not aware of how magic *works*." The wizard waited for the stressed twitch in the pudgy man's face to settle and then continued. "I possess magic, yes...in fact, I was born with it...but my magic is not *inexhaustible*. My essence is in fact *finite*. It will run out one day. For this reason, I require compensation for my services, so when that time comes, I will have the means to retire to normal human life."

"Sounds like a load of rubbish to me." Lew spat the words as if in challenge. "Typical wandering..." Everyone near the little man took a step back. "...merchant..." He looked around. A young girl giggled. "...talk." His eyes darted around quizzically. "What?" No one answered. "What's wrong?" Even as the words passed his lips, a frozen breeze widened his eyes.

A boy of thirteen years or so stepped forward and

3

pointed. "Your trousers, sir. They're on the ground."

Lew grappled with his pants as he thrust a finger in the wizard's direction. "You! You did this—umph." He struggled to pull his pants back up, tripped, and fell face first into a snow bank.

Nervous laughter filled the empty air.

Irulen feigned innocence. "But you said I didn't *have* magic, and I *surely* haven't left this very spot." He noticed the little girl giggling, and a small smile tugged at the corners of his mouth.

Lew scrambled to his feet and dusted himself off. He yelled, "You do, you do have magic!"

"Thank you for vouching for my abilities. Now then, William Steadfrost, I grow weary. Would you like my services or not? I do have to inform you, regrettably, that I must add one silver to the contracted deal, for the demonstration. My magic must be compensated."

The sudden menace creeping over the chieftain's features took Irulen aback. This was not a man to be trifled with. While his body spoke of violence, the large man's words were delivered with surprisingly precise diction. "My daughter Isabel is dead...slain by a beast of unknown origin...and you bring tomfoolery to my feet!"

Irulen pulled down the hood of his cloak and bowed. "You are right, of course. My apologies, sir. I am sorry for your loss. I take it you want the beast identified so that you may hunt it?"

Steadfrost nodded.

Irulen continued. "I would be glad to do so under the agreed contract, then, but night is quickly falling upon us, so the investigation is best left for morning."

An inkling of despair crowded the corners of the chieftan's dark eyes as he nodded. "I understand, so be it. A room has been made for you at the tavern."

* * *

A musky scent lingered in the room, one resembling a

bear den that had been vacated for about a week. The bed sheets had been pulled up, but were still undeniably ruffled. Irulen wondered which of the gorging ruffians he'd passed in the hall below had soiled this living space. Regardless, he reminded himself of why he often slept wrapped in his own cloak.

The room was warm, and for that he was grateful. The wizard offered his arm to Max, who obliged by stepping onto it. Irulen placed the raven on the small table adjacent to the bed, unslung the satchel he carried underneath his cloak and began rummaging through it. Max's uneasiness vanished as Irulen pulled out the pieces to his perch. Once his master finished assembling the perch and backed away, the raven hopped onto his rightful throne and fluffed his wings. A tingle of paternal pride coursed through Irulen. Max was the wizard's one unfaltering source of contentment. In addition, he made a great watch-bird, and Irulen never worried about his belongings with Max there to guard them. No intruder would enter the room without sending the raven into alert mode.

With everything in reasonable order, Irulen made his way down the marble-floored corridor. His footsteps bounced off the stone and wood of the walls. Few patrons filled the drinking hall on this particular night, and for the most part, they drank solemnly. The room stood taller than the rest of the inn, creating the illusion of an unexpectedly large amount of space. Still, as far as taverns went, Irulen figured this one was as good as any to drink away one's woes. Since alcohol loosened lips, and suspects often joined the revelry in order to avoid suspicion, what better place to begin an investigation?

Irulen seldom wasted magic to bolster his hearing. Even without magic, however, his well-trained ears keyed on certain words and ascertained the demeanor of the people who spoke. The death of a young girl did not often promise a pleasant night for any tavern, and this night was no exception. Six souls in all, all men, had split into two groups, a group of four and a group of two. The larger group was engaged in a fierce debate over what creature could have taken Isabel to her miserable fate. The group of two sat off in a dark corner, brooding quietly.

Common people, those whose entire existence was spent within the confines of a single day's ride, loved to throw around words such as "demons", "trolls", and the like. Irulen thought this phenomenon stemmed, in part, from the political nature of these small towns. Town gossip almost never encircled a tangible person. Such speculation and slander could, and often did, lead to irreparable social rifts and even bloodshed. The group's argument, which had previously been kept at a respectful murmur, grew in volume as the patrons plied themselves with booze and pride.

One tall and gaunt man spun a story about how wolves had claimed Isabel Steadfrost. "She was a strong-willed girl, always more independent than her father would have liked. It was naturally unavoidable that she would eventually find herself outside the town walls past dusk. You see," he continued, "The wilderness is the great equalizer of all things. Out there, in the realm of animals, a princess becomes food, as our Isabel surely has."

While the loud mouth had something of a point, Irulen felt his lips loosening in defense of the wild places he crossed routinely. For all his magic and capability, Irulen had never used his gifts to defend himself in the wild. He had, in fact, never encountered an animal that had meant him harm. He found his mouth open and a reverberation forming in the back of his throat when a mug slammed the table in front of him. A dark, frothy wave spilt over the top of the mug and onto the table.

"You look too young to be what you claim to be," said the serving girl.

Her gaze met his, and Irulen was at a loss. A golden hue surrounded her small pupils, and eventually gave way to darker shades of green. Her eyelashes stuck out like spikes protecting something sacred. She wore a white headscarf tied neatly in the back and sported good posture for a young rustic girl. Her plain gray robes were bound by a brown rope. A few beads of sweat streamed down her face, matting loose strands of fiery red hair to her rosy cheeks which were besmirched by the toil of a smoky kitchen. Her face was slightly shadowed in the tavern light but freckles seemed to adorn her fair features.

He found words and responded. "And what, pray tell, do I claim to be?"

"A man of magic."

If there was ever a bane to the conservation of Irulen's magic, it was women. Whether in public or in the bed chambers, when they gave him the look he saw before him now, he would often oblige with a demonstration.

"Here, give me your arm." She indulged him, somewhat cautiously. Irulen ran his fingertips down her shoulder to her wrist. They heated at first, then cooled as he dragged them across her skin. He explored her hand and let go of her fingertips. Her cheeks flushed red. She brought her hand to her face and looked at it as she would a stranger. Then she pulled her hand back and slapped him across the face. The two men sitting apart from the others jumped up at the commotion and approached menacingly.

The taller of the two kept his gaze locked on Irulen while he asked, "Is there a problem, Farah?"

The serving girl stared at the stranger and paused for a moment. "No, I believe I just solved it. Have I not, Mister Irulen?"

Irulen rubbed his jaw and struggled to control a childish grin. "You certainly have, my lady. And please, call me Ire." He said the last bit while looking at the men before him.

"*Ire.*" The name played off the girl's ruby lips. "But your name is pronounced *Ir-u-len*, why *Ire?*"

"Call it a character flaw," said Irulen, nonchalantly. *Truth is, I'm prone to fits of rage, best managed through a simple reminder. Wrath doesn't suit me as a nickname.* He watched her walk away and thought he detected a slight awkwardness in her stride. *Perhaps an urge to look back? Doubtful.*

Irulen gathered up his self-loathing and redirected his gaze back to the men who had risen to defend Farah's honor. "Please," he pleaded politely, "I've been traveling for quite a few days. Would you sit with me?" After looking at each other uneasily, the men complied.

The men took their places at the table with stiff

formality. As they sat, the taller fellow with a familiar face introduced himself as Jorin Steadfrost, William's son and Isabel's older brother. "And this is my friend, Brom."

Irulen nodded his head politely toward the two and then spoke to Jorin. "I'm sorry for your loss."

Jorin cocked an eye. "I appreciate your words, but truth be told, I put little stock in empty utterances. Isabel's corpse still rots in the woods. I've seen it with my own eyes. And yet, you use your magic to impress serving girls."

Brom chimed in before Irulen could respond, leaning in slightly. "You should work to impress *us*, find out Isabel's fate." Tense silence fell over the table as both men held the wizard with frozen stares. Irulen looked from the large black pupils of Jorin's green eyes to Brom's rusty brown marbles peering from beneath his shaggy, dark hair.

The boisterous group of men grew louder in their repertoire. Jorin and Brom redirected their eyes from Irulen over to the ruckus.

Jorin's hand tightened around his mug. "Angus has sure got a gaping hole of a mouth t'night."

Brom nodded. "I'll raise my beer to the thought of smashing in his stupid skull."

Irulen opened his mouth to speak, but snapped it shut just as quickly. He slouched a bit in his chair. "Very well. To the matter at hand. Tell me what you know."

Jorin looked to Brom, who nodded that Jorin should go ahead and start. "Well," Jorin began, "For Isabel, yesterday was as normal as any other day. I didn't see her for most of the day. Brom and I were out hunting, but I did notice her at dinner. She looked especially happy, excited even…but for Isabel this was all normal. She has often been called the winter's sun around here, a reference to her unbreakable spirit."

Brom took over, smiling wistfully at what could only be a fond memory. "Quite the famous one she has always been. Always attracting the younger lads, getting into trouble…"

Jorin, having recovered his breath, continued. "It seems so apparent to me, looking back, that she appeared to be *expecting* something." He took a deep breath, held it, and blew it out slowly. He shook his head. "And this is why I can't accept what those men over there say, that wolves claimed her, or beasts…or demons."

Brom interjected, "Well, you see, wizard, there was a wolf that *had* claimed the corpse before I found it. Blood red in the mouth it was, and it growled at me so that my spine shiver—"

"So *you* found her?" Irulen tried to steer the conversation back on track.

Brom nodded but it was Jorin who spoke next. "We set out to look for her by torchlight last night, but this morning we amassed a much larger party. Much of the town became involved, and we fanned out in search of her."

Brom said, "It was I who found her, in a clearing near a grove of pines. William told us to leave the body be and attached the note to your raven. We covered her body, so it wouldn't be harmed any further by anything wild, and have taken to the mug most of the day awaiting your arrival."

"Will it be you taking me to her at daylight?"

Both men nodded.

A pair of wiry hands came down heavily on the table.

Angus leaned close into Irulen's space. "Why ah you heyah anyway? We all jus' decided over dare zat she was eatin' by da wolf." His slurred speech was difficult to understand.

Jorin's chair flew back as he stood and punched him in the face. Angus fell backward over a chair and hit the ground. Blood streamed from his nose as he took pause. The other three raised themselves from their table quietly with the potential of violence simmering in their eyes. Jorin screamed at them, "It was no wolf! Only stupid fools like Angus would think that. I suppose a wolf snuck through our town walls, grabbed her by the neck and dragged her right past our gatekeeper?" Jorin cocked an eyebrow, and waited for a response.

One of the men mumbled something about a demon under his breath before submitting to Jorin's deathly stare. Irulen looked behind him as a flash of red locks pulled back into the kitchen. Whether it was the commotion, or her curiosity in him, Farah had indeed taken another look. He smiled inwardly.

Irulen stood up with his hands outstretched. "Please, please, everyone calm down. I understand emotions are running high, but emotion is an enemy to reason. We will, in time, lay Isabel to rest and her story with her."

Angus spat blood and wiped it away with a dirty sleeve as one of his acquaintances helped him to his feet. "I'm sure there will be a story, spun from a web you yourself shoot out of your arse...as fake as your concern in our matters." The sudden clarity and bite of Angus's words left Irulen at a loss. Angus and his companions shambled under the stone archway, through the oaken doors, and disappeared into the dark night.

Jorin shook his head as he plodded toward the fire place. A few dogs that were absorbing the heat scattered in his wake. His bulky figure stooped low, picked up a piece of tinder, and placed it on top of the weakening flame. "Angus is an idiot, but his suspicion is not idiotic." He turned the full intensity of his gaze on Irulen. "I suppose, wizard, that suspicion is something you regularly receive. For three days your raven visited our town, like a harbinger of death. Many would think someone like you could easily have a hand in the deaths for which you are hired to investigate."

Irulen smiled. "There is rarely a town that I have visited where I have not been, at one time or another, considered *a person of interest.*"

Brom shifted uneasily in his chair. Jorin grabbed a prodding iron and stabbed at the burning embers.

"As for the appearance of my raven," Irulen continued, "I'm really not sure, but I seem to have a sense—maybe passive magic, it certainly isn't something I actively think about— a compass inside me, if you will. It's as if I'm being steered toward where I need to be."

"People like us only experience magicians like you in folklore." Brom spoke from his seat and raised a long-neglected mug of ale to his mouth.

Irulen hated being called a *magician*, but he let the

reference slide. His mug met his lips. The liquid was dark, frothy and warm…only slightly tinged with the chill of the downstairs cellar. He had to concede Brom's point. "There truly aren't many of us." He shrugged. "If I wasn't one myself, I'd doubt real *mages* existed. I am, after all, a skeptical person. Truth be told, I've had mobs try to tear me to pieces one too many times. My work obviously deals in delicate matters, and I have still not perfected the social element of it all."

Irulen's eyes explored the room. A stone wall surrounded the place, and a wooden roof arched upward from there. There were a good number of tables and stools, and what looked like a small stage for a performer. He imagined how lively the place would be in better days.

"You know," he said to the men, "It has been a while since I've seen taverns such as this one in a state of merriment. Sure, on some occasions people celebrate the dead, usually when it's a man that's passed on honorably. But, more often than not – and especially when it is a woman who's been killed – I find myself in a somber embrace. I think I need a break from it all."

Brom's face wrinkled under his black beard. "I'm sorry that your occupation grieves you so…"

"But…" Jorin interupted, "surely you must take comfort that you find yourself on this side of the living divide and not that of your quarry."

"Quarry, you say? The dead are not my quarry. I do not travel to *find* dead bodies. I do not take pleasure in lingering over a corpse. I hunt living culprits who have caused the deceased to be so removed from our plain of existence."

"You speak in too stately of a manner for this time of night, traveler," Jorin said.

"You are right, of course. Sometimes I get caught up in thought."

"For now," said Brom, "think of good ale and mead, the company of women – though not the serving girl, mind you – and see yourself to rest. Tomorrow will be a trying day for us all. I now depart, good night."

Irulen wasn't one for much resting, too often haunted by

images of the past, but he bid the others good night and ordered two more mugs of beer to keep him company.

* * *

A chill snaked up his spine as Irulen approached the door of his room. The sense that a strange presence was nearby overwhelmed him. He pressed his ear to the door. A slight rummaging sound, and fear for Max, propelled him into action. Irulen swiftly shoved the door in and fell into the room. He stopped dead in his tracks. Farah sat gently on his bed with her feet hanging off the end. Though she was older than her small frame portrayed, she appeared rather childish sitting there. She held Max with her left arm while scratching under his chin with her right hand.

Some watchbird he is. Realizing he may have made a commotion, and being found with this girl in his room would not help his cause at all, he glanced up and down the corridor before quickly shutting the door behind him. Irulen surveyed her, took in the knowledge filling her eyes, and determined that she wasn't as young as he had first feared. *Hard to tell sometimes.*

"I didn't realize I'd made such a good impression," Irulen said, as he moved into the room. Farah's headpiece was gone, and her wavy locks bounced freely about her neck and back.

"Bury your mischievous intent." She placed Max back on his perch, studying Irulen from beneath her lashes.

Irulen's expectations had unexpectedly fallen off a cliff. *So here's a girl waiting for me in my bedroom, in the late hours of the night, and she's not looking for mischief. Well, that can only mean one thing.*

"Well," he said, "it seems we're risking a lot for little. What's the trouble?"

"I'm not sure exactly, but things aren't what they seem." She glanced at the door as if she might be heard. "This is not the first time a young girl has gone missing. Five years ago, before the new wall was built, Angus's daughter, Claudia, was dragged into the woods, brutalized, and breathed her last under a full moon. Angus went on about a demon in the woods that used wolves as puppets, demanding they bring him a steady flow of nubile women to devour, body and soul. The matter was investigated, but nothing was unearthed to refute his story. Angus would not be swayed from his reasoning. Those who listened to him began taking precautions against the demonic forces. *They* built the new town wall. *They* patrolled and even enforced a curfew…" Her voice faded.

"Where did William Steadfrost stand on all this?" He leaned in closer as his interest grew.

"He thought we were trapping ourselves in more so than keeping goblins out. After a few years of his criticism, and a lack of violence, the patrols ceased, and the curfew was less strictly enforced. Then there was Igrain last year…an orphan like me and not much younger." Farah paused, apparently hesitant to continue.

Irulen coaxed some bird seed out of his pocket and placed it in her hand. She held it across to Max who nibbled at his snack gently. Irulen waited. She would tell her story her way, in her time. He watched her gently pet the bird's head, allowing her the space she obviously needed.

She paused, a wistful, forlorn look crossing her features. "People are acting strange and have been for a long time." She stopped and shook her head. "I don't know what I'm saying. Maybe it's nothing particular, but I'm scared. I may be a few years older, but I'm still alone, like Igrain. I live here at the inn. I have nowhere else to go."

"Look, I understand how you're feeling." His heart ached reluctantly with the need to reassure her. He scratched his head. "Ah, you'll be safe. I'll have my business here sorted out tomorrow, and whichever devilish creeps are lurking in the recesses of this town will be ferreted out…You have my wor-" Irulen stopped talking. Max had his head cocked, not at him but *past* him, toward the door. Irulen threw his right hand over Farah's mouth while extinguishing the candles with a wave of his left. They sat in dark silence for many long moments.

Floorboards creaked in the hallway. Irulen held his breath, unsure of how much the person might have heard.

Whoever it was, stood close.

After a moment of silence, the formed shifted weight and continued moving down the hallway. The steps seemed more of a shuffle than full strides as if something dragged behind. Irulen exhaled slowly in relief. The benefits of confronting a possible eavesdropper were far outweighed by the prospects of being caught alone with one of the town's few beautiful flowers. They waited for the sounds to fully disappear before speaking again in the darkness.

She tugged at his hand.

"Oh." He pulled his hand away. "Sorry."

"Sure as snow you are."

"So…what now?"

"A lit candle would be nice."

Sudden sparks ignited against the darkness as Irulen struck his flint stones together. Before long, one candle was lit, and two glowing faces sat in silence. Farah glanced nervously at the door then looked down at her hands.

"Look," started Irulen, "you can stay here if you want, though I would rather no one saw you exiting my room in the early hours."

"How would that work?" Farah asked.

"I'm used to sleeping on stones in the wild. I can sleep on the floor."

Her face convulsed. "Ew! You have no idea what I've seen spilt on that floor."

"Ha, well, I'm sure it is no worse than what's been spilt on that bed…"

Farah studied him, her eyebrows drawn together in a slight scowl. Irulen stewed in the shame of his lack of decorum, feeling as if he had been stripped naked.

He laughed a little nervously. "Well, I don't think you'd want me next to you in that bed, anyway. I'm not a light sleeper. I toss and turn. I wouldn't want to put you in any danger. I'll tell you what – let me have a look outside." Once again Irulen found himself using magic for the sake of a girl. He stared at the crack underneath the door. His foresight, of course, worked best when unimpeded by physical objects. Fitting through a crack took time.

Squatting between the bed and the door, he blurred his eyesight through contracted pupils and pushed it best he could. *Success.* His mind's eye scanned the hallway to either side and even checked around the corners.

He came back to the room. Farah was awe-struck, her wide-eyes sparkled above a slackened mouth. It was a look Irulen often took advantage of. *Not this time, though. Dammit. Not this time.*

"I'm sorry," he said as she snapped back into it. "I forget people aren't used to it the way I am."

"It was weird, like everything between you and the door changed in a way... blurred even... I don't understand. What... what did you see out there?"

"Nothing." He shrugged. "Nobody there. I think you are good to go if you are quiet about it."

She smiled and gave Max a pet on the head as she stood. "Well, I made my way in here, didn't I?" She crept to the door, cracked it open, peaked through, and snuck out. The door pulled shut, and Irulen wondered at the stillness of his room.

CHAPTER 2: MOURNING

A slight ray of sunlight peeked through the shutters that had been nailed down for the harsh winter. Irulen gathered his wits, rolled out of bed, stood up tall and stretched while letting out a bestial yawn. He took the fact that no one had come banging on his door in search of his testicles as a sign that Farah had slipped back to her room undetected. Once ready, he nodded to Max who flew to his rightful place upon his friend's shoulder. Irulen opened the door and stopped just short of walking into a wrinkly old man who was short of stature and bereft of hair. Irulen thought he saw dust emit from the man's mouth as he spoke.

The innkeeper walked with an obvious gait. He leaned on his left leg while waiting for his bum right leg to catch up. *Was that him near the door last night?*

"Did you enjoy your night?" A slight hint of suspicion pressed at the old man's eyes.

Irulen responded, "I spent the night in comfort, thank you. I'm sorry, but what is your name?"

"I'm Samford, proprietor of this public house."

"Oh, well it's a pleasure, thank you for your hospitality. I must be—"

The old man thrust a brown package into the wizard's hand.

"What's—"

"Some salted herring for your travels."

"Many thanks. I must be on my way to meet—"

"They are waiting by the front entrance," the man said.

Irulen walked down the hallway waving goodbye to the

innkeeper. He felt the tingle of the man's glare as he walked away. There was no audible movement from where the innkeeper stood. The uncomfortable feeling of being watched burnt hot on his back.

When Irulen entered the tavern area, he found a group of men sitting around the table closest to the entrance. William and Jorin Steadfrost, his friend, Brom, and the gatekeeper, Lew, were all present. The early morning did no favors for Lew's complexion and general appearance. His fat sagged, bags hung around his close-together eyes, and his posture left his back bent in the shape of a "C". His hefty head hovered inches above an empty bowl of mashed oats, offering only the subtlest resistance to the force of gravity.

In contrast, William stood tall, his pride and rigid masculinity represented by his erect spine and broad stature.

Brom was much stouter than Irulen remembered, and the comparison between Jorin and his father was remarkable. He was a slightly scaled down version of the barrel-chested brute. They all had black hair, although Lew was bald in the middle of his head. They were all outfitted with gear and looked ready to travel.

Even though he was on time by his reckoning, Irulen realized they had all been waiting for a good while now. Their bowls were empty. "My apologies, gentlemen, last night was the first I spent in a real bed for some time." *Which one of them sent the innkeeper with the fish?* Irulen hated fish, especially dried fish. And he hated Lew, or at least disliked him intensely, and the man's voice, especially this early in the morning, grated on his nerves.

"We hope you enjoyed your *rest*," Lew rasped. "There is much work to be done before this day is through."

"I am more than happy to get to it, but we can't all go. Too many feet to further disturb the scene." Irulen saw the discontent etched in their frowns. "I'm sorry, but I have a set of rules for what I do—a system. I need Brom, since he's the one who found her. I'll take one more, and even that person has to wait away from the actual kill site."

Lew volunteered to stay behind and watch the gate.

Jorin and William walked outside and talked privately for a moment. Max stirred on Irulen's shoulder and faced backward. Irulen fished into his pocket and held a rag under the raven's rear-feathers. Max lowered himself and evacuated his vent. Lew and Brom looked on with disgust as Irulen folded the rag inwards. Irulen shrugged at them. "Better than the alternative."

A breeze blew in as the front door swung open. William approached Irulen with quiet purpose, "Jorin will go."

Irulen bowed his head slightly in acknowledgment of the decision. He fell into step behind Brom and Jorin, as they exited the tavern.

Irulen viewed the town differently by the light of day. The swinging of the door startled a rogue dog which skittered away. Walkways intertwined neatly with blocks of housing. The roofs of their homes were formed by interlacing thatch packed with mud, and were supported by wooden walls. A few dwellings of stone, likely belonging to the elders of the community, held positions of prominence. Although a few hogs slept in stalls, probably being saved for festivities, these people survived the winter mostly on dried meat and grain. A few children ran past him just then, playing. They weren't wearing as much as he thought a child should, but these were stout people. *Stout. The word fits them well.*

Soon they passed through the gate and began putting space between them and the town. The sled Jorin dragged to retrieve Isabel's body left a trail in the fresh coat of snow. As usual when traveling this area, Irulen took notice how the village was but a small speck in a vast wilderness.

They didn't go far on the road before Brom veered into the woods. They found themselves in a grove of pines. The ground's snow was littered with brown needles that had been cast off by the conifers above. Brom turned back. "Not far to go, the place is at the end of this grove."

Max, deciding to spread his morning wings, flew from Irulen's shoulder. Brom flinched at the sudden flight, and Irulen caught a flash of metal as Brom's brown cloak flew back. *Probably an axe.* He didn't find it suspicious in this region, but he always kept a map of weapons and their owners in his head. The perpetrator could be anyone. Jorin, as yet, seemed unarmed.

Just when the wizard thought the whiteness at the end of the grove was a mirage, Brom stopped and waved Irulen to him. "It is straight away. There," he said, indicating with this finger. He started to walk forward but Irulen grabbed his arm.

"I need to go on alone. I'll call for you when I'm ready." He whistled for Max to rejoin him, and the raven obliged.

The area Brom pointed out was a small clearing that met with the edge of the pines. There was a refraction of intense light as the sun pierced the canopy and hit the white ground. Small snow crystals floated in the air, a byproduct of the swinging of the nearby trees. The glare was almost blinding, as if some unseen force was illuminating the way for the wizard, or obscuring it.

In the middle of the clearing, on top of a boulder the size of an altar, lay Isabel. Her body was wrapped with snow except for her face. Her face peeked out, crystallized and sparkling. It was one of the most angelic faces Irulen had ever seen. He pushed the wind with a sweep of his right hand. Max flew into the air, startled for a moment, as the gust blew the freshest layer of snow away from the body and surrounding area.

Irulen winced as Max returned to his shoulder. The body was eviscerated, her rib bones poking out, having been opened with the clean cuts of a sharp blade. The older, more frozen layer of snow around her was blood red. The wizard spent a little more magic heating the snow around her, ever so gently, so to tamper with the blood splatter as little as possible. The ice melted, except for one piece inside the cadaver's gored-out cavity. Irulen went to remove it by hand and noticed something strange about it. He cocked an eye. What he pulled out was not ice at all, but a crystal stained with blood. The splatter on the outward facing part of the crystal implied that it had been implanted before the blood flow stopped, before Isabel's death.

He had seen a scene similar to this before. He slung his pack around and rummaged through it for a good ten seconds before removing another crystal with a slightly trembling hand.

He held it alongside the one he'd just found. They looked very similar, almost identical. He pulled out a rag and polished the bloodstained one as clear as he could, then held both up to the sunlight. At the center of each was a telltale black blemish, larger in the newer one. The crystals appeared to be cut from the same source.

This killing wasn't by wolves, as many at the tavern thought. Not only did wolves lack the thumbs to place a crystal into the body, there was little evidence of actual predation. Although some of her entrails had been pulled from her body, they seemed mostly intact. Maybe Brom came across a wolf investigating the corpse. Maybe he didn't.

He put both of the crystals away and turned his attention to the footprints on the ground. There might have been too much foot traffic to determine which were the culprit's, but then again, maybe not. He identified about eight different sets of tracks and gently warmed a few prints from each. On the third set of prints, his patience paid off. Blood drippings, just far enough away for an arm to have hung. The evidence suggested the perpetrator had walked away with at least one bleeding hand.

There was little bathing to be had this time of year, so the dried blood might still be present on the assailant's body and clothes, maybe even his hands and fingers, though this would be doubtful.

Fingernails. Irulen pulled out a little flag from his kit and staked it next to the footprints. He spun back toward the corpse, lifted her hands one at a time and examined them. Bruises circled her wrists. Pieces of skin remained beneath some of her fingernails, specifically, large chunks under the three fingers in the middle of her right hand. Whoever was responsible for this crime had been marked by his victim. *And might suspect that someone would be hot on his trail.* Irulen glanced back, half expecting Jorin, Brom, or both of them to be bearing down on him with axes flailing. There was no such conspiracy.

Irulen pulled out a fresh rag and walked back to the suspicious set of footprints. He brushed lightly around the inside of one of the prints, removing the fresher layers of snow. The amount of frosted snow at the bottom of the print indicated that the track dated back to the night of Isabel's disappearance. He placed the rag over the most well-preserved print he could find and pushed down, gently lining the inside.

Afraid of low heights, Max flew to a nearby branch to look on while his friend worked. The wizard took out some ink and a brush then proceeded to outline the inside of the boot print. This task complete, he let his work dry and then collected the outline of his suspect's boot. Satisfied with the evidence collected, and finding little else, Irulen signaled to his companions that they could come and prepare the body to be transported. They set to performing the grim task while Irulen investigated the suspicious footprints. His raven fluttered from branch to branch behind him.

The killer had walked out the far side of the clearing where the terrain sloped downward. Irulen stood and listened to his own breathing and the labor taking place behind him. Just above the rushing of the blood through his ears he heard the rushing of a river below. The prints headed in the same direction, as he figured they would. *Every killer washes somewhere.* He relished the thought of the perpetrator freezing his testicles splashing around in a winter stream.

As he approached, Irulen noticed a disturbance along the riverbank. Sure enough there was a burnt out fire pit. It was here that Isabel's blood had been scrubbed from skin and sent into nature whence it came. Irulen recalled crossing a small creek on his way into town. Gauging from the direction this water ran, the creek he was looking at was the same one he passed on the road. The killer had scrubbed down and walked back to the main road, using the rocks in the shallows to conceal his tracks. Once on the main road, the path of the killer's prints would be concealed by the increased traffic.

The sophistication of the murder indicated premeditation. The body's positioning on an altar of stone and the embedding of the crystal inside her chest cavity indicated ritual. This killing was a premeditated ritual, perhaps with a metaphysical relation. In Irulen's mind, something had been worshipped here. These sorts of rites were usually carried out by overly superstitious people who feared gods, demons, and the supernatural. Angus instantly became a primary suspect in the matter. Still, Irulen was missing something—something basic—he was sure of it.

The way back was marked by crunching snow and Max circling silently overhead. Flurries of snow peppered the corpse bearers. The hike wasn't a long one, and soon the walls of Frostbridge appeared. The creaking of the large gate lingered in the air as the town swallowed the travelers and their package. Irulen found something symbolic about the gate, but the thought was fleeting.

Inside, the inhabitants had emerged from their dwellings and now stood solemnly out in the cold. The mob's collective breath blew hot across the air. William Steadfrost stood at their head with his wife, Ophelia, a lady whose long jet black hair was matted with snow and whose face was frozen with tears of ice.

Max rejoined Irulen, and they jointly stepped to the side. Rituals had to be performed and mourning needed to take place. A mercenary-investigator had no place in these things. He found himself looking for Farah, but to no avail. Absent beauty, his gaze played over the crowd until it fell upon Angus. A black eye from the night before had settled on the lanky man's face. His eyes were averted, mostly he looked down. Irulen had seen guilt before and was certain that Angus was somehow involved in this case.

"So… Angus?"

Irulen was startled to find Jorin beside him following his scrutiny. Max snapped at the air in between them.

The muscular young man tensed. "What are you surprised for? I've had all morning to sulk in my grief. Vengeance tastes sweeter." Jorin stepped forward while reaching for a weapon under his cloak. Irulen grabbed him best he could. "Wait. Wait!"

Surprisingly, the bull acquiesced. "You may have grieved, but they have not. Angus isn't going anywhere; let me conclude my work. I need to be certain." Jorin stayed put, but the rage on his face wasn't easily subdued. Like a stranded field mouse, it didn't take Angus long to sniff out the murder in the air. He looked up and saw Jorin's contorted face. Like any paranoid animal in the face of certain death, he took off running.

Jorin leapt between the man and the freedom of the open gate. Max cawed loudly as he flew off Irulen's shoulder. Angus turned back to the crowd, grabbed a young boy, and put a knife to his throat. None of this stopped the storm that was William Steadfrost once he realized what was happening. If Jorin was a beast then William made beasts wet themselves. So intensely did he descend on Angus that the man froze in fright, the knife falling out of his hand. William threw him down. Angus was on the ground with his arms pinned behind his back, writhing and cursing. William grabbed Angus's wrists and pulled upward. The skinny man cried in pain as both of his shoulders dislocated.

Angus flipped onto his back. "Stop, stop!" William, deaf to words, raised his mammoth fist with the intent of caving the wiggling worm's face in.

Irulen wedged himself between the men. "Let me do my job!"

Jorin pulled Irulen away and spoke with menace. "You have. This man killed our Isabel!"

"No, no I didn't!" the man cried.

"Regardless, I have evidence to test," insisted Irulen, shaking free of Jorin's grasp. "I'm taking this man into my custody. Please see me to a room or house where we can be alone."

The older Steadfrost, who had regained some semblance of composure, heaved in a deep breath. "Very well, bring him hither." He gestured to two men. "Lead them to the stable."

* * *

Irulen was soon set up inside a stable with his captive while William looked on. Max waited outside.

Interrogator and suspect sat across from each other on large log cutouts. "Please remove your shirt and boots," Irulen commanded.

Angus hesitated, weighing what little options he had, then obliged. Irulen worked silently. The boot matched his print. Scratches and signs of struggle peppered his arms.

Irulen caught his gaze, held it. "I know you were there, and that you were involved. But I don't know why, and I don't know who you were *with*." The silent behemoth behind Irulen shifted upon hearing the wizard speak about the possibility of an accomplice. Angus remained still.

The inquisitor continued, "Isabel had badly bruised wrists. Bruises caused by human hands holding her wrists. She was restrained by one person while another took her life. Only one of the people was splattered by blood, one trail leading to the creek below. I was unable to identify which set of prints belonged to the second person. So tell me, who was it?"

Angus sniffled as boogers dripped from his nose and down his lips. He spoke through the slime. "You don't understand. He has their *souls*. I was trying to *help release them*. He has my Claudia, Igrain, others…"

Deafening silence filled the room.

"I plunged the dagger into Isabel's heart, and Igrain's, but I was protecting the town and the soul of my daught—"

"This is lunacy!" William spouted as he drove his fist into a nearby support beam. The beam splintered inwards without fully cracking. Irulen winced at the power of it.

Angus cowered as he spoke. "He came to me, after my daughter's death, and told me that she couldn't go to the other side, that her soul was constantly being torn asunder and put back again, that she was in perpetual pain. He had immense power. I struck a bargain to keep the town safe."

"A bargain of sacrifice? Why didn't he take the girls himself?" Irulen asked.

"I don't know… It had something to do with the ritual and the crystals."

Irulen moved in close to Angus's face. "What do you know of the crystals?"

"Nothing." He shook his head, pleading with his gaze

for understanding.

"Who is he?"

"He has been among us for some time but not always as the same person. Most recently he was Lew."

"Shit." Irulen stood abruptly and turned to William. "Stay here. Don't hurt him."

"Lew!" Irulen roared, as he ran across the town to the gate. He found it closed and locked, the ramparts appearing vacant. The wizard went inside the tower against the wall and climbed to the gatehouse. Nothing. He looked out over the wall and noticed a pile of something peculiar. Irulen scrambled down with the last of his breath and pushed at the gate. It didn't budge, locked somehow from the outside. His hands heated with rage as he applied them to the solid wood. An outward explosion tore through the gate, blowing it to smithereens. He ran through.

To the left of the road, up against a tree, sat a pile of bodies. Two watchmen lay face up in the snow, Lew's underlings. Lew's long-frozen corpse was propped up against the tree. The chubby man had an eerie smile on his face, his arms frozen and outstretched. At the end of his limbs his middle fingers were displayed in a crude gesture. Irulen had fallen for the darkest of jokes.

CHAPTER 3: THE WOLF AND THE RAVEN

A sharp pain seized Irulen's chest as he looked at the grisly pile and forgot to breathe. *A shapeshifter? A magical culprit? I never considered…*

He was snapped out of his daze by Max landing on his shoulder with a flutter. His hand instinctively raised and ran along the raven's back. The bird purred in his own fashion. Irulen shut his eyes momentarily then turned back toward the town and the crowd standing in stunned silence.

As he watched, the group of townspeople slowly parted and William walked toward Irulen with two things in his hands, a bloodied hatchet and a pouch of coin. He threw the latter to the wizard. "Here is your payment for resolving the crime. Angus has found the justice of my axe." William paused then looked earnestly at Irulen. "There would be more coin, however, if you brought me the head of the person responsible for *this*." The large man made a great sweeping motion with his hand. "This creature," he continued, with teeth clenched, "deserves an unpleasant death for the untold number of innocent lives taken by its grisly hands."

"I'm sorry," Irulen started, "my profession is to investigate, not to kill."

An aged voice creaked from the crowd. "If you won't kill him, who will?" Samford, the innkeeper, stepped forward. "It takes someone like you to kill someone like that…"

Irulen scratched his head and shifted uneasily. "It's just that…" He paused, shook his head. "Magic isn't meant for that kind of work. Using magic to cause death is what twists someone 'like me' into such a monstrosity. I've only killed once – one time too many. I'm an investigator and may even help apprehend a criminal from time to time…but the role of justice is always my clients' to be played. How criminals are treated differs wherever I travel."

A dusty voice spoke up from the crowd. "The face of justice might change for every town you visit, but there are base evils that infect this world. One of them is fleeing this town with haste. He shows a smile through deed, but deep inside he fears the chase. He hopes you won't follow. He is afraid of your reckoning and that…" Samford pulled a familiar brown bag of salted fish out of his pocket before he continued. "And that is why he *took Farah with him!*" The old man threw the bag at Irulen who fumbled and recovered it. "For your travels," said the innkeeper.

"Farah?" Irulen scanned the crowd. The townspeople turned inward on each other searching for her.

"I haven't seen her all day," said Samford. "In fact, the last person to have seen her was *you.*"

Jorin stepped forward, confusion furrowing his brow, anger reddening his cheeks.

Irulen held his hands up toward the mob. "Look," he started, "she was just helping me out with my investigation."

The old man cackled. "She must have offered quite a bit of help, judging from the time she spent in your room!"

The crowd began to grumble, the fire of suspicion spread wildly. Both the younger and elder Steadfrost looked ready to smash Irulen's brains in the name of honor.

Irulen threw his hands in the air. "Alright, alright. I understand you people are scared and angry, but being in such a state often ends in stupidity. Do not be stupid. I don't want anyone to get hurt. I didn't touch her… honest." The crowd began to quiet. Irulen breathed a heavy sigh. "Look…I'll help, but for my own reasons."

Jorin pulled his axe out. He didn't seem so easily convinced.

Irulen waved his finger at him "Don't be a hero. You've seen what I can do. I'd rather not do it again."

Brom joined Jorin's side. He too stared daggers.

William Steadfrost moved to stand in front of them both, his enormous mass eclipsed them. He held no weapons, but his fists looked as large and heavy as any mace.

Irulen stood his ground. "I'm serious. Frostbridge has lost enough already. Bury and mourn your dead. Let me handle this."

The older Steadfrost menaced Irulen with his glare. His bear heart scratched at the surface. Irulen's breath quickened. *What would I even do with this fucking guy?*

Suddenly the brute's shoulders relaxed, as if his human parts had finally started working. The big man turned from Irulen to look at his people.

"I don't want anyone to get hurt," Irulen thought his voice sounded hollow.

Steadfrost's massive shoulders relaxed further as he turned to the wizard. "I want to send a soldier with you."

His son jumped in. "I'll go." Irulen shook his head no.

Brom stepped next to Jorin to signal his intent as well.

Irulen, perceiving the end of the immediate threat, shook his head and waved his hands. "No, no. If this were a normal quest of retrieval, I would allow it, but more people means this man can assume that many more identities. Against this foe, numbers are a disadvantage." The group took a moment to measure the wizard's words and accept them. "If I came across any of you on the road, I'd be forced to view you as an enemy."

More of the crowd began murmuring in a tone of reason, but Jorin remained displeased. "Allow me to accompany you at least, even if I am to be chained to your side."

Irulen shifted. "You want the head of this culprit. I understand…but I alone will collect it. I will send it to you by raven." Irulen looked toward William Steadfrost and continued, "Along with a modest request of compensation, of course." The large man stiffened, and then nodded his acquiescence.

"Very well." Irulen contemplated taking a horse for his journey. He wasn't exactly a horse enthusiast, but in certain situations he would make exceptions and ride the brutish animals. He realized quickly, however, that there was little livestock to be had in this ghostly town, let alone steeds to be spared. Winter was especially harsh this far north and the people relied heavily on their animals. Taking a horse could spell disaster for them, not to mention borrowing or renting something came with the responsibility of having to return. Irulen did not want to return. He had, in fact, worked it out that he would certainly bypass the road and town all together should he head this way north again. *No*, he thought, *this chase will have to be an uncomfortable one. I will have to catch this son of a bitch the hard way.*

Nodding to the townsfolk, the wizard wasted no more time on idle chatter. He grabbed a small packet of supplies and set off on foot. To put Jorin's mind to rest, he suggested that the young man take a band north to make sure his quarry hadn't doubled back. All indications showed that this maneuver had not been the case and that Farah and her captor headed due south toward the city of Northforge, but Irulen could not chance anyone getting in the way of his hunt. If that creature made it to Northforge before he did, Irulen would be hard pressed to find them in the huge city. Once she lost her value as his security, the mysterious person that was Lew would either kill her or sell her into slavery. Time was ticking and the challenge stood unaddressed. The wizard and his raven began their predatory pursuit.

* * *

Someone pulled Farah along, she believed it was Jorin. He held a rope tied off at her wrists. The cord's harsh bristle tore at her fair flesh. She never fathomed that Jorin had anything to do with the murders of the town's girls. He had always taken a fancy to her, and she had always trusted him.

Her abduction was surreal. All she remembered was Jorin outside her door, and then nothing - nothing save a haze of forced servitude. The bitter cold cut through her senses and reawakened her wits. The sharp tugging of the rope and the frozen winter air set her fingers on fire. There was a real chance she would lose her fingers to the frost. Through the blur of swirling emotions and pain, Farah followed Jorin's outline as well as she could for fear of a jerk from that wretched rope. She began to notice distortions in his shape and form. Every time she blinked or wandered in thought, he seemed somehow different. His shoulders seemed less broad, his height shortened. A full-body cloak concealed his features but it just didn't fit right anymore. It fell more loosely around his frame than before.

Suddenly, a raven's call shattered the silence and brought her captor to a halt. "CAW!!!" A stranger turned back and looked upward. *Not Jorin.* The man had a stretched, gaunt face and flappy skin around his mouth that quivered as he spoke. Three black streaks ran from each of his eyes down his cheeks, like a tattoo of dried blood. "Damn sky-rat!" he said. "If only that thing would fall out of the sky and impale itself upon a tree!" His longish, pointed nosed lowered to his captive. "What are you looking at, impudent wench?"

"Why are you doing this?" Farah's voice trembled.

"Why am I doing this? *Why* am I doing *this*? Can you be any more typical? I'm tired of hearing little trollops like you asking *why, why, why...Wahh*! As if knowing *why* would make *your* situation any better."

She tried opening her mouth to speak but found it locked shut. Her eyes widened in terror.

"*When*," he continued. "*When* is the question you should be asking yourself. How long do you really have before your innards are splayed on the ground? How long until I'm wearing your face as a mask? Now shut your little mouth and—"

"CAW!!" The screech ripped through the air above them.

"If I could just grab that raven and..." The goblin-man clenched his fist at the sky. "I wonder how loud he'd caw then."

Farah's hands burned suddenly with a jerk from the rope. The man quickened his pace while glancing backward over his shoulder at the forested path. He looked like a man pursued. She set her mind to desperate thoughts. *He hasn't killed me, but he plans to. I'm being saved for something. If he escapes capture, I'm dead. My only chance is to slow him down.* Farah saw only one way out. *This will hurt.* She closed her eyes and fell to the ground like a sack of potatoes.

The rope jerked and then went slack for a moment as her captor walked back toward her, mumbling. She used the brief moment to blow hot air onto her hands and moved her fingers as best she could. "Get up! Or your time will come sooner rather than later. I'll spike you to that tree." He grabbed the rope close to her hands and jerked. Farah opened her mouth but refused to cry out. Searing pain shot from her wrist up her arm, but she would not move.

A raven's caw sounded overhead. Max swooped and circled.

"Well, it was a waste of effort bringing you this far, and the crystal gets nothing if I do the killing…but looks like I'll have to cut my losses," the goblin-man growled, as he reached under his cloak and withdrew a fiendish looking dagger. He pushed Farah down, straddled her chest, and raised the dagger into the air. Farah clenched her eyes shut tight and fought her assailant. During that moment between life and death, the rickety turning of wheels sounded from the direction they were heading. Farah's captor looked wary at first, and then a smile crept across his flaccid features. His vacant eyes regarded Farah from underneath arched eyebrows. "Ah, the sweet sound of opportunity." He flipped the knife upside down and swung the handle down upon Farah's head. Darkness encroached, and she slipped away.

* * *

Max circled overhead.

"Please, my daughter needs help!" The goblin-man held both of his hands up to halt the carriage as he crouched over Farah.

The approaching merchant brought his two horses to a halt. "Whoa, whoa." He warily climbed down from his perch staring at the crude man and instinctively grabbed the sword at his side. This man was no stranger to ambush tactics, and was clearly off-put by the goblin-man's ghastly appearance.

"Please," the goblin-man repeated, "my daughter."

The merchant's eyes moved from the goblin-man to the body lying prone behind him. "Keep your distance," the merchant declared loudly. The goblin-man nodded and placed himself between the carriage and his quarry.

The merchant approached the girl cautiously, looking over his shoulder to ensure a safe distance between him and the stranger. He bent over to inspect the girl. It didn't take him long to see that she was under-clothed and brutalized. He drew his sword while he stood and spoke to the strange man. "What have you done to this poor girl?"

A sadistic smile tore across the stanger's face. "This is only a sample of my work, my dear friend, a morsel of it. I'd tell you more, but I have little time and less patience. And you're going to help me."

The merchant began to speak but his mouth snapped shut. He scraped at his face as his eyes popped wide. Realizing the situation was fight or flight, he charged his assailant. The marchant flew backward as if pushed by an inexplicable force.

The stranger laughed, pulled out his dagger, and sliced the throats of the merchant's horses. Arterial jets sprayed as the dumbfounded beasts writhed and whinnied. The merchant made another attempt at the stranger but failed to reach his mark, stumbling forward into the air. He cried out in frustration. His eyes were filled with rage and etched with tears.

The goblin-man yelled at him. "I need *you* to kill *her*, or you're next. Cut her chest apart and place this crystal inside before her heart ceases pumping. Do this, and I'll let you live to return to your wife and children." The stranger waved his hand. "Yes?"

Sobbing, the merchant climbed to his feet and picked up his sword. "I won't do it," he said. "I can't." The stranger raised his hand toward the merchant and clenched his fingers together. The poor man fell to his knees and screamed as the fingers on his left hand snapped backward one after the other.

"You will," said the stranger. "I have no time to twist you into it. Just know that if you don't, much more pain will come your way." He laughed. "And when I reach Northforge I'll tear your family to pieces...with my bare hands. I'll return to Northforge wearing your face and body. And I'll roam the streets until your children come running into my arms. Soonafter I'll be stripping them of their flesh . . . delighting in their squeals. You have no choice in this matter, kind sir."

The merchant caught his breath and stood again. His eyes blazed as he walked over to Farah and raised his sword slowly. Uncertainty shook his hands and contorted his face.

Then there was peace, a split second of it. His shoulders relaxed and his eyes softened as he beheld Farah, who was beginning to stir. Before the goblin-man could react, the merchant brought his sword to bear on his own chest and fell to the ground upon it. It was a well-placed puncture, and the poor soul bled peaceably onto the frozen road. The imp cried out and the magical hold on the man's lips removed. The merchant spoke his last words to the sky, "I remembered, an old rhyme my mother told me some years ago, about your threats and all. Demons do what demon's may but a demon shan't have me today."

Irulen crouched behind a tree, breathing hard against the cold, watching his prey. He had seen it all through Max's eyes. The events played out like a memory in the back of his mind. He was winded fom the exertion, but rallied to his feet in a last-ditch effort. Irulen set his mind to the task at hand. *Kill him. There is no time for hesitation. No time...*

The goblin-man was so enraged that he failed to notice the approaching menace. "Damn it all." The fiend scrambled over to Farah with his dagger drawn. He must have considered her a hindrance now. The best he could do now would be to slice her throat and make a dash into the woods, unhindered by a troublesome burden. The goblin-man raised his dagger.

"CAW!!"

He looked up to find the raven closer than it had ever been. Low and behold, the bird sat on a branch just outside of the goblin-man's magical reach. The man cursed, spat, and stooped to pick up a rock. He threw it, missed, and then tried again. Impatience lowered his guard.

"You'll never hit him you know. Max has played this game quite a few times already."

Irulen's prey froze for a moment and then spun with a manufactured smile upon his face. He bowed low. "Allow me to introduce my—"

"No, no that won't be necessary." Irulen advanced toward the creature, his wrathful self in full control. "I'll listen to anything you want to say, once I'm swinging your severed head by your neck ribbons." Although goblin-face was a creature of power, his magic didn't reach half the distance as Irulen's. Irulen reached with both hands toward the carriage and pulled it toward him. Wheels, wood and all the items under the cover flew through the air. Goblin-face had little chance to whimper before being splattered beneath the merchant's livelihood.

Irulen stood, breathing hard against the air for a moment, then looked up at Max who was sitting on a branch staring back at him. "I know, I know, so much for magic economy, but I really wanted to squish this one. I hate imps."

"Imps?" Farah asked, faintly. Irulen turned to find her leaning up on her elbows.

"Hello to you too," Irulen said, relieved. He walked quickly to the wreckage to grab some smashed timber and returned to Farah's side. After sparking a fire for her, he walked back to the debris. "An imp," he said, while removing rubble, "is a manufactured demon—a human that was made magical by a higher power." He moved a wooden wheel out of the way. "Now, most humans aren't made for magic. If they were, they'd have it. Any human that is bestowed magic unnaturally turns septic. They become followers of the person that sired them, but their magic always, always turns black." He found a pair of legs under the pile, grabbed them, and pulled. "This guy is an imp, he can't heal, can't help, he can only kill, cheat, and steal with maybe a few other things thrown in that I don't remember. Of course, the worse the person is originally, the worse the imp he or she becomes - or so I've heard. This fellow is particularly rotten, was probably a thief or worse during his human life."

Farah's voice was faint and far off. "I don't quite understand."

"Well," Irulen pulled again, and this time the body slid out in its entirety. He fell back slowly onto his butt. "This fellow was so caught up in his evil that he even killed his escape – the horses."

He clamored to his feet and turned toward Farah. "Are you warm?"

"Better, thank you, but my hands hurt badly."

"I'll be with you in just a second." Irulen searched around until he found the imp's dagger on the floor. "Do me a favor and close your eyes. Hum something pretty."

"I don't feel very much like humming." She lifted an eyebrow and continued to stare at him.

"Suit yourself." Irulen thrust the dagger into the imp's neck. *Notime for hesitation.* The blade wasn't particularly sharp, and Irulen wasn't particularly practiced in the art of decapitation. The process became ghastly.

Farah closed her eyes tightly and hummed.

Dismemberment wasn't Irulen's thing, and it was some time before he got the head completely detached. The draining blood smelt like rotten death and feces. Irulen fought back his gag reflex as he held the head up to Max. The raven seemed to hesitate a moment, but then swooped down and clutched the ghoulish package. He flew with a fast speed, as if he wanted to be rid of his burden as soon as possible.

Irulen moved closer to Farah and began delving his hands into a snow bank in an effort to clean off some of the blood. "Are you alright?"

She nodded. "I think so. My head hurts, and my hands. I still feel a chill."

"You'll come with me to Northforge, the city isn't far from here. Then I can return you to Frostbridge via horse with a hired escort as soon as possible."

"I do not know if I can go back."

"Let me see your hands," Irulen directed. Farah complied. He pressed her palms together and placed his still-wet hands over hers.

"What's going to happen?" she asked.

"Ha, what do you think? Some magical bubble is going pop up and envelope our hands?"

"Will it glow?"

"No, I'm sorry but it'll be a pretty boring ordeal – no glowing involved. Look, it's already started." A slight heat emanated from his hands and he knew her hands would burn with *frostfire*, the pained feeling of exposing near-frozen parts of the body to sudden heat.

Farah bit her lip at the sudden pain. The moment passed and her teeth retreated back into her mouth.

She's so cute, thought Irulen, *and this thought so inappropriate.*

Speaking in dire formality, he gave her his prognosis. "Looks like we've saved your fingers in time. No need to deal with gnarly metallic instruments and the pains of amputation." Noticing that Farah's eyes wavered with concern, Irulen adjusted the register of his voice. Sounding more upbeat, he continued, "You probably don't understand much of anything right now." Irulen kept her hands locked between his. "You're in shock. Let's get you inside city walls and sit you by a warm fire."

"Where are we?"

"We're near the crossroads where all the roads of the north come together and lead into Northforge."

"How far?"

"If we move fast, we can reach there tonight or tomorrow morning."

Irulen pushed himself up onto his feet without letting go of Farah's hands. They had thawed, but he figured to help her stand before letting them go. She allowed him to pull her to her feet, and they began their trek.

CHAPTER 4: DRAGON'S GOLD

Except for the weather, Northforge was everything Frostbridge wasn't. It was a thriving city. Its walls, where there were any, were porous. Where Frostbridge was virtually run by a single man, Northforge had a burgeoning bureaucracy. There were many politicians and many taxes to be paid. There were more cracks in the system than you could shake a stick at, and so corruption ran rampant.

Blocks of upper-echelon stone buildings sat a stone's throw from squalid slums. Tension ran high at times and the city was known for occasionally violent outbursts and riots. Meanwhile, the politicians who ran the city did not even live inside its walls. Their estates lined Mount Oskney, an extinct volcano overlooking the town. The city itself had been sacked a few times, but the settlements on the mountain were nearly unassailable. Suffice it to say, where Irulen and Farah now walked was not an especially secure place.

The city had always been a good source of income for Irulen. There were always revenge killings that resulted in more revenge killings. Bad blood between gangs and individuals alike ran rampant. If you walked into a tavern though, you wouldn't know it. Taverns were sacred havens of jollity, and citizens from many different walks of life frequented them. The government might have been stagnant and the city streets lawless, but the taverns were protected by an intricate social web of underground loyalty. Everyone was armed, and everyone had a friend willing to avenge. The peace might have seemed tenuous on the outside, but it was pure. The streets and alleys were a different matter altogether. Bandits lurked in the shadows and opportunists lurked behind them with a knife at the ready.

The road on which Irulen and his companions now tread was known as blood alley. In this particular case, the mythological name was worse than the reality. Once upon a time, it was a worse off place, but traffic had increased, and the alley had since been widened into a road. There were too many prying eyes for mischief to take place at levels of a time past.

Max had rejoined Irulen with a sum of money and a note inquiring after Farah's fate. For now, the note rested deep inside one of his pockets unattended. He wasn't sure about his response to them beyond knowing he would hire another raven to give Max a well-deserved break.Irulen stopped by a familiar sign post, *The Roasted Duck*. He looked to his silent companions. "Here we are, time for some good food and drink." For her part, Farah hadn't spoken for the entirety of their trip, and Irulen hadn't tried coaxing her to either. She walked with her hands clasped together as if she had a newfound appreciation for warming her digits. She had worn Irulen's cloak for a time, until he'd found her new trappings at a street market. He thought he could make out her fragrance faintly emitting from his clothes. His nose was soon crowded with an array of fresh smells of roast meat, human bodies, and a roaring fire place. Farah, seeming somewhat overwhelmed, stuck close to Irulen. He in turn made his way, through a maze of large, round, wooden tables and stools, toward the fire place. Such real estate was highly coveted, and Irulen traded coin for a place near the heat.

He sat with her for a moment, while a group of drunkards finished a drinking song, then spoke over the relative quiet. "You won't find the fare of an inn in this place, but they make great potato soup, the type of soup which brings warmth and comfort to growling stomachs and souls."

Farah nodded. "That sounds nice."

Irulen tried signaling a few times for a serving girl before he finally met with success. A dark haired girl with a light complexion made her way over to them.

"Two potato soups, a wine, and an ale please," he ordered.

"Very well, two silver, please."

"You're new here, are you not?"

"Yes, I am."

Irulen fished the coin from his pouch and extended it to her. "I would also appreciate if you'd let Old Quinn know that Ire is here."

The girl's eyes changed slightly at the mention of his name. "Certainly, sir." She bowed her head and ran off.

Satisfied that things would be taken care of, he turned his attention back to Farah. "I've done quite a bit of business in this town. Truth be told, I'd never have to travel if I didn't get sick of the place every so often."

Farah finally spoke. "Even though I was born on the road I have never traveled beyond Frostbridge, with the exception of an annual trip to the neighboring town, Bleeding Creek, for the spring festival."

Irulen listened as he assembled Max's perch in front of him.

She studied his movements. "I wonder where the exact spot of my birth was on that road and whether it was close to where I almost lost my life."

"Life is full of irony," Irulen said. "Each one of us has our own cosmic pattern. And each one of those is chock full of vicious cycles and celestial jokes…things likely meant to remind us all that we are but a small thread in the fabric of the greater universe."

She propped her head on her hands and her forehead furrowed in thought. "I didn't need such a grim reminder of my place in the world. I was happy slinging food and drink."

"That's the irony of it all. You use the word *was*, you *were* happy…as if that contentment has changed. Perhaps what happened to you was a reminder that you were meant for more than simply slinging bread and ale."

"And what's wrong with slinging bread and ale?" A deep voice boomed accusingly from over Irulen's shoulder.

"Nothing at all," Irulen said. "'Tis a noble profession keeping bellies lined and families abused."

Irulen stood up from his seat and lined himself up with a barrel-chested brute of a man. Max cawed his displeasure. They postured for a moment, and the man burst out laughing and heartily clasped arms with the wizard.

"Hello, Quinn."

"Hello, yourself, and who is this little lady that actually has you talking?"

"This is Farah, from Frostbridge."

"I didn't know they grew flowers in that town. It's a pleasure, m'lady."

"And for me as well," she said, warily.

Detecting a little bit of anxiety on Farah's part, Irulen set to putting her mind at ease. "I have known this man for some time and he is perhaps the only trustworthy one in a town laced with scoundrels."

She smiled at this reassurance, but withdrew her wrists from the man's questioning gaze.

"Suffice it to say," Irulen turned to Quinn, "Farah has not had a good day. She was taken by an imp."

"And lived to speak about it?" asked Quinn, while being nudged from behind by the serving girl. There was a new level of respect written in his eyes as he stepped aside. Their drinks were placed before them. "*Her* drink is on the house."

Farah bowed her head graciously. "Thank you. Tell you the truth, I'm usually not much of a drinker."

Irulen leaned in. "You don't say?" He smiled tightly, overly indulgent in his interest.

Quinn, on the contrary, watched her with genuine anticipation. She lifted the glass to her mouth and took a big gulp. It was a long moment before she came up for air. She gasped. "It's good."

The men laughed.

"Ha Ha!" roared Quinn. "Here's to never quite knowing where you will next sit on your ass once you stand on your feet!"

"Indeed," Irulen said to Farah. "You find yourself far removed from your morning bed and the trappings of

Frostbridge. It seems you are becoming fast attuned to city life."

"All I've done is have a drink." Her brow furrowed as she studied him.

"What else is there to do in a place like this?" Quinn laughed. The serving girl returned and placed bowls of potato soup on the table.

"Time for the moment of truth." Irulen winked at Farah. "I get to see whether Quinn's soup is actually good or whether I've just grown used to it."

"Having to grow accustomed to the taste of my soup is like complaining about the ability to fly!" Quinn paused, looked pensive for a moment. "Wait, can *you* fly?"

Quinn's magic questions usually annoyed Irulen, but he found himself in a playful enough spirit to give an answer. "Well, no, I can't. I can levitate but not very high up. It takes a great deal of power."

Both men fell silent and watched as Farah lifted the still-steaming bowl to her mouth and let some of the creamy fluid flow in. She went to put the bowl down but brought it back up before it hit the table.

"Ha ha! Good Show!" Quinn beamed with pride. "By the way," he said, leaning close to Irulen, "I'm not the only one here interested in your magical abilities. That lady over yonder in the corner has been camped out here for two days now asking about you. I don't think she knows what you look like, but she's been eyeing you since you walked in."

"You don't say?" Irulen glanced over at the mysterious woman. Her cloak was drawn over much of her face, concealing the whereabouts of her eyes. A chin of tanned skin poked subtly from the darkness of her hood. "I cannot make her out, is she good looking?" His jest brought a frown to Farah's face. It seemed to be completely lost on Quinn.

"Ohhh yes, she is quite the looker when she lets her hood down. I haven't gotten much information on her, but she's from somewhere south and exotic-like."

Irulen thought he saw a flash of eyes from behind the shadowed veil covering the lady's face. He leaned toward his burly friend. "She looks serious. Should I lift her hood up a bit?" he asked, jokingly.

Quinn raised his head at the ceiling and laughed. Then the brute responded, "Man, if you did that she'd have your nuts. I've seen these types before, and she is definitely not the type you want to screw with. She'll have your tongue in her grasp and your balls on the floor quicker than a hawk snatches a mouse. Ha! You know what? Your meal is on me if you do."

The furrowed wrinkles on Farah's forehead showed serious concern. She'd had it hard today, and the last thing she needed was to watch the testicles of the man who saved her rolling along the bar floor.

Irulen contemplated as best he could the cost of the meal and weighed it against the potential use of his magic. By his best reckoning, the simple flip of the hood wouldn't take much out of him at all. If she assaulted him, though, defending himself might get a little messy. *Hmmm…She was looking for me, and she hasn't tried attacking me yet so she probably needs me for something.*

Suddenly the hood flew back from the strangers tan face. Dark black eyebrows hovered above the tops of wide open eyes. Her nose scrunched in an angry snarl. The moment of surprise was fleeting, and soon her face showed a stone-like repose. The vision of horror had given way to wide olive green eyes surrounded by dark skin and a thin nose. Her lips, when not tightened or pursed, were plump and filled with a natural maroon color. She stood slowly, her posture regal, and walked with a measured pace toward the table where Irulen and Farah sat.

Quinn, for his part, jumped up hastily. "Ah, I have other customers to attend. I shall leave you to your business!" He was gone before Irulen could say a thing.

Farah seemed strangely detached. Perhaps she had hit her limit for anxiety for the day.

A knife swung down onto the wooden table as the woman stood across from them. There was a slight commotion over the gesture in the immediate area, and some of the patrons began to move away. She grabbed a newly vacated seat, still warm from use, and seated herself at the table. "Do that again," she began matter-of-factly, "and I shall part you from your magic wand, Wizard."

Max climbed forward on his perch and hissed at her. He retreated when she hissed back.

"Point taken and not to be forgotten," Irulen responded. "I'm Irulen, and this is Farah. We've both had long days."

"I would like to make your day only a little longer," she said.

Irulen nodded and held his right hand out to her in acquiescence.

"I am known as Kay. I hunt people for bounties."

"I suppose this is where you tell me I'm a wanted man?"

"No, well, not for any bounty worth my while."

Irulen smiled. Farah looked interested in the last bit and turned to Irulen for an answer.

Irulen said, "Oh, you know how towns are with their ideals, honor and such. People often hold grudges over simple things."

"Like drunken brawls and farmer's daughters," said Kay.

"Do tell," Farah burst in, even though her cheeks flushed red.

Kay made to speak when Irulen interrupted her.

"Maybe another time, if you want me to hear out whatever proposition you bear."

Quinn broke into the conversation from behind. "What's a matter Ire? Is the new girl blocking your magic wand?"

The wizard certainly regretted his decision to engage this stranger, and he was all but sure he didn't want to hear anything else she had to say. Farah was looking at him like he was some kind of pervert. Quinn walked off again, his swagger cocky after the witty interjection.

"More like craving its magical essence, unless she has something else to infuse the air she blows," Irulen mumbled.

"I want to make a proposition, a *business* proposition. I want you to help me locate and execute a bounty. This job entails a sizable reward. Two hundred silver, posted by a noble on the mountain side."

The worn wizard clucked his tongue and leaned back on his chair. All the while he eyeballed the woman with suspicion.

"*Execute a bounty*—that's an interesting way to put it. By execute do you mean to execute the job, to apprehend and turn in? Or does *execute* simply mean to *kill*?"

Kay dragged a finger across her neck. "But that doesn't mean *you* have to do that part. I have that role handled." She reached behind her back, pulled out the stock of a crossbow, and let it slip back into its holster.

"I'm not an assassin," Irulen said.

"Nor do I prefer to be," she answered. "But in certain situations, where the money is right and the quarry is evil enough, then I will do what I must. Besides, it will be hard to take this particular person alive."

"Why?"

"Well, he lives deep in the slums."

"Even a place like that should be easily navigated by a person like you." He cocked an eyebrow and waited for her response.

She looked at him unflinchingly.

Is that indecision in her eyes?

She relented and sighed. "He also has magic."

"Ah, there it is." Irulen leaned forward intently. He never ran into other magic users, the past two days had been a rarity.

The word *magic* sent a visible shiver through Farah who had been busy giving Max plenty of head scratches.

"I appreciate your offer and the fact that my name is fast becoming so well known. But really, we have had a *long* day and the 'kill this…magical that' talk is wearing my friend and I pretty thin." He moved to get up, dismissing any further argument she might try.

"The man is a cannibal—eats children."

He froze for a moment, then lowered himself back to the chair. "Oh…well…that lightens up the conversation doesn't it?"

"It's up to you whether or not he continues to commit

these heinous acts. I have some reconnoitering to do before I turn in. We'll talk again tomorrow. Good night."

Farah and Irulen said their goodbyes in return. "I guess we don't have an option on that talking tomorrow thing." He tried to smile, but it felt more like a grimace so he let it go.

He watched the striking woman move fluidly through the crowd toward the door. A hand emerged from a group of men to grab at her rear and retreated with two broken fingers. The assailant's friends laughed belligerently. Kay passed through the front door and out into the night.

"Is she telling the truth? Did that really happen?" Farah asked Irulen.

"I don't think there's much that would surprise me at this point." He ran his hand through his hair.

Farah leaned over and kissed him so gently on the cheek that he flinched.

"I stand corrected, what was that for?"

"Why does it need to be *for* anything, like a kiss is currency?"

"Good point."

"But I don't know—don't get the wrong idea—I just want to have a *good* time *tonight*."

"I'm guessing the whole 'being kidnapped by an imp' thing has had an effect on you."

"Maybe. I don't know. Nor do I care." She held his gaze for the slightest of moments, and laughed. "I have no reason not to give out a kiss and enjoy some good drink. Just promise you'll look after me."

"Ha! Sure. I'm sure you can handle your wine just fine, though. We shall see."

Irulen waved down the serving girl and ordered a new round. She went into the back, but it was Quinn who returned with their drinks. "I have something special for you two that I've been working on, some honey mead."

Irulen was a little disappointed he wasn't receiving the ale he wanted, but his temper was quenched by the look of anticipation on Farah's face. She brought the brew to her lips

Will Bly

almost faster than Quinn could set it down.

Quinn leaned in toward Irulen and spoke. "By the way, your tab starts now, so good luck with that." A grin lit his eyes, and he waggled his eyebrows before walking away.

As Quinn went back about his business, Irulen made an attempt at small talk. "I trust this is the first time you're out late at a place like this?"

Farah nodded, and the sides of her lips lifted into a smile. "I always wondered what the city was like," she said. "All this time it was so close, and yet so far away. No one from Frostbridge traveled here. They—we—always looked at it as a place of trouble."

"Well, you all have that right. It can be a troubling place. Best kept away from if possible."

"Then why are you here?"

"Well," said Irulen, solemnly, "I like to lose myself in trouble."

* * *

It wasn't long before Irulen was showing off Max's wide array of bar tricks.

The raven was busy dancing—his feet pitter pattering on the table—when Farah pointed something out. "It seems like you've both spent way too much time working on this bar routine!"

"Yeah, well, it's popular with the ladies…and men. Everyone, really." Heat crept up his cheeks.

She ignored his slip. "I bet you could earn a fortune on Max's abilities alone."

"Ha, sometimes I do when the pickings are slim. Max is fine earning his keep when he has to, but I don't like treating him like a festival animal. He's my best friend."

"I guess he's mine too, right here and now." She fed Max another treat.

"I won't take too much offense to that, since he can clearly dance better than I can."

It was at just that moment that Quinn—who somehow

always had impeccable timing—came out of the back room with his fiddle.

"Clear some space, need some space."

A little ways from where Irulen and Farah sat by the fire, chairs and tables were cleared to make a dancing area. A bystander dragged a stool and set it up at the head of the circle. Quinn sat upon his throne with his fiddle and began playing an upbeat melody. The circle was soon filled with the stomping feet of jigging patrons.

* * *

Farah noticed Irulen looking a little uneasy. *Maybe he really can't dance.* He nodded his head as best he could to the rhythm while his foot moved awkwardly. Still flushed with a newfound excitement in life, Farah thought about grabbing him and throwing him out to the dancing jackals. As quickly as it flickered into her mind, the thought found itself flattened under the combined weight of alcohol and fatigue. She found the weighty presence of Max, who had somehow maneuvered to sit atop her shoulder, too much to bear any longer. She lifted her left forearm to her right shoulder and he stepped down. She placed him back on his perch where he sat looking at her in cockeyed fashion.

She propped her elbow on the table and rested her chin on her hand. *Crazy day, the craziest of days. The type of day that changes you. I was almost killed today, I was killed today. I'm new, I'm a new person, a new Farah—not that I had much of an identity before. Where the hell am I? Who am I with? What happened? And what the hell am I doing now? Where do I go from here?*

Irulen leaned over and tapped Farah's arm. She looked at him and smiled as best she could. "You look tired."

"I am a bit." Exhaustion beat at her. "A lot, actually."

"Come on, I have a surprise for you."

"I can't handle *another* surprise."

He grabbed her hand and tugged. "You can handle this one, trust me."

And she did. She did trust him.

Max looked on as Irulen led her away. Some ten feet to the left of the fireplace stood a door with an enormous iron lock. "Impressive, huh? This is Quinn's most expensive possession."

Farah ran her fingertips along the cold metal. "Does he really need it?"

Irulen laughed. Farah waited while he fumbled under his cloak and came out with an equally impressive key. He put it in, turned, and leaned his weight into the door. It didn't budge. "The hinges stick sometimes." He thrust his weight in a more serious way. The thing swung open, and he had to catch himself from falling forward. He stepped aside and signaled for Farah to enter. When she passed she caught Quinn giving him a mischievous grin and a wink. Irulen flashed a hand gesture toward him, shook his head, and followed her.

Farah waited in the hallway. To the right was a set of steep steps, to the left a line of doorways. The wall reverberated with the merriment taking place on the other side.

Irulen walked in behind her with his arm stretched to the right. "Right this way." He directed her up the steps. At the top, red tapestry hung from the ceiling, acting as a thin barrier for privacy. Steam poured slowly from the sides. Farah's curiosity was thoroughly piqued before she slowly drew the curtain open from left to right. Her gaze played along a vision beyond her most imaginative dreams.

"Even if you manage to blink, it'll all still be here when you look again." She couldn't tear her gaze away, but she heard the smile in his voice.

He waited a moment and continued. "This is Quinn's life achievement. It's a bath and steam room, complete with expensive stone benches and a large hot pool of fresh water. I helped him engineer it myself a few years ago."

"How?" She asked. "It looks marvelous."

"It is—the chimney is angled so that the fire below heats the water. There are traps on the roof that collect rain water during the warmer months. During the winter months, ice and snow thaw from the diffusing heat of the tavern chimney. This process is a little slower, but we still get to change out the water often enough."

"This is a special place." She looked around and found a curious wooden plank nailed awkwardly against the wall. "What is that there?"

"Well, that's Quinn's special keepsake. He was in a shipwreck once. That's the board of wood that saved his life. He sings about it sometimes, probably the most serious you'll ever see him when he does. Look—I'm gonna leave you alone here. There are robes hanging over there and some soap on the side of the bath itself. I'll call to you from the other side in a while to see how you're doing. Relax, you earned it."

Farah called out her thanks as the curtain fell closed behind her. She paused a moment, listening to Irulen's footsteps fade away then the click of the door closing.

She suddenly couldn't help but smile and shake a little bit. She purred with excitement. A hot bath was rare indeed. Her bashfulness was overpowered by her eagerness; she had never shed her clothes so fast. She walked to the side of the bath and poked at it with the big toe of her right foot. *Ouch!* She retracted her leg like a smote cat. *The only time I've seen water this hot is when I've cooked with it.*

Not to be deterred after such a momentous day, she thrust the entirety of her foot into the steamy cauldron and forced it to stay put. The pain was sharp at first, but gently subsided. *Well, it looks like my skin may stay on my bones after all.* Her left foot followed her right, and she soon stood with both feet planted firmly in the water. She suddenly felt overly exposed in the otherwise empty room, and her anxiety helped push her farther into the water. There was a ledge from the shallow section she stepped into leading to a deeper pool. She sat on the ledge and felt the sear of the water on her legs and butt. She shimmied forward and dropped in.

It was surprisingly deep, the hot liquid rose just above her breasts. Her red hair floated around her like an aquatic plant. She crouched down and submerged her head. She spent a moment under the water, enveloped in womblike comfort. Her head reemerged as she pulled herself back up to sit on the ledge from which she'd entered. Steam rose from her skin and rose to a vent in the ceiling.

She reached for a bar of soap from the bath's edge, wet it, and worked up froth on her hands. She massaged the solution into the pores of her face. Farah splashed her hands in the water to rinse them off and then cupped them full of water. Splashes broke across her face until it was clean and she could open her eyes. She then stood and lathered up the entirety of her body. The action felt powerful, sexual, and feminine. It cleansed her of the earlier victimization. Not only did she feel made anew, she felt like a true woman for the first time. Once suds filled her every crack and crevice, she again lowered herself into the water. This time she meant to stay.

* * *

Back outside, Irulen fought his deviant imagination in an effort to talk with Quinn. The two men sat at the table together separated by Quinn's fiddle, Max, and two mugs of ale.

"Remember the first time we sat in that bath without burning ourselves?" Quinn asked.

"Yeah, you closed the place down for the night and paid your girls to bring the ale straight to us." Irulen grinned at the memory.

"Ha! Yes, we cooked and drank for quite a while that night." Quinn lifted his mug to Irulen, then drank deeply.

Irulen rubbed at his eyes, trying to dispel the memory of the hangover, as well as the images of Farah soaking in the tub. He failed miserably at both. "I still remember the headache afterward."

"I often think that room is the reason you keep coming back here all the time."

"You don't think the wealth of job opportunities does the trick?" He finally gave up and sipped his ale.

"Ha, please, nothing pays well in this piss hole."

Irulen laughed. "There's still quite a bit of work, nonetheless."

"You'll be enjoying more job security soon, I fear.

Things are growing more restless by the day."

Irulen leaned forward and indicated for Quinn to continue.

"The city dwellers and the nobles on the hill are coming closer to blows. The political climate hasn't been worse. Things are getting violent, and armed mercenaries like that wench from before are becoming more frequent."

Irulen stretched backward over his chair until his spine popped and his muscles reached their limit. His body retracted slowly back into position. "An influx of crime means good business for me...and you, for that matter, dishing out drinks to the angry and bereaved alike."

"Trivialize it all you like, these streets are set to fill with blood before Founding Day comes to pass."

"Some people settled a city some four hundred years ago. Who cares?"

"The people festering in the city while the sons and daughters of those founders adorn the mountain side."

"You sound like you're becoming quite the revolutionary, my dear Quinn."

"And the *magician* Ire has become a bit large for his britches."

"Don't call me that," Irulen said, tersely.

Quinn leaned in, pressing the issue just a bit further. "You told me you called yourself a magician when you were young..."

Irulen scowled at him.

But Quinn continued, "..er, and I'm sure young*er* Irulen had more of a heart when it came to the affairs of others."

Nothing bothered Irulen more than references to his past. "Maybe, but maybe he learned a terrible lesson about having such a heart."

"I'd like to think that while the lesson has been long forthcoming, the real moral yet alludes his older, pain in the ass self."

"I must have learned something, since I keep such prestigious company as yourself."

Quinn grinned widely. "There is truth in your lame jest, and I humbly accept the unintended compliment. Enough about you and me, how about the girl? What are her plans, or if you would rather, what are your plans for *her*?"

"Come on, man, it's been a long day." Irulen flopped back, slouching in the chair. He shoved a hand through his hair in frustration.

"It has, and her people have been wondering what has become of her. Did you tell them?"

Irulen slugged back another draught of ale. "Nah, I'm sending a raven in the morning. She doesn't seem to want to go back. Maybe sleep will change her thoughts, or maybe not. Either way, I figured this matter would be best handled in the morning."

"Still…" Quinn smiled. "I think you have a soft spot for this one, what will the local gals think? There goes your reputation, right out the door through which she entered."

Irulen scanned the room. It was starting to empty. "Isn't it about time you checked your doorway for drunken corpses?"

Quinn stretched and brought his hands down onto the side of the table and pressed himself up out of the chair. "I s'pose it is."

Irulen watched him lumber through the front door and could make out his booming voice over the fray, moving along the disabled and disorderly outside.

Irulen shifted in his seat and studied Max for a while. The raven looked as tired as Irulen felt.

There was a sudden, but not altogether unfamiliar, commotion outside. The wizard sighed and pushed himself away from the table. *Damn drunks never want to leave.* He stood and had just started moving toward the door when Quinn came back in. His face was twisted with two looks, one of a job well done and another of stark concern. Everyone paused silently, awaiting the dreaded words Quinn uttered on a nightly basis.

"Time to move along, folks, thank ye for your patronage, but the *Roasted Duck* is cooked for t'day."

Regulars and newcomers alike groaned at the early hour

of closure and slogged away disappointed. Quinn stood next to the doorway as they each passed through grumbling their meek objections. When it was only the two serving girls, Irulen, and himself, Quinn pushed the thick door shut and swung shut the latches. The pride had washed off his face and only worry remained.

"What's the matter?" Irulen asked.

Quinn pulled a rag out of his back pocket and started wiping the tables. "Ah, it was nothing really. One of the disorderly ones said something about coming back here and we wouldn't like it when he did."

"Nothing ever comes of a drunkard's idle threats. Chances are it'll all be wiped from his memory by the time he crawls out of his morning gutter." Irulen and the girls started chipping in on the cleanup.

"Probably, it's just that this guy had a look of certainty, like he'd be swept back here beyond his own power alone. Like it was his fate."

"Damn, that's too heavy for this late at night, man. Who's the new damsel? I haven't had the pleasure."

An older serving lady, Anastas, who Irulen already knew, spoke up. "You shouldn't talk about her like livestock, she's right there, ask her yourself."

"Apologies," Irulen said, bowing low in mock humility. "My lady—"

"My name is Thea, from Snowillow Pass, just to the south."

The wizard raised his hand to his face and stroked his chin. "Ah, yes," he said. "I know the place, very peaceable, not a lot of work for me there. You are doing yourself a disservice coming to this place, there are a lot of ruffians about."

Anastas burst with congenial laughter. "You better listen to him. Who knows better than the king of ruffians himself?"

"Easy with that talk lass," said Quinn, from across the way. "We don't want to ruin Ire's chances with his new lady friend with that type of chatter."

"Ha!" she said. "Why don't we? Save the gal some

heartache…and her innocence."

"Like *you* ever had innocence to lose," Irulen retorted, with jovial hatred.

* * *

Farah, still in her bath on the other side of the wall, tried listening to the conversation as best she could, to no avail. The words were all muffled to her.

Her skin had pruned, her mouth parched. It seemed as if her moment of luxury was ready to pass. Still, she held out a little longer, until the muffled voices died down. She slid out of the bath and hurriedly dried herself. The sound of the door swinging open echoed through the chamber, and Irulen's steps filled the hallway, growing louder as he climbed the stairs. They came to a halt on the other side of the hanging fabric.

"Farah? Have you cooked yourself to death?"

"Oh no, no," she said, as she quickly wrapped a robe around her still-moist body. "I'm in my robe, you can come in."

Irulen swung the curtains open and beckoned for her to come forth. "You can room with Thea, she's new here too."

"Thea?"

"She was the girl that served us."

"Oh." Farah's eyes dropped briefly to the floor.

"Come on, let's tuck you in tonight and figure everything else out in the morning."

He led her down the hall and stopped in front of a door.

"This," he said, as she moved toward it, "is my room, should you need anything."

Her hand withdrew and her brow furrowed at him. He went one more door down.

"Here you are."

"Thank you."

Farah bid him goodnight and closed the door behind him. She settled in and snuggled into her bed. She listened to the restless sounds from the hallway for a while as the others took turns bathing and turning in for the night. Thea came in sometime in the middle of it all, and the two girls fell asleep peacefully. During her final conscious thought, Farah recollected the night before and the long day since. *Hero, drunkard, playboy, ruffian, romanticist.* She wondered what kind of man Irulen truly was. She looked at the wall separating her room from Irulen's, closed her eyes, and dreamt that he lay next to her.

CHAPTER 5: LEVERAGE

The next morning found Irulen walking through a nearby morning market with Max firmly attached to his right shoulder. He was going to send word of Farah to Frostbridge, that she was safe and sound. He had seen her briefly in the morning on her way to the toilet. She had, yet again, expressed a reluctance to return to her old town, stumbled back into her room, and fallen back into a deep slumber.

The young sorcerer's eyes darted to and fro, habitually scanning for pickpockets and other mischief. He was up early enough, he reckoned, that most of the city's threats were still snoring their hangovers away. Irulen came to a halt in front of a raven-master, handed him a few coins and a prewritten note:

Dear Fair People of Frostbridge,
I am writing today to inform you of Farah's safety and general wellbeing.
She has, of her own volition and free will, decided to remain here in
Northforge while she digests the horrible abduction that happened to her. She
is being well looked after, and I will send word if and when she decides to
return to your welcoming walls.

May your ice shine brightly,
Irulen, WZD

Irulen handed the small, rolled up parchment to the scraggly old man. The raven-master slid it into the holster on the bird's right foot and whispered something into its ear. The bird crowed something to Max, who reciprocated in kind. After their short conversation, the raven took off, and Irulen watched the bird's blackness fade into a surprisingly blue sky.

A voice erupted from behind him. "You have a thing for ravens, Wizard?" Irulen spun and was met with the green eyes of the bounty hunter from the night before. The smug look on her face irked him in an ungraspable way. Max hissed, warning her to keep her distance.

"Well, they are good judges of character, are they not? Remarkably intelligent creatures—and great companions to boot."

"Perhaps," she said, "but your connection to them is something more, like a wolf looks to a raven in search for food and sustenance."

"I appreciate the poetry, but I share the wolf's ferocity alone, not its noble soul, I'm afraid."

"Oh yes, you seem like quite the fierce *sorcerer*, damn near have me quaking in my boots."

The old man looked ill at ease with the word "sorcerer" being tossed around. Irulen started to walk away before he caused a commotion. Kay followed in step beside him, her hips swinging just a little bit excessively, a slight smirk marring her features. She was attracting attention, something Irulen hated.

"Why are you busting my balls?" He asked, while picking up the pace a bit. He'd go to *The Roasted Duck* and lock this wench out.

"I could use your help, like I've said."

"Can't you just *stalk* your target to death, like you're doing to *me* right now?" He glanced around to see if they were being watched.

"He's located too far into the Shadow Streets for me to do it alone and possibly too well guarded, even for someone with my skills. The job is worth three hundred gold coins in total."

Irulen stopped short. "Don't talk about money in this place!" He reprimanded her in a harsh whisper, searching the shadows for trouble. "The Shadow Streets are nowhere for any professional to go. Even though I've worked this city every time I pass through, I've never gone into that ghetto—only the outskirts. I am truly becoming even less interes…" Irulen paused as he saw something in the distance. Kay appeared interested.

Farther down the market, without a doubt, Jorin lumbered in an erratic pattern, searching. Instinctively, Irulen pulled Kay with him and moved to a nook between buildings, an alley with a dead end. Kay was pressed tightly against him, though he couldn't help the thought that she had a blade ready at castrating height. He chose not to look down.

Kay disengaged for a moment and glanced outside the alley. She placed herself in the same position she was in previously. "So, what ya hiding from?" She leaned in to his ear and asked in a whisper. "Should I make a commotion?"

Irulen cocked his head and shot her a "don't you do it" look. What had first been an attempt at avoiding the explanation of Farah's situation to a thick-headed Jorin, had now become much more uncomfortable. Irulen's sleuthing skills had long ago led him to believe Jorin had a thing for Farah, a suspicion nearly ratified by Jorin's search for her.

He must think he's so damn heroic.

Irulen cursed the absurdity of his position, pressed against Kay. He would have a lot more explaining to do if caught by his romantic rival. Jorin would surely use this picture as leverage against the wizard, telling Farah all about it. She, in turn, would take the first opportunity to run back to Frostbridge with the man who had saved her from the jaws of degradation. Irulen wanted nothing to do with Jorin, and even less to do with Farah getting the wrong idea. Kay smiled and looked to the street as if ready to make a move.

"No, don't." Irulen's protest sounded weak as he shot his right arm out to usher her back to him.

"But I will, if you don't help me out."

"You don't fight fair."

"I'll take whatever leverage I can get," she said, making to move away from him.

"Okay, hey, wait. Fine." He sighed in resignation. "Sure. I'll help. We'll go talk it out with Quinn. I don't want to be seen by that big guy in the brown coming our way."

"Well…" She looked out into the street. "You better pucker up because here he comes." Then she increased the pressure of her body against his and locked her lips with her surprised conspirator.

His face was obscured as Jorin, who took only the briefest of moments to survey the happy couple in the alley, plodded by.

The kiss was so believable that Irulen found himself running his hand down the outside of her thigh. Then he reeled backward with the cracking of a well-delivered smack across his face. "He's gone." She looked him up and down. "Gee, you are the eager one."

"Like I was the only one with that quality." Flustered by the situation, Irulen was lucky to form a response at all.

"I simply sold the scene," she stated, matter-of-factly. "Apparently, judging from your reaction, a little too well." She laughed nonchalantly, as she slipped back into the crowd. He followed reluctantly.

"I don't take you as a wizard who's afraid of a debt collector or a nemesis bent on vengeance. So, tell me, who was he?"

Irulen wore his best gambling face. "He was no one, none of your concern."

"I guess I'll have to ask around *The Roasted Duck*."

"I really hate you." Irulen sighed.

"Starting with that pretty red head you dragged in last night," Kay persisted.

Irulen knew she had him pegged and so had little to say. Still, she wouldn't relent. She poked and prodded during what seemed like one of the longest walks back from the raven-master he'd ever had. He finally cracked and told the woman about what Farah had been through and why she was reluctant to return to Frostbridge. He kept his feelings out of the matter, but it was clear that Kay was prepared to play her card to the very end. He was either going to help her out with this job, or she'd go out of her way to torturously complicate things with Farah.

When they entered the tavern, Quinn looked suspiciously from bounty hunter to wizard. "And why, pray tell, have you changed your mind with this one?"

Irulen put his hands out toward Quinn in a calming

fashion. "Let's at least hear her out, we could use the cash."

"We? *We?* I'm getting dragged into this? Into the Shadow Streets? Not interested. *Not at all.*"

"Let's listen," Irulen insisted, obstinately.

Quinn crossed his arms in a fit. "Fine."

"The way my...*our* client puts it—" Kay, briefly interrupted by Quinn's scoff, continued, "Deep in the shadow streets, where the easterners dwell, there is an orphanage steeped in dark magic."

Irulen raised an eyebrow at Quinn as she continued.

"The orphanage lies close to the heart of the resistance, and the man who oversees it is working to fuel conflict in the city. His name is Comcka, a dark sorcerer whose magic is magnified by the blood of young children. I found reliable information last night that there is a bone pile hidden in the complex corroborating this claim."

Irulen nodded. "It is a common imp-sign to hoard the bones and possessions of the ones they kill. I call them rat piles. I've never met a true sorcerer of the dark arts, but I suspect their tendencies might be similar. How are you sure he's a full-fledged sorcerer and not an imp?"

"From all the witness accounts I've collected, there are no mentions of imp-sign across his face...no leaking blackness down his cheeks."

"Interesting, but I'm afraid I echo many of Quinn's concerns. Even though the money is good, this seems like a tall order with a lot of risk."

Just then the door opened, and Farah stepped out looking exhausted and confused.

Kay looked Irulen in the eyes. "Would you rather we moved onto another conversation? I have an idea or two."

"No," Irulen answered, and then called to Farah. "Farah! Could you do me a favor, please, and feed Max? He's in my room."

She nodded while yawning and shuffled back through the door.

Irulen turned to Kay. "Now, tell us your plan."

Quinn shook his head in protest and grunted.

Irulen tried to reason with him. "Look, you hired a serving girl the night before another one fell on your lap. That's three gals to house, feed, and pay. Maybe we can use a lump sum of coin to help get by. Especially with winds of strife blowing around these hard times the way they are."

Quinn softened just enough to where Kay obviously decided she could continue.

"The plan is simple, really. The buildings in that section of the city are old stone ruins left over from the Great Conflict. All we have to do is make our way into the ghetto. There's a tunnel, some old catacombs that lead from the edge of The Central Gardens deep into the area. Once in the area, we simply need to scale some of the ruins and drop into the courtyard of the complex. You can check out the bone pile while I cover you with my crossbow. If you can force or lure Comcka out, I'll put an arrow in his heart."

Quinn dragged both of his hands down his hardened face. "Why is it your plan sounds far too easy?"

"A plan doesn't have to be difficult to be effective," she replied, matter-of-factly.

Irulen smiled and shifted in his seat a little. "Well, we haven't seen that part of the city yet have we, friend?"

Quinn sounded exasperated. "Well, it's your ass on the line, not like the gods will let me die anyway."

"Oh?" Kay looked at Quinn quizzically.

"Long story, lass, long story."

"Quinn believes he's cursed to survive any calamity," Irulen declared, in an apathetic tone.

"Pah! I'm going to go grind my axe." He shoved his chair back, got up, and strode across the room.

Irulen and Kay set to talking about supplies.

CHAPTER 6: THE MAZE BENEATH

By later that evening, Quinn had hired two larger gentlemen he knew for the night to keep an eye on the tavern's security. He left the operation of the place to Anastas, who in turn was already bossing Thea and Farah around when the hunting party left.

The first notable place that Kay, Irulen, and Quinn traversed was the Central Gardens, the fairest place the city had to offer. Here, in the center of the city, was a collection of rare, colorful plants and trees native to the northern environment. Many of the tree blossoms were bright red and pink and would routinely part from their branches and float calmly to the garden's cobbled pathways. An increasing lack of upkeep had merged the plants with their manmade barriers to create a unique forest of stalks and sculptures.

Irulen walked as he always did, though he now carried with him a short sword lent to him by Quinn. Kay was decked out in tough leather trappings, a light armament that was dark in color. Irulen watched her disappear into every shadow they passed. Quinn wore a flagon slung over his shoulder and carried a double sided axe in his hand and a pack of supplies upon his back.

Irulen momentarily regretted leaving his raven behind. *Max always loves it here.* Irulen would often take Max to the Central Gardens to spread his wings, especially when they found themselves stationary in Northforge for too long. There were many paths and passages through the park, but main roads ran like a compass through it all. As long as they stuck to their current course, they would emerge on the eastern side of the gardens and on the edge of their mission's danger zone.

An eerie quiet hung over the center of the garden. It was beautiful, but the party knew robbers and transients made their livings in the area. These people were of minimal threat to the three travelers, however. Bandits preyed almost exclusively upon the lonely and weak. The second leg of the gardens was as uneventful as the first, and soon the three were on the edge, staring into a vast, dark corridor in the distance.

People milled about, regarding the group with suspicion. The inhabitants of this area specifically were of mixed descent, and so did not pose much opposition to the group's travel. They gawked at them, nonetheless, sizing up the quarry, and apparently ultimately deciding there would be nothing to gain through bothering the strangers.

Quinn paused for a moment in the space between the gardens and the alley. The others stopped silently beside him. The lunar light illuminated Irulen's and Kay's faces as they watched the large man slide his axe into a belt holder on his side.

"Tis a clear night, and I shall have a drink for the mother moon and her many offspring."

Kay looked across Quinn to Irulen, as the coarse looking man unstrapped his flagon and lifted it to his lips. Irulen shrugged and accepted the flagon when Quinn offered it. He took a draught and breathed a cloud of satisfaction into the frosty air, and then suddenly tossed the container over to Kay. A disapproving look graced her face as she shook her head from side to side. She raised the flagon to her mouth and drained an amount much greater than the two men before her. She flipped the cap back on and thrust it into Quinn's hand. He reattached it to the sling and hung it once again around his shoulder. "So," he said, "What now? Where are the catacombs? Damn tunnels creep me out."

"Nearby, this way." Kay led them on.

Irulen was fairly reassured that most of the prying eyes had rescinded from whence they came, like ants into their hill at the sight of a much larger predator. It was only a short walk into the alley where they came across a secluded passage to the right.

They followed the side passage for only about twenty feet before they reached a locked wooden door hidden among the shadows.

Kay stepped forward and knocked on the door. It swung open before she could completely step back. A white orb emerged from the portal, the bald head of a pale monk with a long face. His brown robes reached the floor, masking his steps and giving the impression that he was floating. An arm materialized from his robes and a hand opened, palm up. He remained silent as Kay filled his palm with coin.

"You didn't mention we had to pay our way through," alleged Quinn.

Kay responded, "If we are to use the property of the Brotherhood of the Third Eye, then we have to provide a donation, unless you want to walk the whole way through the slums."

Quinn looked to Irulen, who shrugged his acquiescence.

The monk's hand reached outward again, signaling for them to move through the portal. Quinn went through first, and stumbled before catching his balance. The doorway was met by stairs heading downward.

"Thanks for the warning," he grunted, and continued on.

The stairs let out into a dark, dank hallway. The group turned to the left as their guide stepped in front of them to lead.

It wasn't long before the glimmering candles illuminated ornamental displays of meticulously arranged bones along the walls. Shadows swirled in the many tributaries running off the main passage, monks moved silently about their business. They lived most of their lives in the subterranean labyrinths beneath Northforge and other cities.

Perhaps the most unnerving thing Irulen noticed as he passed through the Brotherhood's underground world, was the occasional standing skeleton that donned monk robes. It was as if the dead watched the living pass through their realm. Irulen had it on reasonable authority that, through the power of necromancy, anyone who vandalized or trespassed in these catacombs would find themselves face-to-face with the reanimated undead.

He shivered at the thought of being confronted by the skeletal monks. He moved a little faster every time he passed one of them. As if to make the atmosphere purposefully more unsettling, some of the monks standing along the wall weren't dead at all. His heart jumped every time he detected living eyes beneath the hoods, accepting his presence with an unknown disposition. Irulen was well ready for whatever dangerous job awaited them above ground, and swore he would risk all above ground for the trip back to the tavern before he would return to this place.

Kay walked in silence with Irulen behind her. The wizard watched as the pacing of Quinn's steps increased and slowed as he passed the hooded figures, apparently suffering from the same discomfort that plagued Irulen. For her part, Kay walked as she ever did, keeping a straight face on the edge of a smirk. Her seductive walk looked as if it she were trying to coax the old bags of bones back to life.

Irulen was not one to fear darkness. He could, after all, illuminate the surrounding area whenever he pleased. It was from this ability that the wizard harvested his courage. Still, he felt eyes upon him, as if the skeletal monks were turning their heads as he passed.

The tight passageway expanded into a large dome. The openness could be felt in the air. Candles flickered along the far walls, casting light across still effigies of monks living and dead.

As Kay and Quinn reached the end of the room, a curtain of shadow fell between them and Irulen. He lost sight of them. The wizard brought his hands out, intent on lighting his own way while forging onward.

"*Wait.*" A raspy voice filled his ears. It was joined by a chorus of others.

"*Come back.*"
"*Stay, for a moment.*"
"*We know you.*"
"*About you.*"

It was hard to determine one voice from the next. They

shared a similar tone, but the way all of these sayings overlapped each other made Irulen feel like he was in front of many souls. He walked slowly back to the center of the room.

"What do you want?" he asked them.

"We know about what you did."

"Oh? Are we to discuss my heroic exploits?"

"The girl, we know about the girl, the one you ruined."

Irulen's heart skipped a beat. "Lynette?"

The voices intertwined with each other. *"Yes, Lynette, as she was once called. 'Your great sin.' She still roams the world above, restless."*

"I will put her to rest, be assured." His voice didn't hold the conviction he'd been striving for.

He now heard the voices as one. *"You must silence her soul. She travels, tormenting others as she is tormented herself. Her pain affects the world, like the magical abominations, the imps."*

Irulen found himself wincing at the vocabulary attributed to what had been his childhood friend. He buried his feelings deep. Now was not the time to face them. Not yet.

"I have, in turn, rid the world of many other imps in her stead. I hope to atone for what I've done."

"Yes, you try very hard, but imps are made as fast as they can be disposed of. You are chasing the trail of death diamonds, the ones you have been finding in the corpses of victims. At the end of that trail is a man who seeks to upset the natural order. He seeks eternal power at the expense of others, infinite magic and life."

Thinking he had finally caught his break, Irulen began questioning the brotherhood eagerly. "You know this man? Where can I find him? What do the diamonds do?"

"We do not know where he is or what he goes by. He is strong enough to avoid our gaze. The diamonds are the key to the puppet master's making and unmaking. They siphon power to him. The diamond has to be placed next to the heart before its final beat. In order for the ritual to work, a non-magical human must kill a human. So his imps and followers manipulate and force others into committing these heinous deeds.

Deafening silence hung over the chamber, and then the hoarse whispering continued. *"One of the mysterious one's followers roams the city above. This servant was one of us, at one time. We feel the servant, but his location is also hidden from us. The creature's true name is Illithar, and he is a necromancer. Your friends seek your presence, it is time to go."*

"But I feel there is more to learn, here and now."

"If you want to speak to us again, rid the world of the imp you sired."

The pitch black peeled back to the normal level of fluttering darkness. Quinn called to him from down the bleak corridor. Irulen moved quickly as he followed the call.

CHAPTER 7: A SONG OF STRIFE

Farah used a rag to clear her forehead of sweat and matted hair. *The Roasted Duck,* not as busy as the night before, was about half filled. The fireplace, that had just the night before been a place of comforting solace, was now an adversary. She walked through the kitchen door to find Anastas brewing a stew in a giant cauldron, grasping a giant wooden spoon. The way the lady was hunched over her boiling stock reminded Farah of childhood stories about witches.

Anastas looked up, grinning. "How is it out there?"

"Oh, 'tis fairly full now…need two more please." She used the back of her wrist to brush a loose strand of hair from her face.

Anastas grabbed a wooden mug. She filled it, making sure the vessel was full with equal portions of stock, vegetables, and meat, before thrusting the swashing mug into Farah's hands and filling a second. Farah took her order out into the main room, narrowly dodging Thea as she skirted past her near the door.

Farah took solace in her work, for work is normalcy. She lost herself in it, and even found herself bantering with the customers. Her face passed with ease from smiles to concentration as she served table after table. She became so involved, in fact, that she didn't even notice the intense gaze that had locked onto her. A hand suddenly grabbed at her arm, and she spun around to find herself face to face with Jorin.

"What is this?" Anger was written along his scowl.

Farah had little to say. "I'm working."

"I see that. But I'm wondering…you have a job already.

Why are you still here?"

Farah felt suffocated by the proximity of Jorin's mass. Her skin was numb. "Look." She untangled herself from his grip and backed away. "Just have a seat and I'll talk to you more. I have a few things to do first."

Concern softened his features. "I wanted to know if you were alright."

"I know, just sit, please." She swiped at her brow with the back of her arm.

Jorin acquiesced, found a spot at an empty table, and averted his eyes.

Farah turned from him. Her mind raced erratically between random thoughts; dishes and Jorin, drinks and Irulen, customers and her future. She knew Frostbridge was no longer in her immediate future. Jorin, who had always looked after her, had likely seen her as his future bride for some time. *I don't want to crush his world while creating my own.*

The flow of food soon slowed, and Farah made sure her half of the tavern was well stocked with ale. Thea worked busily, but seemed to have everything under control. Farah approached Jorin, who stared at her expectantly. She glanced around, searching for any work that needed to be done, before reluctantly sitting down across from him.

She found his gaze lingering on the bruises around her wrist. She withdrew her arms and placed them under the table. "I'm safe." She met his stare, held it. "The wizard saved me. He led me here."

Jorin leaned in toward her, his jaw clenched.

He's always so intense.

"Then why are you still here? Will you go home with me?"

"No, at least not yet. I wouldn't feel safe there."

Jorin's fingers pulsated in a clenched fist. Agitation tightened his lips. "And you feel safe *here*? This place reeks of danger. Just look at these people." Jorin's wide arm swept across the room. "Frostbridge might not be the answer. But neither is this place. Not for you."

He was right, of course. Deep in her heart, Farah knew that at some point she would find herself in above her head. She had spent most of her time inside the perceived safety of the tavern, but the city outside could be outright brutal. Irulen had told her as much.

Still, she was being moved by a force beyond the restraints of logic and comprehension. *Maybe fate, maybe stupidity.* Regardless, Farah couldn't find the words to explain her attachment to the one who had saved her, the one who had helped her wounds heal. *Love* wasn't it. She did not feel the pang of love, or butterflies rattling her rib cage, when she looked at Irulen. The only word that seemed any kind of right was *destiny.* She belonged near him. For whatever purpose, she had been removed from Frostbridge and the life that had been drawn out for her.

"Maybe not. Perhaps neither here nor there is right for me. But maybe this is just the start of something."

Jorin opened his mouth to speak, but froze, interrupted by sudden silence. A hush fell over the tavern's merrymakers. Outside, a sound like wind chimes grew violently louder. Jorin recognized the telltale clash of steel. He stood up, placing his hands near the hatchets he kept attached to both his sides. For a moment, he locked eyes with Farah.

The door slammed open. "Excuse me! Pardon this insufferable interruption."

Jorin and Farah looked toward the voice at the door. An unassuming man dressed in formal red attire stood there. Even as he spoke so eloquently, the song of swords and strife could be heard out in the streets.

"Attention! Attention please. Ladies and gentlemen, I regret to inform you that, due to recent threats to our domestic security, we are here to collect weapons." He greeted the sound of protests and weapons being put to the ready with outstretched hands and pleas for silence. "Please, please." He held his palms toward the angry crowd, as if he could hold them back should they surge forward in anger, but the people quieted once more. The man looked familiar to Farah.

He continued. "Once the ones seeking to harm the security of our city are identified, your weapons will be returned to you. All you need to do is register your weapon—"

"Piss on that!" Yelled a drunkard. The partygoers started to grumble more.

"We can be civilized about this, surely?" The aristocrat's confident tone wavered slightly.

Anastas, who had come out of the kitchen, spoke up, "S'pose you want my butcher's knife too, since it can cleave a face in half as good as any axe. And do you want my serving knives...that can be thrown as accurately as any arrow?"

She pulled her butcher knife out of her apron and walked toward the man. Two soldiers stepped up behind him, chests puffed, hovering protectively. An unknown number of soldiers formed a line that stretched outside the door. The bodyguards Quinn had hired were nowhere in sight, and were likely dead on the street.

For a moment in time, stark silence hung in the still air. Anastas turned her back to the man as she scanned the tavern's patrons, most of whom she'd come to know as well as any family. Farah caught a glint in the older woman's eyes, something that spoke of indecision.

The orator lifted his left hand over his shoulder, signaling the soldiers to keep their distance and hold in place. Anastas heaved a heavy breath and turned back to the man. She gave the butcher knife a feather-light toss up and caught its metallic head. She offered the aristocrat the handle. He obliged, reaching his hand out and gently grabbed the knife from her.

"Thank you," he said, with a slight bow.

"Anything for our safety," Anastas responded.

Her hand thrust forward with unforeseen quickness. Her strike connected with the man's throat. His windpipe was crushed irreparably. Anastas retrieved the butcher's knife and buried it into his chest. The soldiers surged forward and hacked at her as the tavern folk met them head on. Neither Farah nor Jorin saw what happened to the older serving woman. The mob clashed with the city soldiers as screams and excitement filled the air.

From the mob, Thea emerged.

"I have the key!" She motioned for Farah to join her as she held up a key-ring. Jorin followed as the two women headed to the secured door next to the fireplace. The fighting spread like fire throughout the tavern as she fumbled with the lock. The door unlatched, and Thea pushed it open. Farah followed behind her. Thea looked back outside. "Anastas?"

Jorin paused at the door entrance. "Lock the door. I'll knock three times!"

The urgency in his eyes made her obey without question. She backed up as Thea pulled the door shut and latched it. The silence on this side of the wall amazed Farah.

* * *

Jorin turned toward the fray and pulled out his two hatchets. A soldier charged him. He pulled his right arm back and threw an axe which landed with its blunt end against the soldier's chest. He was not very adept at mortal combat, but he was strong. The sheer force of Jorin's throw shattered a handful of the man's ribs, and he fell backward. Spitting like a wild animal, the soldier scrambled back to his feet and raised his sword. Jorin brought his left axe down on his enemy's face. Blood spouted, as if from a stone-figure fountain, and the body crumpled. Tables and chairs split and cracked as the fighting spread throughout the tavern. Jorin retrieved his right axe.

A brief flicker of indecision split his thoughts between two impulses; knock on the door, or determine the fate of Farah's friend. *More than likely she's dead, and this fight isn't mine.* He glanced at the door that protected Farah for a split second. *She won't be safe until this place is cleared out.*

Jorin threw himself toward the mob. He raised both of his weapons and brought them together on the neck of a soldier whose back was vulnerable. The vibration of the man's collarbone cracking beneath his blades rattled through Jorin's hands. They would have hurt fiercely if it weren't for the adrenaline coursing through his veins. He worked with the mob to press the attack back to the entrance. The soldiers were visibly surprised that these people, strangers and riff raff mostly, had mounted such a powerful and organized attack. Jorin found himself at the back of the herd as it shoved the soldiers out the door, all the while trampling the wounded underfoot. Jorin stood and watched as the wave of people pushed out into the streets to join the larger battle taking place outside. The receding wave unveiled the crumpled pile that used to be Anastas.

Thinking quickly, Jorin cleared the entrance of two uniformed bodies. He slammed the heavy door shut and placed the heavy slab of wood into the notches behind the door. *It would take a ram to get through that.*

Then, he grabbed a cloak from a decapitated patron and laid it over the old serving lady. He couldn't hide the entire scene of carnage from Farah, since more than ten bodies littered the inside of the tavern. A moan from under one of the tables caught Jorin's attention.

He bent down and found an older man writhing in pain. His right arm had a deep wound. Jorin tore a piece of the man's shirt fabric and tied it high on the bleeding arm. The man emitted whispers of thanks. Jorin helped lift him onto one of the few tables that stood undamaged.

Everything had happened so fast. Jorin walked over to the door and knocked three times. Metal creaked as the door swung open, revealing Farah and Thea's frightened faces. Farah had a raven on her shoulder. Max hissed a warning at the intruder, only to be calmed by Farah. Jorin urged the girls back into the hallway and slammed the door shut behind him. He fell to the floor and leaned his back against the wall, exhausted. His head was filled with fumes of confusion and fatigue. Blood stained his shirt and soul.

Jorin was a simple man upon whom the subtlety and need for politics was lost. He had no idea of the state of things in the city. Even if Frostbridge was reasonably close, it might as well have been another world.

The wayward traveler looked up at the girls and raven. "What was that?"

"I have really no clue," answered Farah.

Thea shared what she knew. "I think the mountain-siders are making a move."

"Who are they?" Jorin took a deep breath and tried to wrestle his racing heart under control.

"They rule the city. They collect taxes, keep a standing army, and hold the common people in low regard. There have been many rumors lately regarding rebellion. These talks have been worrying Quinn for some time now."

Farah's furrowed forehead spoke volumes before she ever opened her mouth. "So this was a preemptive attack, you think?"

"Yes, one that's not going away soon."

Jorin groaned at the impossibility of it all. "We've been saved from the cooking pot only to be roasted over a fire."

"Irulen—," Farah started.

Jorin spit onto the wall across from him. "Irulen, Quinn, and that woman they're with…they'll all be back soon. We can flee together."

"To Frostbridge?"

"My home is to the south," Thea offered feebly.

Farah looked from Jorin to Thea, from heading north to travelling south. "We'll figure it out when they get back."

CHAPTER 8: FATE'S FORTUNE

Irulen, Kay, and Quinn watched their guide's face disappear as the outer door slid shut before them. The three companions instinctively turned and looked to the clear night sky that once again graced their vision. For a moment, the moon's astral embrace felt as warm as any summer sun. A chill, wintery breeze swept through the streets, reminding them of their present time, place, and purpose.

"Where to?" asked Quinn, as he looked around. The old, stone buildings in this area were the decaying remnants of a golden age long since passed.

"Speak quietly," said Kay, warily. She left the men standing like shunned children and crept to where their alley connected with the main street. After looking both ways, the bounty hunter moved silently back to her companions. "It's just a little farther."

"Well then," Quinn grunted, while shouldering his axe, "Maybe I'll soon cease being so damn bored." He took a gallant step forward only to find himself blocked by Irulen's arm. The wizard locked eyes with his friend. "We're going to come out of this one clean, all right?"

Quinn's gaze hardened for a moment. "All right, sure," he said, gesturing for Irulen and Kay to go on ahead.

Moonlight guided their way. Irulen refrained from using illumination of any kind. They would be lucky to pass unnoticed through the notorious ghetto, but they would maintain the element of surprise for as long as possible.

Behind Irulen, Quinn tripped in the darkness, and Irulen was both impressed and amused by his friend's ability to rage in silence. Turning his attention back to their path, uneasiness slipped into Irulen's mind. It wasn't all that late, and while he never frequented these streets, they seemed oddly empty.

At some point moving through the darkness, Irulen lost the outline of Kay's figure. A cool breeze blew through the hair on the back of his neck, which already stood at attention. A trickle of sweat traced his spine. He remained alert as he walked, his night vision keen. Still, his eyes played tricks on him. Shadows melded with shadows, creating outlines of penumbral creatures lurking in the darkness ahead of him. Though unnerved by his surroundings, Irulen dared not illuminate the area and draw undue attention.

The wizard put his hand back to halt Quinn. A splayed figure lay only a few feet ahead of them. Irulen cautiously scanned the area as he approached and leaned over a middle aged man with a sword on the flagons near his outstretched hand. He was laid out as if a dragon had tail whipped him from behind, his face against the pavement and his arms flailed outward. It became clear to Irulen that Kay was moving ahead and clearing the way of sentries. The two men may have felt a touch uncomfortable in their surroundings, but hunters like Kay thrived in the darkness.

An unconscious bundle, sometimes two, appeared every so often. After about ten such meat sacks, Irulen heard a sudden noise to his immediate right. He flinched as a rope from above writhed on his head like a wild snake. A second one dropped next to the first. Irulen and Quinn shrugged at each other in the darkness, and then began climbing up as best they could. Quinn used his brute upper arm strength to haul his girth upward. Irulen gripped the rope, leaned back, and walked his feet up the wall.

They both pulled themselves over the wall and were greeted by an unpleasant surprise.

"This one was not so easy... Um, he might be dead," said Kay, of a man sprawled out on the roof before them.

"What do you mean *might*?" Quinn studied the subject.

Irulen stepped over the might-be-dead man. "It should

be a pretty straightforward thing to tell if he is dead or not," he said, and put an ear to the body's mouth. "He's gone. Damn."

Quinn ran a hand over his head. "This changes everything," he said.

"We haven't even investigated the matter we were hired for," Irulen said, solemnly. "This guy could be a hardened criminal for all we know, if he is helping Comcka. We don't know if what we've heard is true or not."

Kay spread her hands. "What can I say? He knew how to fight. I did what I had to do."

Quinn turned to Irulen. "You think we should abandon the job?"

"No." Irulen shook his head to emphasize his point. "No, if we turn back now then this act is simply murder. Let's move on and hope our bounty hunter has her story right."

"I don't like it," Quinn grumbled.

Irulen swiped a hand across his mouth. "Nor do I." He turned away from the corpse. "Lead on, Kay."

They moved silently along the rooftop, watching from above as figures lurked in the street below. The long roofline ended with a short gap between it and the next. The moonlight shone more brightly on the rooftops, and they moved quickly. They came to an eave overlooking a complex with a long house in the middle surrounded by a courtyard. Irulen figured the heavy plume of smoke rising into the air emanated from a fire pit at the back of the house.

The three of them looked into the courtyard as Kay spoke. "That's the orphanage he uses to harvest the kids. He should be near."

"We need to go see what's for dinner," said Irulen.

"This guy must like his meat tender." Quinn fell silent when Irulen and Kay stared at him in mixed disappointment and disgust.

"Go ahead," Kay ordered, "I'll cover the area from here."

Kay secured two grappling hooks to the edge of the roof, letting the lines down. Quinn and Irulen descended to within a few feet of the ground and then jumped. They crept across the cobblestone yard—weeds pushing up through every crevice—and arrived at the smoldering pit behind the house. The ropes were left behind, swinging in the darkness.

Quinn peeked through a crack in the shutter at the back window. He walked back to Irulen who was shining light from his right hand on the smoky debris. He used his left hand to prod the pile with a rod he'd found nearby. Charred bones and wood clicked together softly in the quiet night. Irulen grunted with displeasure as he sifted through the debris.

In truth, what Irulen found was disturbing. The bones were *not* human. There were no clavicles present, for one. It seemed that there had been little more roasted here than pigs, certainly no children. In order to confirm his findings, Irulen stood up and moved quickly around the grounds. He was searching for what he called a *rat pile*, a hidden stash of items collected from the victims—a common practice of imps. He figured there wouldn't be a huge array of hiding spots for the imp to use in such an urban dwelling. He approached a shed in the back and pushed an unlocked door open. He illuminated his right palm again and scanned the room, but found nothing more than basic tools and supplies.

In that moment, Irulen cursed himself for agreeing to this cloak and dagger mission. Dragging Quinn along only made it worse. There was a reason he always kept things above water and in the public's eye. Now a man was dead based on flimsy evidence, and nothing pointed to the sort of cannibalistic practices that were supposed to be happening here.

He had made a second mistake within a matter of days, this time with fatal consequences. Either Kay had lied to him, or she had been lied to. Perhaps a little bit of both. Regardless, Irulen decided he wouldn't press an investigation with a dead sentry only a few rooftops away. He needed to grab Quinn and get out of the area faster than dragon's breath. If they were found out, their business in Northforge would likely come to an abrupt, and unpleasant, end.

He beckoned to Quinn and met him halfway.

"We have to go, this is all wrong."

"Shit."

"I know, we need to leave."

"Post-haste," Quinn agreed, glancing around erratically.

They had just finished creeping back to the wall where Kay was stationed when Irulen paused and put his hand out to stop Quinn.

"We've been found," he stated, solemnly.

At that moment, a slew of torches were lit, and the two men found themselves facing a small mob of unknowns.

"Who are you?" Came a thickly accented voice, commanding, gruff, and strong.

It was Irulen who spoke. "My name, sir, I shall not give willingly. My purpose, however, I shall gladly set forth. You see, I've been commissioned with a task—a faulty task—based on what I now see as flimsy evidence and now regret my current position. With your permission, we will withdraw, peacefully."

"Still," said the man, "you did not request permission to come here and do not yet have my permission to leave. I would have more words concerning your purpose. It is disturbing that you are here looking in windows at children."

Irulen couldn't make out which of the men spoke. There were too many of them, and they all stood militaristically still. The wizard decided to take a shot at coming clean. "We have been sent here to investigate a matter of infantile cannibalism. Ridiculous I know, but we couldn't leave children to be munched on like crackers, could we?"

"And who is supposedly munching on them?"

"A sorcerer called Comcka."

Laughter filled the night.

"I have no taste for human flesh, let alone that of a child. These orphans are products of the abject poverty imposed upon my people by the mountain dwellers. I am no sorcerer, just the leader of my people and of the resistance. Who makes this accusation?"

"Funny you should ask…" Irulen's voice trailed off as the speaker stepped forward from the crowd. He also found himself once again aware of Kay's lingering presence, crossbow in hand, perched like an angel of death on a roof above. He wondered how much she could hear of the current conversation, and whether she believed what Irulen was saying or took his angle as a ruse to lure their target out into the moment. At any moment she might make her presence known, maybe by shooting the man where he stood.

"Stay back!" Irulen yelled.

A bright flash and concussive reverberation shook the ground. Kay must have managed to squeeze the trigger, but her shot missed high. Irulen and Quinn didn't wait to see what had happened.

They ran, hoisted themselves up over the wall, grabbed Kay, and urged her on. It was clearly time to leave.

CHAPTER 9: DEAD RISING

"Gather and pack anything important," called Jorin, as he opened the door to check on the wounded stranger. He shut the door quickly behind him. He didn't want Farah seeing such a grisly scene until she had to. He loathed seeing how she would react to such carnage after what she had already been through.

Farah, having no possessions of her own, went into Irulen's room to see if anything needed organizing, and collect anything that might have worth in the event an escape was needed. Thea walked back and forth between packing her own things and scavenging some of Anastas's belongings. She gathered Anastas's personal effects into one pile and supplies that could be used to travel in another.

Jorin held his head over the old man's mouth. Breath passed softly and spread across Jorin's ear and cheek. He stood up straight, walked to the front door, and listened. Farah had suggested sending Max to alert his owner to their plight, but it was a risk just opening the door to let the raven out. It was hard to tell whether the dull sounds of combat were figments of his imagination or not. He believed they were real, and the risk of opening the door was best left not taken.

Confident in his decision, Jorin walked straight back into the kitchen. He began assembling cooking utilities and any preserved food he could find. He rummaged around clumsily and took hasty stock of the food stores. He would insist on waiting out the outside storm as long as they could. Traveling as they were was not an option. Perhaps if Farah's beloved wizard and his friends came back the story would change, but for now their best bet was to stay put. It seemed Anastas kept a good deal of salted meat on hand. Some raw meat sat out on a wooden slab nearby.

He found it surreal that he would be doing this, but he used a candle as a pilot light to start a fire under a grill. The fumes would carry up into a chimney and spill out over the city, but he was willing to bet no one would pause fighting at the smell of it. He was awkward in the kitchen, but wasting the meat seemed out of the question.

He had no sooner placed the meat over the fire, when he heard a terrible noise. It sounded like something between a gurgle and a scream—a ghoulish noise Jorin never wanted to hear again.

He instinctively pulled out his right axe and headed back into the main room. The thing that hit him hardest, that clued him into what was going on, and that terrified him to the core, was the isolated sounds of slurping, tearing, and chewing. The dead were rising, chewing on the meat and breaking their teeth against the bones of the wounded man Jorin had saved.

The scene was a morbid mockery of a drinking festivity shared among comrades. Except, there was no ale or mead pouring forth—only a trickling waterfall of blood leaking between the cracks of the table and pooling on the floor. There was no laughter, only the guttural sounds consistent with corpse eating.

Jorin pulled back inside the kitchen before any of the ghouls noticed his presence. He pressed his back against the wall next to the kitchen's swinging door. It wouldn't do to try barricading himself where he was, the racket of moving things might attract them faster than his ability to seal the entrance. Besides, the one thought in his mind terrified him. *Farah*. He had already feared she would open the door to the outside slaughter. Now that the dead were rising, his fear had ratcheted up beyond comprehension.

He'd run to the door where Farah and Thea were and hope it wasn't locked. If it was, he had to hope they would reach the door and open it before the ghouls took him. It was more than likely he would have to fight. In the folk stories he had read as a child the undead only fell when their brains were bashed in. He grabbed his axes and took a deep breath, as the swinging door began to creak open. Something was shambling through. Jorin's hands tensed against the wooden handles of his axes. The thing's face came through slowly, looking straight ahead with a lack of awareness. It was Farah's friend, Anastas.

Jorin waited for her to come through and show enough of her back for him to take her out. He waited to see which way she would turn. He was to the left. She turned to the right. The decrepit thing that was Anastas shambled over to where the steak Jorin had put on was burning. With hands mangled by defensive wounds and without using any sort of utensil, she flipped the meat.

Watching her perform this last human act gave Jorin pause, but he knew what he'd seen. The swinging door was still, and there were no other followers. Jorin crept behind her, wavered a moment about which way to swing, and decided to go with a single strike with his right axe. He raised his arm and brought it down with all his might. The axe made a deep *thud* as it contacted her skull, and she fell to the ground. The bone of her head definitely split, but Jorin hadn't done enough damage to the brain.

Fearing anymore racket would see his life forfeit, Jorin held her down with his foot. He placed a hatchet inside her mouth and stomped down as hard as he could, successfully separating the brain-holding half of her skull from the rest of her body. The move worked, the body laid limp, but the eyes in her severed half-head still moved. It had landed awkwardly from the strike, and it now looked as if Anastas were buried in the floor up to her nose. Jorin placed himself above the grisly thing, lined up his axe with the crack he had made before, and finished the job.

The fire cooking the meat had dimmed to smoldering embers.

Jorin was as ready as he'd ever be. His mind focused on the door as he launched himself through. The door slammed against the wall as he burst forth. The dead were more spread out now, some had become disinterested in their grisly meal. One, an exceptionally large male soldier, sniffed around the door that sheltered Farah and Thea.

The door opened a crack, and Jorin held his breath, but bodies had piled up against the door and the women couldn't push it open. "Don't!" he yelled as he moved into the room and started toward them. Jorin, busy running and fighting for his life, saw the door start to move again. "Don't!" he repeated. "Don't open it!" The door sealed once more. It was no longer an option for him. The cat and mouse game he was playing with his shambling foes couldn't carry on for much longer. His only way out was through the front door, the one barricading the tavern from the battling outside world.

He ran to the entrance and lifted the heavy slab of wood barricading it shut. He swung the wood with all his might into his pursuers, knocking many of them back, and jumped out into the night. Tripping over who knows what, he fell face first into a street puddle of mud and blood. Even with the adrenaline coursing through his veins, Jorin's body grew tired. He lifted his head to find a pair of legs facing him. His spine contorted with the anticipation of a back crushing blow—one that never came.

"Come on now, you don't need to be kissing my feet."

Two massive hands grabbed him by the shoulders and pulled him to his feet. A large man steadied him from behind as he stood face-to-face with Irulen. A shadowy outline of a woman stood behind him.

"Jorin, meet Quinn and Kay. Where is Farah?"

Jorin pointed into the tavern and managed to fit a word in between the compression of his breaths. "Careful."

The wizard led the way with his two companions behind him. Jorin was left outside to listen to the inner commotion. He looked around and listened closely. Fires burned, casting waves of illumination across the darkness. The streets were lined with dead, and the song of strife echoed from a distance. He saw, whether through reality or his own paranoid lens, bodies pressing themselves up by their hands and legs. The cloud of war began to lift as Jorin walked briskly toward the tavern.

Once he stepped inside, he saw that the job he had started was finished. *The Roasted Duck* found itself disguised in gore and a history of violence. Blood splattered the walls, limbs littered the floor, and headless torsos slumped on the floor frozen in the varied postures of insomniacs in bed. These three people were efficient killers. Jorin retrieved the slab of wood he had thrown previously and once again barred the door.

Quinn fell to his knees in distress at the state of *The Roasted Duck*. His head was lowered in cosmic defeat. Kay surveyed the carnage with professional detachment. Irulen pulled at the pile of corpses Jorin left near the door to the living quarters. After moving the first one, the wizard paused. "You know, it takes a powerful necromancer to summon this amount of wights, even if they are low in power."

"Wights? Power?" Asked Jorin. He had only heard of such things in folk tales.

"Usually wights are used as undead guardians of their master's treasure. You are likely to run into them if you trespass on hallowed ground. They exist at differing levels of power. Some necromancers choose to invest large amounts of power into one entity, or employ many entities of lower power."

Irulen stopped talking and strained to lift a second body. He succeeded at pulling it out of the way.

"Whatever they choose, these creations of the dark arts will often roam the planet much longer than their masters. What you see are wights in an *initial* phase, they have just started becoming what they will become. Eventually their corporeal presence will recede in favor of a wraith-like existence."

He reached down to grab yet another corpse. "A little help?"

Quinn sat at one of the few seats left standing upright and ignored the request. His face remained buried in his hands as he experienced untold grief. Kay looked around lackadaisically.

Irulen met Jorin's eyes and pointed to Kay. "She's a little hard of hearing right now, got in the way of one of my spells, she did. Would you mind grabbing her and then coming over here to lend a hand. Maybe just tap her on the shoulder? Careful, mind you, she's known to show some spunk from time to time."

Jorin winced in untold pain as he stood. He approached the woman and stopped a few feet away from her, a little unnerved by how well she took the carnage around her. "Hey," he called. No response. "Hey!" Not knowing much in the way of caution, he stepped forward and tapped her on the shoulder. In an instant he was kneeling on the floor, his finger in her firm grasp. He felt his pointer and middle finger separating and thought for a moment they would snap like a wishbone. To his relief, she stopped.

"WHAT?" She asked, her deaf voice raised. Jorin pointed to Irulen, who in turn beckoned for them both to come over and help. They obliged, and before long the doorway was cleared.

* * *

The number of corpses piled near the door served as testament to Jorin's valiant effort at getting through to where Farah and Thea had been waiting. *So this is his love for her,* thought Irulen, *a pile of gore.*

In a separate strain of thought, the wizard also wondered whether Kay would have disappeared by now if the blast hadn't left her partially concussed and hard of hearing. There wasn't much room for her in the hall of the wizard's good graces, but he'd decided to make use of her while he could. While the initial effects of the spell he cast at Comcka's orphanage would have worn off by now, Irulen practiced magic on the bounty hunter in particular. As he walked away from the door, he quietly elongated the new spell that bound her ears. As long as he kept her in need of help, she wouldn't be going far. There were questions he would need answered when the time came.

One thing was certain—compensation was required for this ruse of a job. Perhaps if he found out who had hired Kay he could then collect his magic's weight in gold. In the meantime, he would keep her as close as possible.

Jorin knocked on the door three times. No answer. Irulen reached into his pocket and tossed Jorin his keys, and

Jorin opened the door only to find the hallway vacant.

"Farah!" He called.

The door to his immediate left started to move. A familiar set of eyes peeked through the slit as it opened. Once recognition dawned, the door swung open faster and Farah stepped out with Thea behind her. Max flew out after them, landed on Farah's shoulder, and eyeballed Jorin with suspicion.

The young women came out with their arms knotted together. They gasped and turned their heads away from one horror just to see another. Their intertwined arms shook from shock. The scene was surreal, the splatter abstract, and the destruction complete. The place which had not so long ago been full of merriment and music was now little more than a slaughterhouse full of flayed corpses and splattered walls. Kay scoffed at their visible fright at the macabre surroundings. Irulen walked over to them while they took in the scene to try and calm them down. Jorin wasn't a good speaker, and so stood looking on silently while words choked him.

Quinn, who had come back to his senses somewhat, wandered around what was left of the peaceful life he had etched out for himself. He walked into the back and found Anastas. She was unrecognizable except for her cooking attire. He pressed his bulk through the swinging door and back into the main room, relighting the dimming candles scattered about.

Quinn paused over one of the corpses. He placed his right foot against its cheek and moved the face into view. "Hey, Ire, I know this one."

"That's the one that Anastas killed." Farah gagged.

"He was the leader." Thea averted her gaze.

"A well-spoken son of a bitch," Jorin confirmed, bringing his eyes to bear on Irulen for just the slightest of moments.

Quinn spoke as Irulen bent over the corpse. "This is the guy I had words with last night, though he was slurring and not so well spoken. The bastard said he'd be back." Irulen waved Kay over and asked loudly, "Is this your client?"

Kay shook her head no. "But," she said, "He was at the

man's castle."

Irulen spoke more to himself than to anyone else. "An advisor or messenger of some sort, then."

The man's body was crumpled within his cloak. Irulen peeled the cloak back and untied a brown satchel attached to the man's belt. The content of the bag was startling. The others watched intently as the wizard crossed the room, pulled out something shiny, and held it up to a freshly lit candle.

"What is that, a diamond?" asked Jorin.

"No, not exactly. These are tools of black magic, although I'm not sure exactly how they are used or, for that matter, what they are used *for*. I often find them hidden in corpses of the murdered. I am beginning to suspect they are used to harvest something from the dying."

Thea spoke up. "Then this guy was here to kill all of us, whether people surrendered their weapons or not?"

"No one would come into *The Roasted Duck*, or really anywhere in the north, and expect a request for a mob of people to willingly lay down their weapons to be followed," Quinn declared pointedly. "No, this bunch came for blood. Maybe he thought he could increase his odds if he could intimidate and disarm a soft crowd or two. Pompous bastard, this one." He spat.

Irulen tied the satchel next to the one he had already filled with death diamonds.

"We packed what we could," offered Farah.

Quinn perked up. "Packed? To leave?"

Silence lingered in the room.

Quinn breathed deeply and continued, "Well I s'pose so, this duck is cooked. Been getting a little boring around here lately, anyway." He laughed suddenly. "Ha! So, any ideas as to where to go?"

"We could go to Frostbridge," Jorin offered, eagerly.

"Frostbridge has had enough trouble," responded Irulen, "there are certain people on both sides of this conflict that may be looking for us. I don't want to bring that to their doorstep. We'll need to keep moving."

"What do you mean both sides?"

"There was a slight misunderstanding with a rebel leader called Comcka. He thinks we're working for them." Irulen pointed toward the corpse-soldiers. "We had a *small* job offer from Kay, here, and it turned out to be a part of a much larger plan."

"You maybe, but not Farah, or me. They don't know us."

"The lad has a point," affirmed Quinn. "Might be time to set Red loose."

"And does *Red* have a say?" Farah asked obstinately.

"I'm not hearing everything you're saying," Kay interjected, "but if you're talking about where to run, well, just know that what has started here is a flame that will spread throughout the region. Nowhere nearby will be…*safe*. The only way to keep from being burned is to keep out of the flame's reach. Travel far, and travel fast."

"Thank you for that *insight*," said Irulen, facetiously and loudly. "You know, I spent a lot of magic fighting my way back here, not to mention the botched job itself." Irulen couldn't tell whether Kay heard him or not through his spell. She wasn't looking at him. He sighed. "Whatever we do, we don't have much time. How about you Thea?"

Thea twisted her hair around her finger. "My hometown is four days south of here. I'd like to go there."

Irulen decided to level with the others. "I'll tell it to you straight, there's something I have to do, someone I have to find, and since we are as far north as we're going to get, I need to head south."

The wizard paused a moment, and continued. "And for that matter, I agree with Kay. This skirmish is just the first of a war, and wars tend to pull things in as they expand outward. I doubt Frostbridge will be any type of refuge in the days to come. Perhaps if the town leaned one way or another and joined arms with the winning side, whichever that may be, then you have a way out. I'll be heading south."

Irulen looked at Jorin and Farah with earnest. "If you

want, I don't think Max would mind guiding a safe passage for you to Frostbridge."

Quinn interjected. "We shouldn't split up." He pointed in the direction of Farah, Jorin, and Thea. "You haven't seen how it is outside. It's like a tidal wave washed everything away save for the gore and misery."

Jorin made to open his mouth but was superseded by Farah. "I want to go south. I'm not sure why, but I feel like I'm bound to it. My fate is not meant to be spent in Frostbridge, or here. I've had enough of the North's cold heart and its bleeding of red ice."

Everyone in the room looked at Farah for a long moment before Quinn finally spoke. "Did you know she was a poet, Ire?"

The wizard clucked his tongue against the roof of his mouth. "Gee, well, it seems like we have our very own bard to write and sing our heroic deeds into the annals of history. Jorin, what say you?"

Jorin seemed a little off and a bit annoyed. He huffed out a breath. "I'll help you all to the southern limits of the city," he stated. "There I shall turn back and circumnavigate the city from the outside. I will return to Frostbridge, be there for my people, and do what I can."

"You are a heroic son of a bitch, aren't you?" Irulen asked, with a grin.

Jorin winced as if he had been pained.

Irulen tried to pacify the enraged bull caged behind Jorin's eyes, "Oh! Calm down, calm down. I'm sorry." The beast, at present, withdrew into the distance.

The next few minutes were used to gather up what food could be salvaged from the kitchen and grab the bags Farah and Thea had packed. Jorin warned them off of grabbing the steak he had tried to cook earlier. Irulen moved Anastas and put a sheet over her before the girls set about checking the food stocks. Quinn pushed all the wood he could up against the fire place. "One last fire for this tavern," he said. In his hand was a small pot filled with oil, something he kept on hand for hazardous occasions. In this instance, he planned on using it as an accelerant. He was going to burn *The Roasted Duck*, and everything with it. The last piece of wood Quinn threw on the pile was the very plank that had once saved his life. He wanted to bring it, but decided that there were times when the past was best left to burn. Why not try flipping two pages of his life's story all at once?

Once the baggage was stacked neatly by the door, Irulen and Jorin began moving it all outside. It was quiet. The street was clear. The song of strife had all but faded. For the first time, however, Irulen found himself bothered by a *lack* of bodies. That state of things suggested the necromancer had come through and conscripted the deceased into his services.

* * *

Everyone was outside waiting for Quinn when the shadows seemed to close around them. Wights began pouring out of the alleys and moving like ants toward a picnic. A quick glance back at the *Duck* showed the front entrance brimming with brightness. Quinn's fire had begun, and the tavern no longer offered them shelter to retreat. Irulen called for the barkeep to come outside. He emerged with a large sack of globules slung over his back. The bag clinked and clanked as he moved. He set it down, looked around, and whistled.

"Seems the hard part of the night has just begun," he remarked, dryly.

Weapons were made ready as the wights closed from both sides. To the south, the wight closest to them stopped and all the others followed suit. "I reckon the *hard part*," the wight jawed lifelessly, "was waiting for you all to come out of there! Like clowns from a crate!"

"The 'mancer is here." Irulen glanced around, loathe to take his gaze from the creature, but more worried about the threat the necromancer posed.

Another of the wights stepped forward, a girl of maybe ten, pulling his attention from his search. Like a puppet drawn by a string, she curtsied and spoke in a shrill voice. "Indeed, might I introduce myself? I am—"

The introduction was cut short by a bolt from Kay's crossbow piercing the girl-wight's head. She crumpled to the ground and there was a moment of silence. As if a puppet master transferring from one of his creations to another, the previous wight ceased being slack, came to attention, looked down at the dispatched wight, and laughed.

"Ha! Ha! Ha! I like the shooter from the shadows. She's my favorite, a real black soul in that one there. I think I'll keep her as a pet after we're through."

"Tell you what," said Quinn, as he began rustling through his bag. "If we're going to have a show, would you mind if…" he pulled out an oil pot in each hand. "… I provided the fireworks?"

Realizing his friend would need an igniter, Irulen looked into the *Duck* and pulled a broken chair leg to him. It flew through the air, barely missing his old friend's face, and landed in the wizard's hand. He ignited and tossed it back to Quinn. Thea and Farah handed Quinn the pots as he threw them. Before the puppet master could react, his horde of undead to the north was engulfed in flames. Kay picked off the scattered few that had managed to shamble through. The wights to the south immediately moved toward the group.

"Listen," called Irulen. "He's in the back somewhere controlling them, looking through their eyes. If we kill them fast enough, he won't be able to react."

"Well then," smiled Quinn, vacating his oil pots and heaving his broadaxe onto his shoulder. "Let's get to reaping!" With those words, Quinn the berserker led the charge. So fierce did he appear that Irulen was caught watching him in awe. Quinn's axe retracted as he approached the front of the mob and sprung forward. His massive arms pulled the axe through multiple wights like a scythe through corn. Irulen's eyes then found Kay's face for the slightest of moments. Her eyes glimmered in admiration and excitement. She withdrew to the shadows along the wall, and from those shadows flew bolts from her crossbow.

Irulen pulled out the short sword and set a spell upon it. Radiation passed from his palm as he ran his hand over the cold metal. The sword began to glow a dull green. Jorin was fighting to the right. Quinn was to his left, greedily severing spinal columns, cutting down the wights in giant swaths.

More wights had emerged behind them, and Kay was hardly able to put them down and reload her crossbow fast enough. Irulen released the binding spell on her hearing, and she paused for a moment, seeming perplexed. She regained her composure as a wight bore down on her, driving a dagger deep under its chin. Farah and Thea had taken over the oil potting duties, Thea lit while Farah threw. They couldn't keep up the pace as before, though, since their friends moved to and fro. Farah also couldn't throw nearly as well as Quinn.

Irulen set his purpose to attack the middle with his imbued sword. Nothing made of flesh could withstand its corrupting ability. He ran up to an elderly, female wight and slashed it across the cheek. Instantly the skin started sloughing off its face. The flesh melted off of the bone, and soon there was nothing left save the skeleton and mush. The wizard moved quickly through the center. At times he spun wildly and five or more wights would find themselves corrupting rapidly. By the time Irulen pressed through, the necromancer appeared to be gone. The wights were acting less coordinated and more random.

Irulen's attention was caught by a familiar "Caw!" Max had perched on a window sill above, nodding his head in a southeast direction. Irulen nodded his understanding, and Max took off into the night.

Irulen began working back toward his friends so the wights wouldn't overtake them. The process of cleaning out the street only took a few minutes, but it seemed much longer. Fearing accidentally touching one of his acquaintances, Irulen dispelled the sword once the situation was in hand. Soon Kay was walking around retrieving her bolts, Quinn was taking stock of his oil pots, and Jorin, Farah, and Thea sat resting against a wall.

Irulen stood in the middle of them and spoke. "Listen,

this 'mancer was working for someone, he was looking to harvest something, maybe the spirits of the living. But for what purpose I don't know. He was using the same death diamonds I've been finding inside many of the victims I've come across. If he can't harvest the living, then the next best thing for him would be to create more dead. A common modus operandi of necromancers is to cause death on a mass scale by poisoning the water supply, and that was the direction in which Max indicated he was heading. I need to catch this guy. Max is tracking him for me. I'll go after him. Travel outside the south walls with our supplies and then get off the road. Max or I will find you there."

"Do you want me to go?" asked Quinn.

"No, you stay with the others and get started. I'll catch up with you soon."

CHAPTER 10: UNCEREMONIOUS DEPARTURES

Irulen could tell by Max's calls that he was gaining on his prey. He would be hard pressed to catch the necromancer in time, even though it seemed like the enemy was intent on taking his sweet time. Irulen was aware of where the mouth of the river was, though, and even in the dark was making good time. The moving water grew louder as he got closer.

"Hello, Irulen, Lynnette asked me to send you her regards."

Irulen froze at the edge of a clearing. Across from him, near the water's edge, a jester sat upon a rock. Black streaks ran down his pale face. The black and grey jester's outfit he wore shone dull against the moonlight. His face was stretched in an exceedingly large grin. "I bet you're wondering why I took so long to come here and why I haven't yet poisoned the water. Or have I? Well, I haven't. And I'll tell you why. I need you to do it. I need a corpse with power to pull off my plan B."

"How do you know Lyn?"

"Come on, I'm talking about how I need to turn you into a corpse so I can kill off the entire city of Northforge, and all you can do is ask is 'How do you know Lyn?'"

"I plan on doing a lot more, but I'd like to know that first."

"She's doing our master's work."

"Master? But you are no imp. From just using the moonlight, I can see the streaks on your face are running from sweat."

"As if I need to be an imp to choose a master?"

"And you chose to leave the brotherhood, why?"

"They live in another world; I wanted to get involved in this one." The harlequin laughed. "And what, pray tell, did my brothers of the cloth tell you about me?"

"Not much, really, that you delved deep into the necromancy they are known for, took what you learned, and hightailed it out of there."

"Did they tell you my name?"

Irulen paused, perplexed. "Actually," he feigned, "they didn't."

"Well, then, allow me to—" Something whistled through the air, and the necromancer went limp and tumbled off the rock. He landed face first against the ground with his hindquarters sticking upward toward the sky.

What now? Irulen walked over to the man. He placed his foot upon the jester's ass and pushed. The body fell over and revealed the edge of the bolt sticking out from the man's left eye. The face was still smiling, though blood had leaked from it.

"Kay?" Irulen called.

"Yes?" She stepped out of the shadows.

"Why did you do that? Now I'll never know."

"What? His name?" Her eyebrows drew together in a scowl.

Irulen shoved a hand through his hair. "No, forget it."

"How do you think he was going to go about killing you?"

"Well, I guess we won't get to know that either. Where are the others?"

"I left them soon after you did. They should be hidden outside the city walls by now."

Irulen whistled and Max came down. He whispered into the raven's ear and it flew away again.

"Well," he sighed, "Max will find them, let them know we're coming."

"I wanted to apologize." The words fell awkwardly from Kay's mouth.

"What? Now? Why? For what?"

"I've cost you and Quinn a great loss of magic and coin. I'd like to repay that debt."

"Well, you *did* just one shot an evil necromancer looking to use my corpse to create dark magic that would wipe out human existence in the surrounding area."

"Yes, but financially. I made a grave mistake on faulty information. This man here, he was the one who hired me, I can tell looking through his makeup." She stood over the man and rustled through his clothing. She pulled out a bag and threw it.

Irulen caught it and opened it. He had expected more death diamonds, but what he found was a bag full of gold coin.

"That should be a start," she said.

The wizard laughed. "Well," he declared, "if you are going to hang around, then I want you to follow my lead. Consider yourself temporarily banned from the contractual element of our little business venture."

"Agreed."

Irulen found it very awkward that Kay was being so straight with him. There was no sexual façade or casual apathy. She seemed almost vulnerable. He found himself wanting to escape the situation. She seemed to pick up on the vibe.

"Shall we go?"

"Yes."

* * *

Farah's eyes were on Quinn, who hummed softly as he sat against a tree. They had been off the road now for the better part of an hour. There had been a pretty steady stream of soldiers marching out of the city, likely preparing for a pitched battle in the morning. When it was silent, refugees could be heard meandering through the woods.

Farah shimmied close to Thea, who sat close, her knees folded inward to her chest, waiting. Farah fought the overwhelming urge to sleep. She looked at Jorin and found him watching her. She squirmed under his accusative gaze and slowly moved forward to confront him. It was only when she reached him that she realized something was wrong. His eyes were vacant, his skin pallid. Quinn joined her at her side as she slapped Jorin across the face. Quinn put his hand to Jorin's mouth, waited a moment, and grabbed Jorin's wrist.

"His breath is weak, and his pulse is even weaker."

Farah drew back from the two men in fright. She was caught by Thea, who had moved forward to help.

Quinn ripped open the man's shirt to reveal a wound near his abdomen. "Not a wight, at least, not at first," Quinn whispered. "The initial wound looks like a single puncture, as if from a thin dagger. Must have happened earlier, at the tavern," he pointed out.

What he isn't saying is that Jorin had looked after my safety with reckless abandon, and might lose his life for it. Who knows how long he's been bleeding.

"It looks like, from the way the surrounding skin is pulled outward, that a Wight must have sniffed the hole out and tore at it with…" Quinn stopped his diagnosis once he met Farah's eyes. She felt her face contort with pain and regret.

Quinn softened his expression. "Maybe Ire can help," he said. "But he doesn't have long."

As if on cue, a flapping black mass came to rest on a branch nearby. It was Max. Farah knew that wherever Max was, Irulen would soon follow. All she could do was apply pressure against the wound and hope he made it in time.

* * *

Irulen followed in the direction Max flew. The raven would come back from time to time to adjust the course, but the wizard hadn't seen his friend for some time now. He figured this meant he was heading in the right direction and that soon he would be among his friends again. Kay followed silently behind him. She had gotten them into a sticky situation, but he felt she was sincere in wanting to make amends. She was also a damn good shot with the crossbow. He had a feeling that Kay would come in handy no matter the situation.

The woods were quiet save the crunching of fresh snow underfoot. They were fairly close to the road when Max came flying full speed. Irulen put out his hand and the bird landed. He cawed loudly and flew away once more.

"Something is amiss," said the wizard, unceremoniously. He ran after Max and was surprised when Kay blew past him in a blur of black and kicked up snow. Her speed pushed him to dig into his reserves and run faster. Although designed to keep him warm, his attire worked against him during sudden bursts of activity. His core heated rapidly, his lungs ran short of breath, and mucus began to build up behind his nose and throat. His sweat froze and broke free of his face even as the salty liquid pulsated from his pores. It was a rarity for Max to give the sign of death outside of their profession. Irulen expected the worst.

The road wasn't as close as he thought, and it took a good deal of broken branches, fallen logs, and torn skin before he reached it. The wizard paused in the middle of it and looked left and right. There was no one.

"Ire!"

Irulen matched the familiar voice with Quinn's face in the woods. He ran to him. "This way." He led Irulen to Jorin's side. Kay was already there squatting next to him. Jorin was awake and was asking Farah to break the news to his father and family. "Please, just let him know that I'm sorry I won't see the family again."

"No," she whimpered, holding her free hand against his cheek. "You tell them yourself."

Irulen saw the wound and knew there would be little he could do.

Kay continued speaking. "I fed him a vial of a potion derived from the blood of a frightened horse. The fear fuels him for the moment, but not for much longer."

Irulen could see that the adrenaline was already wearing off, and that Jorin was too far gone. To save him now would be to owe death a favor, a debt that Irulen wouldn't want to pay.

Jorin fell silent, and Farah turned her head to Irulen. "Use your magic!"

"I cannot." He lowered his head. Though necessary, the refusal did not come easy.

"You can use it however you please." Her cheeks flushed crimson against the cold…or, more likely, with anger.

"I may, but then I have to accept the consequences. For me to save him now would be the first step down a dangerous path. Magicians who play with death and life end up like the necromancer who made the wights. I can't save him now just to hurt others later."

Farah stood up and walked over to Irulen. Kay took her place pressuring the wound. The young woman came to a stop in front of the wizard and slapped him across the face. "Bullshit."

"He's right lass." Quinn winced at the look she shot him. "I was hoping he would say something different, but he's right. Power, even if used for the best possible intentions, will corrupt the user if he changes the natural order of things. For Ire to rob death of a life would be to invite darkness into his soul."

"I'm sorry," said Irulen, his voice little more than a whisper.

Farah walked to where Jorin lay still, knelt in the snow, and placed a hand on his cheek. Thea joined the troubled girl's side, and held her tight. They sat there huddled against the frost as the steam of Jorin's last breath escaped his mouth. All was quiet save the sobbing of the two young women. Irulen gave them what time he could, but they were still perilously close to the trail. Still, he felt Jorin needed to be honored.

Quinn helped the wizard carry the body a little farther away from the trail. They used oil to melt a surface area and took turns using the only shovel they had to excavate a hole. Kay moved back and forth between the men and the women, obviously not comfortable in either's company.

They worked tirelessly, and before long Jorin rested in his grave. Kay leaned over and put her hand over his mouth and checked his pulse one last time. It was an uneasy thing, double checking a man's death. She retreated and stood by Quinn and Irulen.

Quinn, who looked surprisingly proud for the situation, declared, "It is as fine a resting place as any lad could ask for."

"What now?" Kay remained stone-faced.

"Should we have a ceremony?" Irulen searched their expressions, unsure what was expected of him.

Kay shrugged and went to retrieve the young women.

Quinn unloosed his flagon, which he had restocked at the *Duck*. He also had plenty of alcohol stored, which made for heavy baggage. "Well, I'll tell you one thing," he said, as the women rejoined them. "This man had honor and bravery. He had balls that clanked as loud and metallic as the mightiest of them."

Farah's mouth fell open, visibly taken aback by the words.

"Everyone has their own way of coping with death." Irulen spoke quietly, but poignantly. "Quinn is a ruffian, but his words are well intended."

"Here, here!" cheered Quinn as he poured a drought of mead from his flagon onto Jorin's lips, then tossed the container to Kay.

The bounty hunter stepped forward and lifted the flagon. "Here lies a good fighter, unknown to me, but loved by his friends and family." She drank and tossed the flagon across to Thea who fumbled it clumsily.

"Like most of us," she started off shakily, "I had just come to meet this man." She took a deep breath. "He helped save my life, and I promise to honor his death until my own."

"Well said," Quinn praised.

Thea handed the flagon to Farah on her right.

A strand of Farah's red hair stuck frozen to her cheek.

"There are too many things to say, but the words won't come."

Silence hung in the air. Irulen shifted a little, but waited her out nonetheless.

Farah soon spoke again. "Even if I spoke about how we grew up together, or how Jorin was my first kiss, what good would it do? You all don't know him. Here is Jorin, being buried, and none of his friends or family know of it." Her tears flowed warm, and the stream thawed the strand of her frozen hair. It floated in front of her, free in the thin, frigid air.

"He was a good man," she stated coldly, and fell silent. She sipped at the flagon and handed it to Irulen.

"I am sorry." He shook his head. "I'm not really sure what to say. I hope he's living the life he wanted in the afterworld, with whom he wants and where he wants to be."

"Living?" Farah searched his gaze. For what, he wasn't sure.

"Well, it's just something an old lady in my village once said about life and death. She was something like a shaman, or seer, and she believed that death was a final canvas, our one true freedom and reward for persevering in this world."

A frown creased her brow, and it took Irulen a moment to realize his explanation was insufficient, so he elaborated. "You see, the final moment between life and death is the key. She believed that in that moment you are given godlike power, that you are able to create your own afterlife through nothing more than your own imagination. You build everything from the meadows to the gate of entry. When you breathe your last breath in this world, your very own afterworld awaits you with infinite possibilities. It all comes down to that last instant. And something tells me that Jorin, who saw Farah before drifting into his eternal sleep, is living a life kinder than this one could ever be."

There was a heavy silence, and Irulen suddenly found himself feeling exposed. He drew his cloak around him.

"I don't recall you ever talking about where you grew up." Quinn cocked his head, obviously waiting for some sort of answer.

"Yeah, well, it was a pretty bland place." Irulen rubbed a hand over the back of his neck, hoping to ease some of the tension settling there.

"What was the old lady's name?"

"Wha—oh, her name was Lynnette."

Kay's eyes perked up at the mentioning of Lynnette, but she remained silent.

"Sounds interesting, that one," said Quinn.

Irulen paused. "Nah." He forced a smile. "She was

pretty bland too."

"Come." Quinn moved away from the grave. "The glow of dawn will be upon us soon. Let's settle and rest best we can."

* * *

Some hours later, after getting what little rest they could during the early hours of a cold morning, the group packed up and started south. The road, which only a short while ago was burgeoning with horse-drawn traffic and foot soldiers, was now surprisingly clear. Max flew overhead, lazily swooping to and fro, checking ahead and behind for other travelers. Farah had quit sobbing, but tears were still freezing to her cheeks. Thea walked to her right, their arms once again interlocked. Everyone remained silent, as if the first person who spoke would be breaking some kind of unwritten law.

The gradient of the road began to increase as they headed toward the south mountain pass, a place Irulen wanted to pass through during the day. Even in the frozen north there were different degrees of cold, and it didn't get much colder than in the high altitude mountain passes at night. It would be a victory if they could be on the other side by sundown and be spared a torturous night of wind and frost tearing at their skin.

Whether they were eager to leave Northforge behind, or whether they couldn't wait for a warmer climate, the group moved at a brisk speed. The terrain gradually grew rockier as they gained altitude. The road was well worn, and the snow had been compacted into slippery ice. The woods were quiet save for the rustling of some white-furred squirrels digging up their winter caches. The sound of birdsong was so distant that the listener would sooner think it was an echo of the mind. Birds didn't make a habit of hanging around where Max traveled. It wasn't because he was especially fierce, although he'd been known to chase off a bird from time to time, he was just different—as if he were less natural, perhaps.

The sun was near its highest when Thea looked behind her. "Oh my." She stopped short, and the others turned around, awestruck. They were high enough now where they could see across the valley. The city was to the left, but she stared at something far more menacing. Across the tops of the surrounding forest of conifers was a plain used for farming during the Great Defrost. And on this plain, two expansive armies stood across from each other.

"Looks like the Necromancer can kill from beyond the grave," said Irulen.

"Even with a bolt through his brain?" said Kay, straight-faced.

"Nah," grumbled Quinn, "This isn't his doing alone. This city has been a cesspool of politics and violence for some time now. The 'mancer just road the wave of it all."

"And drowned," Kay added again.

Quinn studied her for a moment, as if expecting her to laugh. When she didn't, he turned to Irulen for a lifeline. "What do you think?" he asked the wizard generally.

"I think it's best we use the vacant roads to make haste and get over this mountain before dusk."

Thea spoke up. "What about them, down there? Shouldn't we tell them—"

"What?" Irulen interrupted her, "That they have fallen for the ploy of a necromancer that was outcast by the brotherhood lurking underneath the streets of their city. Maybe we should tell Comcka and his folk that we're sorry for all the misunderstanding? How much luck do you reckon we would have passing through their sentries and ranks without being accosted?"

"You don't have to tell them anything," said Farah. "You have the power to prevent it, or end it."

"No—"

"Why not, for the same reasons you didn't help Jorin?" Her petulant comments stung, but there was nothing he could do.

"That isn't fair. And no, not for the same reasons. My power is finite, mind you. If I went down there and put on a display for, for what? Delaying a conflict for a few more years? Wars are natural, and if I'm going to descend like a god onto a battlefield, raining my magic and bringing to a halt—erasing—a historical event…if I am going to spend the lump sum of my magic it has to be worth it, because after that, I will never have magic again."

She tilted her head and lifted an eyebrow, obviously unconvinced.

In the valley far below, the armies of speckled dots began moving slowly toward each other—blocks and squares moving at different angles.

"There are battles a dime a dozen during this dark age," he continued. "How am I supposed to tell which one to alter? And who am I to intercede? Nature must take its course. Northforge will rise again united and washed clean. But for that to happen, sadly, blood will first be spilt."

The groups of ants below crashed mutely save for the perceived clash of steel being carried by the wind.

Kay stepped in to act as both mediator and expediter. "Come on," she said. "No reason to waste any more time. He'd not have made it in time anyway. They're already dead."

So it was that they ascended the south mountain pass with the blood of the north at their backs.

CHAPTER 11: COMING DOWN

Passing through the mountains was relatively uneventful. The road itself did not raise even half the height of the mountains bordering it. The road was rocky and moderately treacherous, and a fresh coating of snow hid potential pitfalls. More than a few times someone stumbled over a hidden rock iced into place beneath the granulated surface.

Soon after they found themselves descending to the other side, Irulen prepared Max to do his thing. He attached the sign around Max's neck and tightened up the leather straps of the bird's message holster. He lifted Max up on his hand into the air. The bird nodded his good bye and used his altitude to glide into the world below.

"Well." Irulen watched him go. "If we have to walk another three or so days, might as well see if I can pick up a small job along the way."

"We really ought to get horses." Quinn rubbed at his chin.

"Bleh." As if Irulen didn't already have enough responsibility. "Horses are a lot of work, and expensive…and it is not like we're traveling to the edge of the known world. We make due well enough."

"S'pose there is some truth to that. But I demand we get a pony or a mule at least, or else I'll buy one myself, and it'll carry nothing more than my personal belongings."

"Ha! Well, let's take a look whenever we're in town."

Quinn looked pleased with the compromise, and began whistling while he strolled. He clutched his fiddle to his chest underneath his tunic. Afraid that the instrument would be damaged because of the cold, he had moved it from a bag and was trying his best to keep it warm.

Farah and Thea, wrapped as tightly as could be, walked close together as if trying to bounce the heat between them back and forth.

Kay was as stoic as ever.

As he walked, Irulen fantasized about traveling alone with Max. His longer treks had usually, or always, been solitary, and he liked it that way. He enjoyed spending time with, looking after, and being responsible for, himself. He saw his companions like weights attached to chains running to his arms and legs. The only chance for him to get some space was through finding a job.

Hopefully, Max would return soon with news of a momentary respite, an investigation of a murder or theft. He huffed out a breath. *As if I'm ever hired to solve a theft.* He would much rather track down missing cattle than scrupulously analyze morbid scenes of death and decay. The wizard could never get over the way bodies tended to contort, bloat, and even burst when left to their own rot. He had smelt enough of loosened death bowels to last him a thousand lifetimes.

He fantasized about walking alone in a forest of icicles.

* * *

By Irulen's reckoning, they continued to make good time, and by the late afternoon found the ground beneath them beginning to even out.

A little further along, Quinn spoke up. "I reckon we've made good progress. I say we get off the road a bit and set up camp for the night, this time all comfortable like. We have time to actually set up camp proper and have a nice fire."

"I can go hunt for fresh dinner," Kay offered.

"Alright." Irulen searched each of their faces and sighed in resignation. "Sure, let's go find ourselves a nice patch under some heavy pine trees. There will be less snow under them and the boughs will help diffuse our smoke. I think I saw a patch to the western side of the road when we were higher up."

The wizard led the way with Quinn, Thea and Farah

behind him. Kay left straight away to hunt. It was another five minutes of walking through deep snow before they came across a grove of pines. Irulen found a spot with relatively clear ground save for old, browned pine needles. It was this place where they set camp for the night.

Within a half hour the tents were up, and the fire wood was stacked high. Irulen set about clearing an area for a fire. Ideally he would always surround a fire with rocks, but on that day he decided to safeguard the area by clearing it out of flammable debris. There he dug out a modest fire pit, filled it with light tinder that the women had collected, and sparked it to life using a knife and flint. While Irulen stoked the flames, the other three set about arranging logs and even their travel bags as seats.

All four of them were sitting quietly enjoying the flames in their own paradise when Kay returned with three rabbits strung to her back. She swung them forward haphazardly, spraying some of the blood across the snow.

"Look at the size of those," said Quinn. "I would pay a nice penny for game like that at the *Duck*."

"You can consider yourself in debt, then," Kay put the rabbits down.

Quinn, Farah and Thea each set about preparing one for dinner. Before long, three juicy and crispy flesh kebabs were roasting over the open fire. The rabbits' juices dripped on the fire every so often, evaporating instantly and sending puffs of edible pheromones into the party's olfactory systems.

"You know something?" asked Quinn

"What?" Irulen questioned his friend's question.

"This is nice."

"Ha! Really?"

"Yeah, I haven't been on the road for some time. Right now, with the flesh crisping and the fire…and the company. I'm happy."

Irulen laughed at his friend's simple truth.

"Yes, I guess you are right, what say you ladies?"

"Hungry," Kay uttered.

"Those are some big rabbits. They smell nice," offered Thea.

Farah played the word off her tongue, "Nice." A forlorn look pulled at her eyelids.

Thinking he divined her thoughts, Irulen spoke. "A fire has the ability to both elicit and obscure the truth."

"Truth is much like fire," Farah leaned forward and stared into the flames. "Hard to understand, ever-changing. Do you think Jorin would be sharing rabbit with me tonight, had I headed north?"

Irulen winced. He did not want, could not, respond.

"And both fire and truth burn to the touch," added Kay, her face edging on a smile.

"I would have truth." Shadows flickered across Farah's face. "I see lies and secrets in the darkness around us. But I see Jorin's face in the flames. His world ended because of the one I chose to build. I would have truth around this fire. Truth to join its warmth."

"How so?" asked Irulen.

"By divulging stories and secrets. I have little to tell, and few secrets to hide. But you all…" She dragged her finger across Quinn, Kay, and Irulen. "You all have things inside you I'd rather hear."

"How come you didn't point at *Thea*," Irulen protested, lamely, earning a cold glare from Farah.

Irulen shrugged. "*Secrets* are our only truly personal possessions. They are also our most prized possessions. We carry them because we don't want to be controlled by them."

"Still, I'd like to know more about who I'm traveling with." Farah singled out Quinn with her stare.

"P'raps she's right in this one." The flames moved as the brute bellowed. "'Tis a great night for good stories, don't you reckon?"

"Fine." Irulen cocked his head at his long-time friend. "If you tell them about Aldo then I will consider divulging something myself. But first, Farah should offer us—"

"It was Jorin who I gave my virginity to," she said,

plainly.

Irulen was stunned by the interruption. "What? Couldn't you have started with something else? I thought, I thought you were more...*innocent* than *that!*"

Kay laughed, and everyone grew silent for a moment. Her laughter was awkward and halting, like someone who had long failed to exercise the proper facial muscles needed for such cheer.

Quinn involuntarily showed her how it was done. His belly rumbled as he took in the scene.

"It was two years ago, when we were sixteen years. It was curiosity more than anything. You see, the truth can be disappointing," Farah said, "but now you are closer to knowing the *real* me, like it or not."

"I like it not," the wizard declared.

"Ha!" Quinn wiped a tear from his cheek as he reigned in his laughter. "Well folks, nothing makes a campfire better than having good stories told, and I have the first tale to tell. Grab yourselves some meat, drink, and prepare to be serenaded."

Irulen sighed. Whenever Quinn told a story, it tended to be much more detailed and longer than it needed to be.

"It all starts to the west of here; off the coast, over the sea, and along the shores of a distant Isle named Fogmorrow. It was there, in an unnamed fishing village, that little Quinn was born. My father, of course, was a fisher. My mother was also, in fact, in her own right. Legend in the village has it that my mother birthed me while they were out fishing. The sun was setting and my mother's screams spread across the waters like the screeches of a gull. Some elaborations have it that my parents *used* the waste of my birth as bait to *fish* with on the way home. Imagine that!"

Irulen dropped his head into his palms. Once Quinn began, there was little that could be done to stop him. What happened for the ensuing hour was a meticulously crafted rendition of Quinn's childhood. His listeners were equally bored and impressed at the amount of detail he pulled from his memories.

Through all his stories one name kept popping up, Aldo. Irulen knew who it was, but the women were intrigued by the lack of detail attributed to a name that seemed to intertwine with Quinn's every memory. Eventually, their curiosity was satiated, and once it was, they would never look at Quinn the same again.

"Would you tell us about Aldo?"

"Aldo?" Quinn raised an eyebrow at Farah's question about his friend. "I'll tell you about Aldo. Showed me what it meant to have friendship, he did. He was ever present in my life, in anything I ever did. Whenever I fished, I fished with him. When I got in trouble, he'd share in it. When I told a joke, he'd build off it. We had our own names for people and things. Heck, we practically shared our own secret language."

"The thing is, I spent the first eighteen years of my life in an interlocking existence. I was with him so much that the other children colored us gay and made fun." Quinn put his hands out, quick to dispel their curiosity. "That is, until we beat the snot out of all of 'em."

"Our relationship wasn't like that. It was in the way that we shared everything and often knew what each other would say before we said it. But as for sodomy, well, I'm sorry to disappoint you. It's more than possible to have an intimate relationship between men without that sort of thing."

Quinn stood up and gave Irulen a pat on the back. "Just look at Ire and me! Best of mates, now, aren't we?"

"Indeed, but please, do continue." Irulen removed Quinn's hand from his shoulder.

"Right." Quinn paused, seeming to search his head for where he had left off. "Right, OK, so we were what we were and we grew older as such. Soon it was time for us to look forward to our futures. I was always the imaginative one, and I always dreamt of travel. Aldo, not so much. He was more than content fishing away for the rest of his life. There was a local girl, by the name of Henrietta, and he planned on making an honest woman out of her. But…"

"But I had other plans. I wanted to travel, like I said, but I didn't want to go it alone. We were of fighting age by then, and

I knew my large stature could be my key to a grand adventure. I'd see the world, lay with exotic ladies, experience exotic drugs, and sleep under exotic stars. I wanted someone to share it with, because if you don't share these sorts of things with someone then who is there to say they really happened? Who would be there to separate your imagination from reality?"

"So I talked to Aldo. I convinced him that joining a battle party and crossing the sea would be beneficial to him and me alike. I'd get everything I wanted, and he would raise enough money to support his would-be wife for years to come. He was unwilling at first, but he had just enough youth left in him for me to exploit." Quinn paused, massaging the bridge of his nose between his fingers. "He agreed. We spent a fortnight saying our goodbyes. I to my family and he to his family and girl. The lass agreed to wait for him, and we were all happy."

"We set off, packs on our backs, to the King's hall. King Eoric, was the name. The realm wasn't all that large, but the area was known for fierce warriors. We met with the king, pledged our fealty to him, and soon found ourselves sparring and making ourselves ready for the next great adventure. I remember how grand the king looked, with his gold and finely crafted beard. He looked like a god, and in him we placed our trust. This was the man who could give us everything we had ever wanted. He was a strong man—a good man."

"For weeks, stretching into months, we trained in killing, drank, and trained some more. We would help harvest timber to build ships and revisit the lumber sites at a later date. We would then sort through the wood mulch for magic mushrooms. This was how we coped with the strenuous cycle of labor and sleep. Regardless, time seemed to travel at lightning speed. Before we knew it, the eve of our departure was upon us."

"There was a great festival with music and the smell of cooked wild boar in the air. It was that night I decided I wanted to play music. I ended up bartering the last of my coin for a fiddle I would practice during the downtime of our journey."

"Oh," he said, poignantly, "that was the night I lost my virginity, at *eighteen*, a more proper age for that sort of thing I think."

Farah scoffed.

"The next morning," he continued, "we were all set to go. We were assigned to a long ship, one of ten I believe, and we took our places at the oars. We met the captain, a man called Ore, and he put us to work rowing out of the harbor. Soon the labor paid off, the weather smiled upon us, and we set our sail to the east. The ship darted through those waves like a spear through a spleen."

"Every hard day was washed away by a beautiful night. After dusk, the lights of the night sky dazzled our eyes while we rested. It was during this time that I found a musician willing to start teaching me the fiddle. Although, I wasn't allowed to play much, since the terrible sound of my playing would wake the others."

"Soon we received word that landfall was expected within a day or two. Seagulls circled overhead and the waves began to grow more active. It seemed that even as we approached land, something else approached us—a thing much faster than we could ever hope to be."

He paused for a moment as if steeling himself for the next part of his story. "I never knew a storm could up come so quickly. If I was ever taught anything, it's that there are clear signs and indicators of oncoming tempests. In this instance, we never had a chance—for there were no signs. It was a rogue wave that did us in. I remember very little of the actual event, of the boat being tossed and smashed on rocks hidden by the water's surface. What I do remember was all of us being tossed like ants from a hand. The ship broke apart and shattered, and it was then—when the real storm hit, that I saw a monster. It was one tentacle that retracted from the boat and into the tumultuous sea. One large tentacle of something hideous, but that's all I saw of it."

"I figured myself lucky at first. I had found a sturdy piece of driftwood and even managed to pull Aldo safely across from me. We clung to the piece best we could and collected more debris as it came by. We had the ingredients of a makeshift raft, but no means with which to fasten it together. That night was the worst night of my life. We held on as we were tossed to and fro, and hoped beyond hope that the current was taking us into shore."

"But our endeavor was not fated to end happily. It was during the stormiest part of the night, as lightning flashed and thunder boomed, as rain splattered our already drenched faces, that Aldo lost his strength. For whatever reason, he fell unconscious and slipped downward into the water. I reached across, grabbed his arm, and held it tight. For untold hours I held on as best I could."

He paused to strip a piece of rabbit off the fire. "Don't forget about the rabbit, it's starting to burn." Kay took the rabbits from the fire and staked the bottom of their spits into the ground.

"Between holding together the debris on which we were floating, and holding onto him, my muscles began shaking uncontrollably. I offered my own life to anything listening if Aldo simply woke up and climbed further atop the raft. My muscles ripped and my body shivered from the cold. Eventually, my hand gave out. I don't remember making the decision to drop him. I just remember my hand opening. And I remember, just before his head hit the water, his eyes opening and meeting mine. Then he was gone." A visible shiver ran through him, and he shook his head, obviously battered by the pain of regret.

"Much of the debris loosened with him and I couldn't keep it all together. I ended up clinging to a single piece of wood. You all have seen it, but it too is gone now. The day after the next I found myself washed ashore on this side of the sea. And since that day I have lived with the knowledge that I had persuaded him to come on that journey. I imagine the face of Aldo's young Henrietta as she looked out to the sea day in and day out, waiting for his return. The image of that face is what has kept me from ever trying to return to that Island. The Quinn that island knew, like Aldo, died on that day."

"I don't know what to say." Farah lowered her gaze to the fire.

"That story gets me every time," Irulen quipped. He dodged as rabbit bones flew at him from an unseen source. It seemed like they came from Kay's direction, but the wizard wasn't sure.

"Well, now you know about me, and the lives I ruined," muttered Quinn. His demeanor lightened suddenly. "But it feels good to share, truly it does. Ha! So who's next?"

"Kay." Irulen threw down the challenge and stared at her.

Kay looked at him sideways. "I've never spoken about my life before," she said.

Irulen saw much of himself in Kay. Mentally, he felt, they were in very similar stages. She and he were closed off and distanced from other people. The main difference between them, as he saw it, was that Kay was moving toward people while he was steadily drifting away. At the campfire they were also at a crossroads, and Kay went on ahead to where Irulen was not yet ready to tread.

"Alright." She shifted, before settling in to tell her tale. "I'll share. Firstly, 'Kay' is not my real name. 'K' is actually the first letter of my name."

"Do we get anything for guessing?" asked Irulen.

"Yes, you get the prize," she stated, sardonically.

"I was eight years old when I last went by my old name. I'm from the southern lands of the summer forest. The weather is mild at its coldest, and snow…" She waved her hand around her. "Snow was something that never happened. Our winter was full of rain and typhoons."

A novice story teller, Kay spoke at times haltingly and at other times hastily. But the sheer imagination of a warm place had the northerners enraptured.

"The rainy season had come to an end, and the weather was warm that day. The constant rain was quite unpleasant. Only the most durable crops could survive the torrential downpours, and hunting was much more troublesome. Still, spring brought days longer and drier, more enjoyable and fair. The flora sprouted in full and the tropical forest filled with dazzling displays of bright colors. The cycle of nature might not be as drastic as in the north, but the wheel of life revolved there just the same.

"I remember sitting in a field. The weather was pleasant. A light breeze caressed my cheeks and bees skirted about the flowers. My hands sorted through the grass and picked out the very best flowers.

Father was off on a hunt and mother was in the distance tilling soil. Seeds were being sewn and soon we would be provided with fresh fruits and vegetables. The winter harvest had been nice—I liked raspberries very much—but it was the spring and summer that provided my favorite bounty, apricots." A wistful smile played at the corners of her mouth. "A good apricot was truly rare—they never kept well for long and so tasted the best soon after being plucked from the ground.

"Being out and about on my own…I was new to this freedom. Being eight years old, I was now responsible to look more after myself. All of the village children had been trained to look for snakes in the grass, and our eyes were honed to detect the slightest shimmering of a snake in the grass. Perhaps it was because I paid so much attention to the grass near me that I did not recognize the larger threat. A great shadow cast over me, and I thought that perhaps a cloud had covered the sun. I looked up as a sack came down over my head. I found myself caught in a world of darkness, chaos, and confusion. I fainted."

"I will always remember the words with which I was awoken; 'Let me see those nice pretty eyes.' I blinked against the bright sunlight hitting my face."

"Atta girl, how are you feeling?"

"A blurry shadow lingering over me came slowly into focus. The face was an older man with a balding head and a skinny, wrinkly face. He had disturbingly large black pupils and a single black streak ran from the bottoms of each of his eyes down his face.

"'Who are you?' I asked. 'And where are my…'" Kay's voice drifted off as if she were reliving the exact moment.

"'Oh dear child, my poor child. Your parents are

missing. Your village was attacked. I found two men here in the woods, carrying you away in a potato sack. I slew them and saved you. Dragged you from them so you didn't have to see the blood, I did.' He smiled wide with yellow teeth. His breath was foul."

"My eyes began to tear, 'I don't know,' I said."

The stranger spoke to me again, "'The thing is, I'm a hero, Prince Erik is my name. I'm on a quest.'"

"'Can you take me home?' I asked."

"'No, it wouldn't be a good idea. I'm not even sure where your home is—lots of raiders wandering about these woods, we have to move and be quiet.'"

And this is how I came to be a slave. The man called me princess and kept me in his hovel a few days' walk from my hometown."

"I'm so sorry." Tears pooled in Farah's eyes, but she struggled not to allow them to escape. This woman was too strong, she wouldn't want sympathy. She shivered.

Kay nodded before she continued. "For four years he kept me, raped me, and used me. I knew how many years because he would celebrate the day he abducted me. We'd have a party once a year to celebrate our 'union' as he called it."

"After three years, he started trusting me with walks to the market and such. He told me he knew everyone there, and that they knew I was his. If I told anyone, they would hit me and bring me straight back to him. I believed him, until life became unbearable enough that I didn't care."

"At just about that time, a strange man came riding into town carrying a sketch of a man. He said the subject of the sketch had a bounty on his head for robbery. No one wanted any part in identifying my captor. Small towns in the south don't like people invading their privacy. *Perhaps*, I thought, *if they knew what he did to me. They didn't care about robbery, but just maybe they'd care about me.*"

"I did the bravest thing in my life, I stepped forward. 'He stole *me*,' I said. A few of the townsfolk who were familiar with the man stepped forward. Perhaps he wasn't lying about them knowing after-all. The bounty hunter jumped from his horse with a crossbow drawn in his left hand and a sword in his right. 'Careful, now,' he said. His warning wasn't enough, and three men charged at him with meat cleavers and the like. One took a bolt to the neck, and the other two fell to the ground in diced pieces. The rest of the people portrayed either feigned or real ignorance."

"The man once again straddled his horse and held his hand to me. I grabbed it. With that choice, my life began to change once more. We road to the horrible hermit's dwelling and dismounted. By the time my feet hit the ground, my captor was running away into the woods. He fell over onto the ground as a crossbow bolt impaled his hamstring."

"'Don't try moving again,' said the bounty hunter. 'My name is Evan, and I am here to collect you for a bounty in the town of Sunshadow.'"

"'What for?' *Prince Erik* whined."

"'For stealing a pig.' The man spat on the ground." Kay paused. She used the back of her arm to swipe the sweat from her brow.

"Evan walked up to the man and tied his wrists, and then he turned to me."

"'You know what I need girl?' he asked."

"'What?'"

"With that, Evan pulled out his sword and sliced the head clean off my tormentor. I never knew a head could be parted from a body so easily. I've still not quite figured out the trick. I saw the man's death as if time itself slowed. The life shedding from his eyes, his head falling opposite his body, it was all poetic and beautiful. To me, his death was the closest I've ever come to that day picking flowers."

"'I need a witness to say he fought me,' Evan said, as he untied the man's hands. He checked the wrists to make sure there were no marks."

"'When I shot him he turned on me and ran at me with this knife,' the bounty hunter pulled out a knife as he talked. 'I had no choice but to, with my expert dexterity, part his head from his body.' Before I said anything, Evan stabbed himself in the right arm with the knife. 'Not before he grazed me, however.'"

"I nodded my pledge to verify his story. And I did, some days later when we made it to Sunshadow, I repeated everything he asked me to. He tried pawning me at an orphanage but I refused. Eventually, he agreed to keep me on. I was a handy instrument; it was much easier for a young girl to snoop about than an attention grabber like Evan. He became my mentor, and he taught me everything I know. Sadly, one job went terribly wrong, and I lost him some ten years later. But that, at least, is a story for another day and another campfire."

Kay's story was much shorter than Quinn's but had an equally heavy impact on the audience.

"I'm sorry for what happened to you," Thea offered.

"Thank you," Kay replied, "but don't be. I've learned to own all my experiences, good or bad, I channel them to strengthen myself."

"Still, that sounds awful." Quinn's gaze held hers.

"That shit-eater is dead now," Kay said, vehemently, "and if Irulen's words about death hold any weight, he is forever caged in a realm of terror. There will be no peace for his spirit."

Irulen spoke. "Sadly, there are too many creatures like that, human and other, in this world. So, your true name, is it Katherine?"

"No."

"Is it—"

"And before you annoy me to violence, you can only guess once a day."

"I want to ask you something else," said the wizard. "Why did you tell us all that if you just met us? Seems quick for me."

Kay seemed a little abashed at the question, and she hesitated before she answered. "Because I've never *known* anyone for *long*, and you happened to draw the lucky number. It's been a heavy burden. I wanted to tell someone."

"Fair enough," he said.

"Well," Farah said, as her gaze found Irulen. "How about you?"

Farah's face glowed fair across the fiery pit. For a moment, Irulen thought he could either kiss it or punch it.

"I can't," he answered.

"Why not?"

"You just wouldn't understand."

"Make me."

"Quinn and Kay's stories are in the past, they are healing. Mine still walks the earth." Irulen was surprised at how clear the sentence came out, as if it was pressing against his lips this entire time.

Farah offered her rebuttal. "Well, it seems that we're all stuck together, and at least I have no idea what we're doing once we bring Thea to her village. We need to know what's going on. In there." She pointed at his head.

"I'm beginning to hate the person that brought you into this mess," said the wizard.

Quinn interjected into the conversation, "I think that person has hated himself for some time now."

"Oh, now you're going to jump in?" questioned Irulen, surprised at the betrayal.

"She has a point. Though Thea is going home, Farah and Kay's futures are in the air. You know I'm bound to help you with whatever you need to do, but they should know what's what."

"Just," said Irulen, as he stood. "I have to piss. I'll be right back." He heard them speaking as he walked away but their words were not clear.

CHAPTER 12: TRUTHFIRE

Some time passed before Farah stood up. "This is a rather long time he's taking."

"Maybe he had to feed the dung beetles as well," responded Quinn. "In which case, should you ladies have need...I packed a bunch of cleaning leaves..."

"Thank you, but—"

"Don't mention it," Quinn said, as he handed stacks to each of the women.

Farah sighed and sat back down.

Kay spoke suddenly. "It has something to do with this Lynnette character."

"What does?" asked Thea.

"Whatever's bothering the wizard. Just before I put a bolt into the necromancer's eye socket, the man mentioned Lynnette to Irulen. She said 'hi', apparently."

"So she isn't some old lady from his village?" asked Farah.

"Whether she's from his village or not, I can't tell you. But she is clearly not some old, kindly woman if she is in league with that like."

Farah turned to Quinn. "Who is Lynnette truly?"

"I don't know." He shrugged. "As long as I've known him, I've never heard that name mentioned."

"Is he a good man?" Farah surprised herself with the question.

"Ire? Well, I don't know if I'm an authority in the *good* man business. But, yes. I think so. Though, doing what he does takes a toll on him."

"How so?" Farah asked.

"Death...decay...evil in its many forms great and small, he lives in it... It is difficult to be alone, submersed in darkness, and resurface clean of stain. It leaves him...a tad...*cynical*." Quinn laughed to punctuate his drawn out thought.

Feeling satisfied with his insight, the burly man continued unprovoked. "For me, I shun my demons with booze, women, and good food. While he has often joined me in such noble endeavors, he carries *his* demons like little pets. He cares for them and keeps them well nourished. They can often be glimpsed, lingering right behind his eyes." Quinn brought a flagon to his mouth as if marking an end to his illuminating insight. He tossed it to Kay, who was quickly becoming a preferred drinking companion.

As she removed the flagon from her mouth, Kay offered a plan. "We could torture it out of him. I'm sure I could get the jump on him out there in the woods."

"Tempting," said Farah. "I'll give him a little more time, then I'll drag him back and hold his cushioned end to the fire myself."

* * *

Irulen had finished urinating and now stood in a small clearing. He found a suitable trunk along the edge and sat looking up to where the treetops met the stars. His gaze traveled far beyond the stars and into the darkness that lay beyond. The world fell away around him and he found himself in another time and place.

"I think it's dead," Irulen said, as a frown contorted his young face.

"Let me see," said Lynnette. She grabbed a stick and poked at the salamander. "Ewww, I think it is."

Just moments ago Irulen had held the salamander in his hand, keen on showing his friend how the reptile detached its tail when it was threatened. The salamander was slimy to the touch and proved to be faster than Irulen thought. It had squeezed out of his hand, landed on a hard rock, and remained still.

"I feel sad," Irulen said.

"Death is sad," she responded.

"I feel bad also, I killed it."

"Well, let's not do it again. In fact, let's *feed* the next salamander we find."

The wrinkles of Irulen's forehead pointed downward in thought. "But then we'd be killing whatever we feed it," he said.

"But all life must consume life. Old Lady Barnaby told us that."

"I remember," Irulen said, defensively. "Let's just not feed anything to anything or touch anything, OK?"

"OK. But what about your magic?" she asked.

"What about it?"

"Can you bring it back to life?"

"No."

"Why not?"

"I'm not allowed. *Nothing that messes with life or death*, mother said."

Lynnette looked disappointed. Irulen hated when she looked disappointed.

"I'll tell you what," he said. "I'll do it."

Lynnette smiled widely and clapped her hands in anticipation.

Irulen made a dome shape with his hands over the salamander. His friend's eyes widened as a glow began to fill the young boy's hands.

The girl's eyes darted as Irulen was suddenly pulled away. His mother had him in hand. "What are you up to?" she asked.

To answer her own question, his mother surveyed the scene. She saw the dead salamander where he had held his hands.

"Go back to the house, Ire." He opened his mouth in protest only to be met with his mother's glare. He began to slowly back off as he heard his mother tell Lynette to go home.

"Please," Lynnette started to plead. She never wanted to go home. "Please, no!"

"Go home to your parents." Lynnette saw Irulen already

walking, and complied.

Irulen was alone with his thoughts, staring blankly, when a loud crunching sound roused his senses. Someone was closing in on him. He cast a spell that melded him into the shadows. It was the one spell he used liberally. It didn't take much of his power, and he often found himself in the need of avoiding people.

* * *

Unfortunately for Irulen, Farah had a knack for tripping over things.

"Damn it," he yelled, as she fell on right on top of him.

"What the—where did you come from?" she asked.

"Apparently I've come from privacy to intrusion." He disentangled himself from Farah and sat beside her.

His face looked as if it shimmered in the moonlight.

Tears? "I'm sorry," she said, softly.

"It's fine."

"What's the matter?"

"What? Oh, nothing." He brushed the shimmer from his cheeks.

"Okay." She sat next to him calmly.

They remained in silence for a long time. Crickets and owls serenaded them.

Eventually, Irulen broke his silence. "The irony of it, I knew all about what would happen if I messed with death, but was ignorant to the effects of divesting magic. I mean, I suspected, but I was blinded."

"Divesting magic? Are you telling me that…?"

"Yes."

"That you…?"

"Created an imp once and it still crawls about today—leaving a trail of misery in its wake."

Farah was horrified at this secret. "Just like the one that took me?"

"More powerful than that one, but very similar in looks I'd imagine."

"You never saw it?"

"I've never gone after it."

"Why?"

"I'd rather not talk about it." He stood and dusted himself off.

"Are you going to tell the others?"

He shook his head. "What do you want me to say?"

"Just the truth," she said, "as much as you can."

He'd started walking back to the camp when Farah grabbed his arm.

"I trust you," she said.

"Well, that's your problem."

She threw his arm down in disgust and started walking away from him toward camp.

"Wait," he said. "Just know, I'll do my best for you. Your quest is different than mine, but I'll help—"

A momentous roar shrieked across the silent night sky.

"Quinn!" Irulen yelled, as he ran toward the camp. Quinn's battle cry was soon joined by clashes of steel and screams. He cursed his complacency. Without Max, extra vigil was required.

Irulen was about halfway there when he ran into someone full force. It took him just a moment to recognize Thea. She was as wide eyed as an arrow-pierced doe. Farah ran up behind them.

"Five." Thea pointed the way. Irulen pulled out his sword, handed it to Farah, and ran toward the chaos. He pulled out his knife as he drew close. In a flash, a creature came charging across the front of Irulen, toward the campfire. His reflexes were quick—he grabbed the thing and stabbed into its throat. Irulen looked it in the face. The creature was no creature at all, instead it was a soldier of Northforge that Irulen straddled.

Irulen arrived at the fire just in time to hear another bloodcurdling scream. Quinn had buried his axe in the inside of an assailant's shoulder. The blow shattered the man's collarbone and split his heart in clean halves. Like a sack of potatoes, the body crumpled before the berserker named Quinn. "Come get a taste, if it's a taste ye want, ye mongrels!"

Kay, bleeding from an arrow wound, stood over another.

"Mercy!" he cried.

"You shall have mercy," she answered. She raised her crossbow as he ran into the darkness. A single bolt followed him into the shadows, followed by a terrified scream and ensuing silence.

"That's three, I stabbed the first one with the roasting spit." Quinn indicated another slouched corpse on the ground. Its hand had landed in the fire and filled the area with the aroma of freshly cooked man meat.

"Smells little different than pork, don't you think?" Quinn waggled his eyebrows.

"Four, actually," Kay said. "I put the one down that shot me earlier. He should be out there with his friend, rotting as raccoon food."

The three of them turned at once to find one of the bandits holding a knife to Thea's throat. His hand trembled fiercely. Sweat ran down his brow, and his eyes darted sporadically.

"Please," he said, "I just want some food and I'll go."

A single bead of blood ran down Thea's neck from the bandit's shaky hand.

Irulen held his hands up as if in surrender. "On my word, you let her go, you walk free."

Kay smiled coolly from behind the wizard. "And if you do not, you will die here, slowly."

Almost immediately Thea was released and ran behind the party.

"Well, it seems you made the—" Irulen froze.

The bandit fell to his knees with a shadowy figure behind him. The sharp end of a sword protruded from his chest.

"Not his choice, after all," Irulen said, as he saw the fire light play over Farah's face. She had run him through as he held her friend. The man's mouth was trying for words that weren't to be found.

Quinn sighed and walked over to suffering man. "That's enough carnage for one night, poor fellow." He dragged the man and his gurgling blood fountain into the darkness of the woods. There was a heavy sound, like that of wood being chopped. Then nothing for the space of time it took Irulen to take a deep breath. Quinn's return was indicated by the crunching of snow underfoot.

"Did everyone get to eat?" he asked. "My axe is full." The big man surveyed the scene and looked to Irulen. "You take care of things here, I'm going to scout near the road." Irulen nodded his agreement.

As Quinn walked out into the blackness once again, Irulen set his attention to Kay and her wound. Farah sat beside Thea, both in shocked silence. Farah averted her gaze. "They came quick, but not quick enough," said Kay, as Irulen looked her over. "They were amateurs, fortunately."

"Deserters by the look of them," said the wizard. He stood up and looked around for metal unstained by blood. He found a small hatchet and walked over to the fire. He kicked the overcooked arm out of the way, and set the hatchet head to the fire. Kay didn't like where this was going.

"I'm going to need help," he said.

Thea stood up as a willing assistant.

"Come grab this a moment please."

The serving girl glided over and ceremoniously grabbed the hatchet handle. Irulen walked back over to Kay and examined her wound further.

"What we're going to do is easy. I am going to first break off the arrow head," Kay winced. "Then," he continued, "I'll pull this arrow out from the back. When I do, I need you to bring the hot steel over here and burn the shit out of one hole while I plug the other with a finger. When you're done searing the first hole, I'll get out of your way so you burn the second. Ready?"

"I knew you wanted to get inside me," Kay said. Irulen tore the arrow out. She joked through the grit of her teeth. "The method you've chosen, though, sure is surprising."

"Now!" Irulen called to his assistant as he put his thumb into the exterior hole on Kay's arm. Thea brought the glowing hot metal over and pressed it against the bleeding puncture on the inside of the arm. After a period of few seconds, Irulen grabbed the hatchet from Thea and finished the job himself. The metal had cooled fast in the wintry breeze, but Irulen was satisfied that the cauterization was complete.

"I always wanted get my skin inked." Kay used her healthy arm to support the wounded one. "I guess getting branded counts well enough."

"It is a beautiful thing." Irulen winked at her. He looked to Farah. "What about you?"

She looked up solemnly and spoke in an even voice. "What about me?"

"What happened, what you did…is not something to be taken lightly."

"I'm *not* taking it *lightly.*"

"I'm not saying…I mean, I know you aren't. I just—"

"I know," she said, quietly.

"How did it feel?" Irulen shot Kay a *not now* look which she ignored. "I take it that was your first time? I know what you're thinking. How final it was—and how easy. Killing is very mechanical, much like turning a knob or spinning a wheel. You have a poke here, squeeze there, and *bam!* Death. The light of a life, extinguished."

Farah glared at Kay with a brew of contempt and curiosity.

Kay laughed. "It is quite ironic, isn't it? Look at one of these corpses. Just an hour ago they were yammering, walking, pissing—God knows what else. But now they're broken. We broke a few integral parts and they are dead. They lay there, like rocks."

"You are quite the ghoulish one, aren't you?" asked Irulen.

"Maybe. I guess I am, but can I help it? I was quiet and sweet once, like Thea the flower girl here. Could I ever be again? Is it something I even want to be?"

"You are strong, I envy that," alleged Thea.

"By what measure?" asked Kay. "*Strength*. Such a murky word. Is it physical? I doubt I could beat many men in brute force, although I'd like to arm-wrestle Irulen."

Kay took a moment of self-reflection, and spoke again. "*Fortitude. Resilience.* I like those words better."

"You are strong of mind," said Thea. "Fierce."

"I'll vouch for the ferocity," offered Irulen.

Quinn lumbered back into the fire's light. "Looks clear for now, saw some stragglers but they seem to be sticking closer to the road. How is everyone?"

"Farah is soaking in her first kill. Thea is cursing herself inwardly for being the victim. Kay's arm is fine, but suddenly she won't stop yapping." The wizard cringed as the three women scowled at him.

"Ha!" Quinn laughed at him.

Traitor.

Quinn bent to grab an arm, then stopped and looked back up at Irulen. "You want to give me a hand putting these corpses out for the coons to chew on?"

"Yeah, sure."

There were only two corpses left near the campsite. They retrieved the one with the roasted hand first. This was the man Irulen saw Quinn cleave asunder, and his torso wasn't in the best of shape. They decided to each grab a leg, they and dragged it into the darkness. The camp was soon cleaned up, and the fire crackled peacefully.

"I reckon it's time for some true rest," said Quinn. "Time for us to start turning in, and take turns keeping an eye out."

"I'll take first watch," Kay offered. "The adrenaline still has me going."

"You'll crash quickly when it runs out," Irulen pointed out. "No, you should get as much rest as you can. As tough as you are, that wound is wicked."

Kay shrugged her shoulders.

"I'll stay up first, I have to cool off the nerves," Irulen

said. "Quinn is a different sort of human. He can sleep whenever, after experiencing whatever. Adrenaline doesn't affect him. He can sleep now and I'll wake him later."

Quinn, returning from a pee, overheard the last of what Irulen said.

"Suits me fine," he agreed. "Just finished watering a tree and am ready to place my head upon my pillow."

Nearby, Thea shook her head at Quinn's vulgarity, she stood and offered her hand to a despondent Farah.

"Ready to get some sleep?" Thea asked.

Farah nodded her acquiescence, grasped the hand offered to her, and pulled herself up. Thea leaned back and successfully helped Farah gain her footing. Arm in arm, the young women made their way toward the tents.

"Oh, you two should share the one on the left, it'll suit you just fine," said Quinn. A look of remembrance passed across the big man's face. "And before we all disperse," he continued, "I'd like to introduce you all to a little invention of mine." He began sorting through their supplies until he found what he was looking for.

"Ah, yes, here it is." Quinn smiled as he lifted what appeared to be four flat squares of wood. "My portable throne," he said, with pride.

"Your *what*?" asked an increasingly tired Kay.

"Each board is connected by a hinge, and the two end pieces share a latch. So what you do is…" Quinn demonstrated as he talked. "You fold the pieces inward so they make a proper square with a vacant middle."

Thea and Farah scoffed and rolled their eyes as they saw where Quinn's demonstration was heading. Kay looked bemused and somewhat interested. Irulen shook his head at Quinn's exuberance.

"Once you have the foundation connected and on sturdy ground, you apply the seat." Quinn held another flat piece of wood in his hand. It had been carved out in a horse shoe pattern. "You simply place your butt cheeks on the seat and, like magic, you have the comfort of an outhouse right here in the wilderness!"

Irulen offered facetious congratulations. "Some fine work you've done there, friend. And to think I've been leaning against tree trunks this whole time."

Quinn, failing to grasp the sarcasm, beamed proudly. "Well then," he said, "I'll leave it here for anyone who may find their bowels in need of relieving."

"To think," said Thea, as she led Farah to their tent, "I'll be home soon and missing out on portable privies."

Quinn spoke to Kay and Irulen as Farah and Thea entered their tent.

"I guess this leaves the problem of who shares the other tent for two?" Quinn pointed out, "Irulen and I can't fit in there together, so alas, lady, whose hot air would you prefer to keep the tent warm?"

Kay's nod indicated Irulen.

Quinn sighed. "Well, I guess it's hard to go toe to toe with a wizard."

"He's not as large," she said. Then, turning her head toward Irulen, she spoke again. "Which suits me, because I like my *space*."

"That's my type of gal," Quinn said, and slapped Irulen on the arm. Quinn lumbered over to the solo tent and sighed as he crawled inside. "Too bad, really," he muttered.

CHAPTER 13: PASSING FANCIES

On the eve of Irulen's thirteenth birthday and a week after the passing of Lynnette's mother, two teenagers sat on a boulder overlooking a forest stream. Irulen had his hand to Lynnette's cheek. His hand glowed hot as a fresh bruise disappeared from her face.

"My father is thankful he has you to cover these up." She rubbed the rejuvenated flesh under her eye.

"I'm sorry."

"He's gotten worse since mother died. He can't keep his hands..." she burst into tears. Irulen put his hand on her back and rubbed for some time. There was little he could do as long as she was under her father's roof. Comfort and healing was all he could offer. Eventually her sobbing subsided.

"You know," she said, "before my mother passed, she said that death could be anything you make of it. It is our one chance to remake the world in our own vision. The one last freedom afforded us."

Her words resonated off Irulen's ears, and he would build off them for years to come.

"How do you see death, Ire?"

"I don't know. I don't like thinking about things I'm scared of."

"I'm not so scared of it, anymore. I grow less scared of it every day."

He didn't like the implications of her words, but he was young with little to say.

"Don't die," he said.

"Why not?"

"Because I love you."

"Do you truly?"

"Yes."

"Then free me from my father."

"How? We can't marry for another three years."

"How, indeed." She echoed his thoughts, disappointedly.

Feeling his answer was somehow a disappointment, Irulen scrambled for words.

"I can offer you hope," he sputtered, "…and a promise. I will marry you, if you'd have me, and in three years' time we'll leave this place."

"Let's leave now."

"I can't right now, my family needs me, my brother…"

"They won't be any better off in a few years than they are now," she said, coldly.

"If we are a legitimate age, and can make a good living for ourselves, I can send them money, at least."

"Fine, but promise me, when we're sixteen, we can be together."

"I promise." Irulen sealed the pact with a kiss.

* * *

Irulen lurched forward as he was shoved from behind. It was all he could do to keep from falling face first on the ground. The world was covered with a fresh dusting of snow. The flakes clung to and toned down the red circles of blood from the previous night's skirmish. Irulen was left looking like a mythical ice creature.

"Some good lookout you turned out to be." Kay stretched her arms. "It's funny that you don't close your eyes to sleep. Never met anyone like that before."

"I was awake," he said.

"Maybe, but you weren't here, now were you?"

"I guess not, not just then anyway, I was up and alert for most of the night."

Quinn's groggy head stuck out of his tent. "Then why

didn't you wake me?"

"Didn't want to, was restless."

"Can't you mix up a potion for that sort of thing?"

"I'm a wizard, not a witch."

"Well," Quinn said, with a look of concern, "how about we keep an eye out, anyway."

"It's not all the time—just when things get hectic. I'll be fine." Irulen yawned as he looked around groggily, "No Max?"

Quinn and Kay looked around with him. "No," they said, in close to unison.

"Too bad." Irulen climbed to his feet and stretched. "I was hoping for some work. We still have a day and change left before we arrive at Thea's village—what was the name again?"

"Snowillow Pass," answered Quinn.

"Pass?" questioned Irulen. "I've been down this way but I don't recall walking through a Snowillow Pass."

Quinn scratched at his beard. "Well it's funny, you see, the town isn't really much of a pass at all. It is set back away from the road and its people take care not to wear trails to and from. They live among the trees, of which they clear very little. They are a secretive bunch living in a secretive place. It is a simple yet effective means of survival."

"That's right." Thea climbed out of her tent. "We've never been waylaid or pillaged in all our years. Only a few people, like my father, ever venture from it. The village is full of weavers, which is a much more quiet profession than smithing or milling."

"Aye," Quinn cut in, "and her father travels to Northforge every now and again. He always visits the duck when he does. You've met him, Ire. His name is Terrowin, a rather small fellow with a…stern personality. I consider him a friend."

"Is he the reason you hired Thea?"

"Yes, in fact, he asked me about a job. Said money was getting tight at the homestead."

"What's he look like, I can't seem to place him." Irulen stretched again, trying to work the stiffness from his cold muscles.

"Oh, I'd say he's about yay tall." Quinn held his right

hand up to his chest. "Squinty-eyed, slightly hunched," he continued, "often wears bright-colored robes to show off his wares."

Irulen's eyes lit up with recognition. "Of course! The little disgruntled fellow. Good for business because he drove people to drink." Irulen's eyes floated over to Thea and he caught himself. "A good man though," he stammered, "he was, is, truly."

Farah, the last to rouse, emerged into the morning light. Her hair was matted from sleep. Bags adorned her eyes. Every facial feature on her was slack. She looked, in every definition of the word, disheveled.

"Ah," said Irulen, as he took witness of the pretty mess. "Fair maiden! A lovely sight to welcome a lovely day."

"Rub your face in snow," she said.

"My, my." The wizard grinned. "Haven't you changed over a short time."

"Or maybe I wasn't as timid as you may have thought," she retorted.

Quinn, who was rustling through some supplies, pulled out a loaf of bread. "Is anyone hungry? I have bread Anastas baked." The group fell into a pit of silence at the unceremonious remarking of Anastas's name. Quinn, not one for subtleties, realized his folly. "May the fallen rest," he added. "It's hard to believe she won't be around to break Ire's balls or cook such delicious bread. Who wants a taste while we may?"

Quinn was, in fact, making it harder for the travelers to come forward and claim their share.

Irulen voiced his uneasiness. "I feel like you're offering us a piece of her body."

"Well I dare say her body wouldn't smell or taste as fresh," quipped Quinn, as he tore off a piece and chewed it, "but suit yourselves."

Irulen sighed and relented. "Toss it here."

Quinn tossed the loaf to Irulen, who tore a piece and passed it on to the others. The silence grew louder as they ate, and Irulen would do anything to quelch it.

"Quinn, did I ever tell you about the forest goblin I saw?"

"Only about ten times."

"Well, I never told the ladies—"

"Who are quite interested," said Farah, her attention seeming genuinely peaked.

"My father said such things don't exist," said Thea.

"There is much to be believed in this world," said Quinn, "and yet very little to be understood. I never believed in any magic or myth at all until I met Ire. Now, nothing surprises me. My mind just goes for the ride."

As he talked, Irulen pointed about the campsite so they could imagine how things were arranged. "I was on the trail, in between jobs…camping. It was deep into the afternoon, and the sun was looking ready to set as I pitched the tent. I had a fish over the fire. I was just about finished setting the tent and ready to plop next to the fire when Max starts squawking like a lunatic and takes off into the trees. Then…everything falls silent." Irulen paused dramatically, but then continued. "I hear a rustling sound, much like a squirrel or a hog rooting around. I grab my sword and quietly creep to the edge of the camp. I couldn't believe it, still can't really, but there it was. The thing was on all fours and was hairy like a hog, but there were characteristics that set it apart from that animal. Its head was humanoid and oversized, and its elongated snout was rounded at the end. The long nose was being used to root around the dirt. Its nostrils only took up a small portion of the snout, two ever-gasping holes close to the face. I watched with interest as the creature successfully pulled out a mushroom from the earth and began gobbling it up. Jagged teeth gnashed against each other as crumbs of food escaped the goblin's mouth."

Thea giggled nervously at Irulen's description.

Quinn chimed in. "Every new version of this story grows increasingly vivid in its detail."

Irulen, ignoring Quinn, continued. "Suddenly, it stopped eating mid chew. The mouth of the thing hung slack as it looked around cautiously. It stood up on its hind legs, rising perhaps two feet tall in total. It was then that I knew I had a goblin, a male goblin, looking at me. Its hair and penis dangling in the wind…"

Quinn laughed. "Ha! I like that addition!"

"I think we understood that a wild goblin's penis wouldn't be covered up," said Kay.

"Whatever," said Irulen. "Anyway, it stared at me for a moment, and just for that moment I thought he was friendly. I started over toward the creature as it eyeballed me suspiciously."

Irulen balled his left fist in the air and used the fingers of his right hand to walk toward it.

"I was a mere body length away from this critter when it unleashes a hideous scream. It seemed like air came out of everywhere. Snot blew out of its nose-holes. Next thing I know, the thing is running through woods with piss flying all about it. And so, I guess that's what it's like to scare a forest goblin."

Farah could not fight the smile on her face. "Full of crow, you are," she said.

"Whatever you say," Irulen said, defiantly.

Farah laughed, waited a moment in silence, and then took a step toward the wizard. "Wait, are you serious?"

Irulen nodded.

Farah pressed more. "This happened?"

"Do you not think it did?" he replied, coolly. "I guess you'll never know."

Farah looked from Irulen to Quinn, who shrugged his shoulders. Then she looked to Kay, who also shrugged, and whose eyes betrayed the slightest hint of amusement.

Thea spoke next. "I thought goblins were supposed to be larger and green-like…with reptilian skin."

"That's just in fairy tales," said Irulen, matter-of-factly. "Not the well-detailed oration of a wizard's travels."

Farah and Thea looked at each other dubiously. The moment was shattered by the clattering of supplies as Kay set about packing up the camp. She was soon joined by the others and together they made short work of the packing.

* * *

Before long, the group was again treading upon the open road. Farah shivered and wrapped her arms around her middle. They were joined by no others; the initial wave of refugees and deserters had washed past them. The exodus would have carried news of northern conflict, and so the group didn't expect to pass anyone heading north anytime soon.

It was an especially warm day for the far north. Snowy trees bled water and a breeze offered the slightest resistance to the walk. Irulen walked in front of the rest. He and the group traveled throughout the morning in relative silence. "I can almost guarantee that today will be an uneventful one."

"What makes you so sure?" asked Quinn, though he probably already suspected the answer.

"Max hasn't come back. We'd know through him if trouble was coming from the south."

"I wonder how our feathered friend is getting on, must be lonely, flying from town to town in search of work."

"I think he likes it," said Irulen. "Probably spent last night chasing a tail feather or two."

"More than likely, I suppose," the large man conceded.

As she walked, Farah found herself scanning the woods with rekindled interest. The story of the forest goblin had keenly stoked her imagination to life. Her eyes played along the forest floor and climbed upon the trees. She was subject to a common trick of the mind, simply that a listener believes there is a greater chance of something when they hear about it. It was as if Irulen's words were magical, and the mere mentioning of a forest goblin would summon the creature before Farah's very eyes.

It was a fanciful distraction, seeing the forest through imaginative eyes. She felt twelve again. Memories of Jorin, Brom, Isabel, and all the others flooded behind Farah's eyes. She remembered playing hide and seek. Isabel counted to thirty while the rest of the children hid. Farah remembered wedging herself under a bush and listening for any sign of discovery. She waited with baited breath as Isabel's plodding feet drew near. *Crunch, crunch, crunch.* Then everything was still. Farah thought that perhaps her footprints in the snow would give her away, but the entire area had been thoroughly well-trodden throughout the day. *Crunch, crunch, crunch, crunch*...the sound of the steps slowly dissipated into the cold air. Then, a scream.

Farah scrambled out from her hiding bush, scratching her face in doing so. Just a short distance away, but still not visible, Isabel shrieked and fell silent.

Farah paused.

Crunch, crunch, crunch, crunch... Footsteps came running toward her. The young girl braced for what came her way. Her muscles tensed, and her body shivered with anxiety. But it was no monster or assailant that came barreling through the woods. Isabel, wide eyed, crashed into Farah's arms. "Goblins!" she said, and grabbed Farah by the hand. "We have to go!"

Farah complied and ran with Isabel as she pulled her along. Branches and twigs scraped at their heels as they ran. The frightened girls entered a clearing and stopped suddenly. Brom and Jorin, holding masks they had fashioned from leaves and branches, stood there laughing. The memory began to blur, and was soon carried away on the frosty air. Older Farah watched as her younger self disappeared. She blinked, and it was gone completely. Still, she felt she had reclaimed an essence of herself, and held on to it tightly as she walked.

* * *

Irulen pulled off to the side and waved for the others to go on ahead. He unhinged his member and watched his steam rise off the snow. Truly there wasn't a large volume of liquid to be unloaded, and soon he was catching up with the others.

He was bored, and his boredom often elicited darker shades of thought. Ideas of a sexual nature carried him as he walked. As he looked at Farah, he thought of the first night he'd met her—they had even shared the same bed. He felt her warmth against his left leg, as if she was pressed against him at the present.

His thought jumped randomly to Thea. He wondered if she was a virgin. He'd once thought of Farah as being such an unspoiled flower and had been bitterly disappointed to find that fantasy extinguished. Jorin, who had grown up with Farah, knew her more intimately than Irulen likely ever would. Especially with the bitterness—the bitterness that seemed to fill her eyes at random. Even at her happiest, he often spotted sparks of anger emitting from her gaze. The reasoning, as he saw it, had much to do with her perception of his power. She had, at first, seen him as something he was not. A hero perhaps, but he was no hero. A hero would have saved Jorin. A hero would have done his all to stop the battle of Northforge. A hero would not have stood idly by, nor would he have run away from people who needed him.

She had been entranced with his magic, and her entrancement had been broken by his decisions. But who was she to judge him? She had only been welcomed to the world just a few days before. Still, he regretted the volatile status of their relationship—if it could be called a relationship—and found himself looking forward to the promise of reconciliation that is often offered by more peaceful times. The wizard laughed to himself. *We'll find little peace where we're heading.*

He thought back to Thea, who to her credit seemed less harsh in her judgments. And if she felt ill-will toward Irulen, she hid it very well. She kept her reservations to herself, much like everything else. Thea was not the attention grabber of the group. To the contrary, she was very much the wallflower. Irulen felt something of a pull toward her—not necessarily romantic, perhaps, but much like a snake charmer looking to coax her from a basket. He had even less time to get to know her and felt a little sad that the chance to do so would soon pass. She would be at home, safe, and he would be on his way to find Lynette.

Lynette. It had always bothered him that they had never shared sex. The wizard spat bitterly onto the frozen ground. He hadn't realized the harsh sound he'd emitted, and he smiled and waved his hand as the women turned on him. Different shades of curiosity graced their faces. They were still fifteen paces or so ahead of him. He smiled and waved his hand to go on, and they did. *I would have never thought I'd be more likely to kill Lynette than to be found in, and chased from, her bed by that bastardly father of hers.*

He blinked away tears. Truth be told, he felt no

emotional attachment to them. Irulen did not own the few tears that escaped his lower lids. There was nothing in him signifying sadness. He thought quickly to a time in Quinn's pub when he was so twisted on mushrooms and ale that his body purged itself. The wizard had just a moment before been chattering merrily. Then, without warning, he felt chunks erupting from his throat. There had been no warning or decision. His body had fully rejected the toxins he had injected it with. *What did my eyeballs expulse just then?* The wizard pondered at the thought for a little more than a moment.

Irulen realized his darker imagination was getting the better of him. When he snapped to from his fog, it was as if his senses had been unclogged. He saw, heard, smelled, and felt more clearly. In his mouth lingered an inexplicably foul taste. He found himself analyzing all the feminine curves and features through the fabrics of the women's clothes. The wizard suspected he had found out why Quinn so often stopped for pee breaks. There had been no time to stop and smell the roses with which they traveled. All three women were beautiful in their own way. Irulen found himself craving the company of a female form.

It was Kay, though, who most demanded his attention. She wore her clothing more tightly than the others, and somehow managed to lightly swing her hips as she walked with seamless effort. If any of them could divine what was on his mind, it was her. Kay had an assertiveness about her that appealed to the wizard's baser self. It passed through his inner ape and entwined itself cordially with his lizard brain. She was a sexual being and reminded Irulen of a succubus meant to invade ones dreams, or a forest fairy luring wayward travelers to their doom. She walked as straight as ever, but had her wavy dark hair hanging loose in the slight wind.

The nice part of his brain interrupted the tribal drums beating in his head. He realized that much of what Kay knew about sexuality had been learned from a man by whom she had been enslaved and brutalized. He wondered if he could ever let her please him without thinking of where she'd learned to please. Feeling guilty and fairly disgusted with himself, Irulen sped up in an attempt to catch up to his place in the group.

* * *

Irulen regained his spot at the front of the group, and they carried on for a while in relative silence. The journey's fatigue was starting to settle in, and the walkers spent the next few hours concentrating at the task at hand.

Irulen stopped. He lifted a hand to halt the others, blinked his eyes hard, and squinted into the distance.

"Someone's coming," he stated, coolly.

When the others startled at the news he was quick to add, "Just one."

Kay, whose vision was even better than Irulen's, confirmed and elaborated. "One person is right, but he has a mule. The beast is pulling a cart."

Irulen scratched at his scalp while digesting the details. "I may know the man," he concluded. "A wandering merchant I often meet during my travels."

"Merlane?" Quinn asked. "He comes by the Duck from time to time…always wearing those bright robes."

Irulen pitied the way Quinn spoke as if he never lost the tavern. In his mind, perhaps, it was still there, lively and well. "Yeah."

"I could use his services about now." Quinn failed to elaborate on the nature of his needs. His face looked wanting with a slight tinge of desperation. His large eyes looked hungry.

"Maybe we have stuff he'll want to buy." Irulen indicated the large sacks of supplies they were pulling around.

Quinn looked at him. For a minute he seemed uncomprehending, but then he sprang into action. "Yes indeed," he said, "perhaps we should take some time to look through our gear while he approaches." Quinn set to sorting through their supplies with vigor. "Seems to me we could spare some cookware."

"Perhaps," Irulen replied, "but we have coin enough so let's not get crazy about it."

"Still," Quinn pointed out, "this could be a great time to

lessen the load, lugging all this crap around."

To which Irulen responded, "Fair enough—for a fair price, though."

The man drew near.

"Oh, I also know him," said Thea, "he's one of the few merchants our village trusts with the secret of our location. He knows the landmarks we use to find the place. I've seen him often trading goods from other villages with my father for clothes and fabric. As children we'd call him the colorful merchant, named so for his colorful dress and personality alike."

The wizard always thought of Merlane's attire as an eyesore. Due to the nature of both their professions, the merchant had at times traveled alongside Irulen. At the best of times Irulen found Merlane as amiable company. At the worst of times the merchant was so overbearingly happy that the wizard wanted to punch his face out through the back of his head.

Merlane always said that being together with Irulen represented something divine. He was a believer in what he called the balance of nature. There were two sources of energy in all things, which he called sha and rha. Sha was creation and life. Rha was disintegration and death. Neither, however, was seen as good or bad. Everything was a necessity, and as the merchant always said, everything evens in the end. And so it was that, in the great balance of the world, Merlane and Irulen evened each other out. Irulen was often sardonic, brooding, and depressed. Merlane, some ten years older than Irulen at the least, was habitually optimistic, overzealous, and happy. He also had a habit of wearing pointed hats, which he often tried to sell to Irulen.

* * *

Irulen noticed a single shiver run up Farah's spine.

"Are you alright?" he asked.

"It's just…just uncanny is all. That man looks familiar…in the worst of ways."

"Oh?"

"He reminds me of my captor."

Irulen turned back to the man and analyzed his likeness.

A matching, bright-yellow pointed hat sat atop a long, gaunt face. He studied him for the shortest and longest of moments, and he agreed with her. The instant passed, and he realized all differences in the man.

"I can see it a little in the face. But no, this man is much taller and lankier, his face is old but far less worn, and his smile is genuinely rooted in benevolence. Trust me."

Farah nodded and smiled.

"Hello there, Ire!" the Merchant hailed, once he was close enough. He waved his bright-yellow clothed arm back and forth in the air. "Call me a cretin! Never thought I'd have such luck traveling this road at this time."

"Luck, indeed," Irulen mumbled under his breath. "Hello, Merlane," he said, reluctantly, but louder so that the merchant could now hear him. "Pray, why risk such a dangerous road at such a time?"

"Ha!" The merchant laughed, spoke a few words into the ear of his mule, and walked over. He lifted his right arm to Irulen's left elbow in a sign of greeting. The wizard stood rigid against the formality. Merlane laughed again and gave Irulen some space. "Everything destroyed needs to be replaced, does it not? The grisly events of soldiers make for prosperous times for a merchant."

Slightly annoyed at the merchant's naiveté, Irulen responded, "Only at high risk are you going to reap any type of reward in such a venture. Are people in need of your wares? Likely. Will they pay you for your goods or stab you for them? That, my friend, is less clear."

Merlane laughed again and spoke to the others "The mug is always half full, when it comes to Irulen. Tell me, Ire— who are your friends?" The merchant walked over to Quinn and greeted him while speaking. "This man I know, of course, but some of these ladies' faces also seem familiar."

"I am Thea, sir, from Snowillow Pass."

"Ah yes, of course, I remember you now, even though it's been a while."

"I'm Farah, from Frostbridge."

"Longer of a while still," said Merlane. "I haven't been in Frostbridge for some time, but I'm sure I've come across your face before—so it must have been there."

The merchant turned to Kay. "And you," he said, "I don't know."

"Nor shall you now," she said bluntly.

The merchant laughed. "As you wish, my lady, as you wish."

Kay removed herself a small distance and leaned against a tree as the merchant set to talking business.

"Irulen, I have something for you," he declared.

"I can't wait," Irulen said, facetiously.

Thea and Farah moved to the mule and began petting him as Merlane rifled through his goods. "That, is Suzy," the merchant told them.

With girlish giddiness, they gave the mule the best petting it had received in a long time. Suzy eagerly leaned into their touches.

"Ah ha! Here it is." The merchant pulled a tubular object out of a bag. "This is an enhancing glass."

"Glass?" Irulen asked, obviously intrigued.

"A true rarity in the north," said Quinn.

"Truly, any type of glass is rare in this region," Merlane agreed. "But this type of glass is rare to the world! It enhances things you point it at, makes them larger and more clear. You simply have to look through this opening, called a lens."

"Is it magical?" asked Irulen.

"Perhaps, in a sense, but it takes no real magic to use," Merlane replied. "You simply need enough light to use it. So you either need the sun, or the radiation of your own wizardly skill. The sun is high, and the sky has somewhat cleared, so now is a perfect time for a demonstration. Bring this end toward my cloak and look through the front hole."

Irulen followed the order, brought the contraption close to the man's cloak, and looked through it. It took him a while to process what he was seeing, and it would have taken him longer if the merchant hadn't told him. "Those are the threads and fibers that make up this stunning attire."

"That is really something," Irulen had to admit. "But what good is it to me?"

Merlane was drawn aback. "What use?" he asked, mockingly. "I've dragged this thing a thousand leagues to sell it to you and you ask 'what use'? The nerve of you."

Irulen shrugged.

Merlane took a deep breath and sighed. "Very well," he said, ready to explain. "You can use it in your profession, of course. To witness details otherwise obscured from you. This can help you greatly."

"Not interested," said Irulen, feigning disinterest.

Merlane looked hard at the wizard for a long moment. His mouth hung slightly agape. "You haven't even asked how much."

"I'll think about it," said Irulen. "Quinn here is a little more enthusiastic today. Talk to him."

Quinn beckoned for Merlane to come walk with him. Showing the girls where Suzy's food was, and grabbing a satchel out of his cart, the merchant complied. The two strolled down the road a little and conferred closely. Thea and Farah were still engrossed in the innocent bliss found only in the feeding of an animal—the communion of man and beast.

Kay lifted herself from the tree upon which she'd been leaning and sauntered over to Irulen who was looking after Quinn.

"So what's the secret?" she asked.

"It's not worth using my wizard-sense to listen," said Irulen, plainly. "Quinn is getting supplied with his medication. Merlane is many things; one of them being a drug dealer and Quinn's prime source of happy pills. I'm not even sure what herb goes into making them… Still, it's one of Quinn's ways of coping with the loss of his friend. It has been years, and yet he still feels responsible—responsible and guilty. Sometimes I think he hates himself more than I do."

"You hate yourself?"

"Maybe." He wiped the sweat from his brow. "Didn't

mean to say that."

"What reason do you have?"

"I need one?"

"Does it have something to do with Lynette?" The words sounded innocent, too innocent to sound sincere when coming from Kay.

Irulen found himself taking an involuntary step toward Kay. A wave of rage splashed against his insides and withdrew. He held himself up even though he wanted to strike her in the face. Something would continue to bother him for some time to come; she was smiling.

"Do you wish me harm, my lord?" she asked, in a sarcastically noble accent. She leaned in close to him and whispered, "Would you like to punish me?"

Her sexuality again coaxed the rage back into his chest. Irulen spoke without thinking. "You would want that, knowing where you've been." He regretted the words instantly and even more so when he witnessed their effect. Her face was set in stone, but there was a deep hurt in her eyes. *Whatever, she's learned her lesson.* Irulen wasn't about to let Lynette haunt him in the words of others as she already haunted his mind. He bit back the impulse to explain away everything to Kay, and to apologize. *It's when you apologize that people often think you did wrong. She knew what she was getting into. Damn it.*

By the time he opened his mouth to speak again she was back leaning against her tree, staring silently across the road and into the woods. Irulen cringed inwardly to think about what she was seeing there. His annoyance with himself turned toward Quinn.

"Quinn, you slow bastard! We've gotta get going!"

Quinn, who was still engaged in his secret conference with Merlane, waved for Irulen to leave him alone. The wizard threw his right hand up and down as he spun away in anger. He locked eyes for a moment with Kay, thought of the many things he could say to her, but came up empty.

Instead, he huffed over to where Farah and Thea stood petting Merlane's mule. He told them that the beast's name was

Elmira, and showed them her favorite spot to be scratched. Reaching behind the mule's head, a few inches down and at an equal distance between her ears, Irulen showed them the sweet spot. Thea scratched vigorously at the newfound source of pleasure. Elmira leaned her head into Thea's chest, almost knocking the human clean off her feet. There was a moment of pure joy shared between man and beast that included all those who witnessed it. Even Kay—who had watched from a further distance—smiled again as sadness seeped slowly from her face.

Quinn soon concluded his business with Merlane. He put something into his mouth and washed whatever it was down with his flagon. He was as cheery as ever as he walked back to the others. They bartered with Merlane as a group, and were able to unload a large portion of the burden from their backs. Much of Quinn's cookware was sold, any of Anastas's belongings that had made it into their supplies, and other odds and ends. By the end of their dealings, both parties were satisfied. The company would have much less to carry, and Merlane had all the more wares to resell once he reached Northforge. He tried, as he always did, to sell Irulen "more wizardly attire"—such as a proper pointed hat much like the merchant wore himself—but as usual, his efforts failed. After the business was all but completed, Irulen begged Merlane for a private moment.

"It seems I sell secrecy along with my other goods!" the older man quipped, as they wandered away from the others. Irulen saw Farah and Kay eyeballing him more suspiciously than the others as he walked his old acquaintance away from them.

"Listen…" He glanced back to be sure no one could hear him.

Merlane laughed as if he knew what Irulen would say, and cut to the chase. "You aren't going to try selling me diamonds now are you? Of the darker variety?"

Irulen's eyes opened wide in surprised and then narrowed suspiciously. Somehow, he was alright with Merlane knowing his line of enquiry. He wondered if he had been loose lipped about his investigation. The old merchant's knowledge was wide-reaching, and he was always a step ahead of everyone else. But Irulen remained wary of his words nonetheless. "Not sell, but these are diamonds—"

"That you've found inside the bodies of recent victims?"

Irulen stuttered "H-how, how did you know?"

The merchant put his hands into the air. "There have been others, quite a few actually. I travel places. I hear things."

Irulen pulled the sack of diamonds from under his cloak and tossed them to the merchant. Merlane's long fingers snaked through the pouch and drew out a single gem. He walked to a spot where the sun shown brightest and held it up into the rays. The light refracted off of the outer parts of the diamond, which was clear as could be. The elder man's eyes were locked on the center, however—a black spot. "It's almost as if it was suspended in an embryotic state," he said and elaborated, "waiting to be birthed."

"That would make me the hen, sitting on these things," Irulen responded.

Merlane laughed. "The thought of you with feathers is funny indeed, but these—these are dark magic, as I'm sure you've supposed."

"You suppose right." Irulen nodded.

"You know, I heard a story once. It was just before the Great Conflict, and a certain magician found himself obsessed with an impossible problem. Outside of his first time, this man had never used his magic for fear that he would lose it forever. So, instead of entering the world of wizardry he chose to become a scholar. This man dedicated his life to defeating this…great fear of his. He scoured every codex or scroll he could find. I sincerely doubt that anyone, ever, has read as much as he."

"So?" Irulen asked as they stopped walking.

"So…he found it—the answer, supposedly."

Irulen shook his head. "No, it isn't possible to accomplish unending magic. I'd know."

"Would you? You use your magic more wantonly than any wizard *I've* met. You don't fear the loss of your essence because you have a plan beyond being what you are. It seems to me, in fact, that sometimes you can't spend your magic fast enough!"

"You know a lot of things, Merlane, but you don't know me." Irulen scowled.

"Maybe, maybe not, but maybe." The geezer winked. "Nonetheless," he continued, "whatever you choose to believe, I heard this man found the way to do it—magic for life. However, it wasn't easily gained, physically or emotionally—the process was an enduring one, there was no single answer, but rather a consistent existence. There was a way to harvest the essence of a person's spirit and to channel it into oneself."

"Impossible."

"Not if you ask the Brotherhood."

Irulen paused for a moment and looked hard at the man across from him. He tried to decide whether Merlane knew about his encounter with the Brotherhood or not, whether he was screwing with him, or if he had come across similar information through another means. To this question, the wizard wouldn't receive an answer.

Instead, Irulen continued his line of questioning. "If it's possible, then how?"

"A special stone, a relic left over from the very origins of the world. It exists within and yet outside the natural order of things. There are, in fact, very few places to find it."

"What's it do?"

"In a way, it's a rock that is alive, both organic and inorganic...an enigma. Somehow they are connected through the ley lines of the planet. These magical lines lay gently over our world like fabric against a babe's skin. They criss-cross and radiate magic, not just to and from each other, but in between as well. You've heard lore as to how you have a greater chance of being born with magic the closer you are to such a line when you are birthed and other myths like that. But what he found, whether through ley lines or other mumbo jumbo, these rocks were all *one*. As in you may separate them physically, but in some other way they still *feel* the same."

"So rocks have feelings now? Where are you going with this?" Irulen's patience was dwindling fast. He didn't have time for this nonsense.

"That even though they are separated by space, these diamonds share time. They exist as one, even as they are scattered individually. Let me put it to you like this… Let's say you ingested metal and died—"

"I love where this is going." Irulen rolled his eyes.

Merlane continued unfazed. "So you are dead, and your body rots, eroding back from whence it came… Eventually you would be dust, and the metal would be left alone laying on the ground. These rocks work similarly within the confines of this world—if our world disappeared, then they would still be left…floating in the darkness between time and space."

"OK, let me unravel your riddle so far. So these rocks—diamonds—exist beyond our world and yet in our world, and even though they may be seen as severed limbs from the body they still share the same nervous system. They still feel and interact with each other as one?" He cocked an eyebrow and tilted his head. "This is heavy stuff."

Merlane laughed. "Yes, well, now you are ready for their significance." The old man's face tightened with graveness. "This man found the way to channel the spiritual energy of souls in dying bodies. He kept a book full of his notes on how to do it. The summation of his work boiled down really to the placing of these rocks next to the beating heart of a human. As the heart dies, the essence flows through the magic stones. The one harvesting the souls has to have one of the stones buried deep next to his heart as well. He drags the victim's essence through the magical fabric of the world and into himself."

Merlane paused, squinted. He studied Irulen's face closely before continuing. "Effectively, as long as this person is able to harvest souls, he'll have magic for as long as he lives. Who's to say he wouldn't live forever, or for a long time, using magic in such a way? The consequences are beyond my understanding."

"So did this man do it? Is he the one I'm looking for?"

"No," said Merlane, solemnly. "He could not accept such a price for unending magic. He lived out his magical days as he could and dedicated himself to new technology and different forms of power. Nowadays, he travels as a merchant, peddling his gadgets and gizmos."

Ah, so this is the true reason for the merchant's trek north. Irulen more than raised an eyebrow at the old man. "Are you saying—?"

"I'm saying that while this man could not go through with such an action, he had a much harder time letting go of his work—his book of research was the achievement of his lifetime. As much as the discovery had stung in its ramifications, the man was still proud that he had solved the riddle. The book stayed with him for a long time."

"You lost the book, didn't you?" said Irulen.

Merlane smiled, but kept his composure. "This *man*, became lonely in his lifestyle. Traveling from village to village, region to region, life on the road became tedious and wanting. He never found the love he was looking for—although, let me tell you, he's had his fair share of romance—and became desperate for company. He decided to take on an apprentice. A young boy named Ithial who had been orphaned. The boy was bright eyed and intelligent beyond his means, and it turned out he was magically gifted as well. Not as naturally endowed as you are, mind you, but he showed a little spark from time to time."

Merlane paused, his face twisted slowly and softly, as if two emotions were filling his head. "The man would always remember fondly as he taught the boy to save his magic...that the boy shouldn't waste it burning bugs and lizards..."

Fatigued, Merlane sat on a nearby fallen tree. "Even then, the boy was so cruel. Whether it was because the world was cruel to him..." He shrugged. "Maybe. But it is what it is."

"The boy found the book, then?"

Merlane shook his head. "You know, you are a very poor person to tell a story to—with the interrupting and all."

"Well?" Irulen pressed.

"OK, fine, yes he found the book, to cut a *long* story short. He found it and disappeared."

Irulen's heart rate ratcheted up. "Where is he?"

Merlane exhaled deeply and shrugged. "I don't know, south, somewhere. I think."

"And what about the wandering man whose book he stole?" A jolt of sympathy shot through Irulen, but he quickly suppressed it.

"Oh, I suppose he might appeal to someone stronger than himself to remedy the problem. He has never seen Ithial since, but he supposes that Ithial will find him when he so chooses. The boy is no longer a child and has been creating imps and causing pain now more than ever. It seems that the boy waited many years before actually *using* the book. Even in his dark soul there is a lightness… though it fights a losing battle."

The two men stood in silence. "It seems that you and I both have created monsters Irulen. But I suppose finding yours might lead to mine, and I must ask you to take care of both."

CHAPTER 14: HOMECOMING

"Why won't he?" Lynnette asked.

"He just doesn't want to give you up yet," Irulen said, lamely.

"But I've waited so long to be sixteen."

"Just a little longer, please."

"We need to leave," she decided.

"We'd never be allowed back if we go now."

"I have nothing to come back to," she yelled.

"I'd rather not elope, perhaps if my parents talked to him. I could get them to disregard any dowry."

"If you loved me then you would do whatever it takes."

"I will. I promise."

The next day Irulen's parents passed to him the bad news. Lynnette's father had denied them, and Lynnette had been there to see it. The girl had run off, and the townsfolk were out searching for her.

Irulen rushed to their favorite stream. There had been a rainstorm overnight, and the rivulet had expanded into a full-on roaring river. He found her with her feet at the river's edge.

"Lynnette, please!" he screamed. She gave no indication that she had heard him over the running water.

She was leaning forward toward the river as he grabbed her from behind. She punched him in the face, his teeth chattered together, and he fell backward onto loose soil.

"You lie to me just like him!" she shrieked. Pain grated her voice.

"No, please, I promise. Anything you want. Tell me."

"Kill him for me!"

"Not that."

She scoffed. "If you can't kill him then give me the power to do it. Or I'll kill the only person I have power over."

"There's no telling what this sort of thing could do to you."

"Nothing is worse than what he's done. You don't understand."

She ran toward the river and threw herself in. Irulen's will rejected the disappearance of her hair under the water. He jumped into the turbulent water after her. In a lucky stroke of fate, he found her in his arms. Once he had her, he pressed with his magic against the current. He dropped with her to the slick riverbed, cocooning her as the water rushed overhead.

She spit up water. "Now do you understand?" she asked. Her wet body was limp and defeated. Irulen paused for the briefest of moments. He felt his magic weakening. He had no idea how he'd created this safe space for them under the river, but he knew time ran short. To finish the rescue, he needed her to want to survive. To do that, he gave her what she wanted. He committed the worst mistake of his life.

"Yes," he said, as he applied his hands to her heart. He had no knowledge of how to do what he was doing, but his hands became dark blue and her eyes soon matched the color. Whether it was a sixth sense, or something else entirely, Irulen had divested her with magic. He blacked out after that, and found himself washed ashore, alone.

Irulen called out for her and received no answer. He began following the river back toward the town. So began the worst walk of his life.

It wasn't long before he started finding the bodies of townsfolk sent to find Lynnette. Their bodies were treated furiously, torn to pieces and tossed asunder. The reality of what happened began to sink in. Irulen ran as fast as he could back into town. He stopped by his family's house and was relieved to find they were in good health. He told them to keep out of sight until he came back and then went to where he knew Lynnette would go.

He arrived at the dwelling she shared with her father. He had never been inside it before. A grisly picture greeted him once he'd entered. Different pieces of Lynnette's father hung from an array of chains. Blood dripped from every bit. There was a piece of parchment left out on the table. Next to the sheet was a feather with blood on its tip. In blood-red font there was written three words:

Thank you, Irulen.

* * *

Leaving Merlane behind, the group tried to make up time by moving twice as fast. The lightened burden helped their progress. Still, they came up a little short of their goal for the day. Irulen maintained, however, that they could make Snowillow Pass by the following day. He had never been in the town himself, but he knew the area well enough. They ended the day in typical fashion, and were able to sleep peacefully as the night passed silently by.

As far as weather went, the following morning was the most miserable of the trip. Rain decided to join the night's snow and left much of the gear soaked through. The stormy weather had ceased for the present, but angry, dark clouds loomed above.

There was still no sign of Max, but Irulen maintained that Max would check in if the bird had no luck procuring work that day. Thea's village was in an area with a low density of population, so Irulen wasn't at all surprised at Max's lack of news. It's why he often worked north of the city instead of south.

The group's morale was as damp as the sloshy ground they trod on. Farah walked quietly, seemingly lost in thought. Irulen wondered briefly if her thoughts were of Frostbridge...or Jorin.

Quinn walked with one hand holding a large sack slung over his massive shoulders. He leaned far to the right and left as he lumbered along the path, much like a ship swaying among waves. A forlorn whistle escaped from his mouth as he walked, but it was more sour than sweet. Irulen imagined the melody as a melancholic ghost singing from the deepest recesses of Quinn's soul.

Kay was stoic as ever, though her injured arm still hung limply. The wounded muscle had stiffened up, and so she shied away from using it. She had refused when Farah suggested Irulen use his magic to hasten the healing process. The reluctant look on his face betrayed the high cost of such a spell, and Kay was far too proud to pursue the issue.

For hours they traveled, and it seemed that every hill they conquered was followed by another that looked just the same. The woods started changing in their makeup. The bristled conifers had retreated deep into the forest. The trees now were mostly oak and maple, not quite as large as the pines, but large enough to provide a decent canopy—had their leaves not been shed for the long winter. The snow wasn't quite as oppressing; the recent mix of rain had small erosive cliffs of mud bordering the track.

It was Thea who soon became the light in the darkness. Thea, who for as long as everyone knew her tended to be a quiet person, was becoming much more outspoken. She had a lot to say about her home village, and her talking grew exponentially as they drew closer to their destination. As they drew near, she clucked as loudly as any chicken.

"My father is probably worried. Oh, I bet my mother will be so happy to see me. Maybe you will have a chance to gnaw at my family's crawfish boil—we pull the little suckers right out of the cold creek and mix 'em with secret family chowder. Use up all the juices. Sure, the crawfish might not look so delicious upon first glance but I assure you you'll be licking up their innards like pudding."

The others shared knowing glances as she paused speaking. "Quinn," she called, as the large man's shoulders flinched. "I'm surprised you never learned about the Thadmore family recipe. My father never spilt the beans? Perhaps during one of his more drunken nights?"

"Nah, lass, can't say he did, and I'm truly sorry the secret of the crawfish boil has not passed through these ears."

"Well," she said, satisfied. "Mother will be happy to hear it. She'd have his pelt hung above the fireplace if he had."

The air was silent for about ten steps as Thea gravitated toward Kay.

"We are a village of weavers, you know," she was saying. "I could find you a new cloak Kay. I mean, if you want one."

"What's wrong with this one?"

"It is a bit…worn is all. We could get you a new one, maybe even with a brighter color?"

"A brighter color?" Kay scoffed. "I don't think having a pink cloak would help me much."

"Yeah, how is she supposed to lurk in the shadows wearing something beautiful?" asked Irulen. "Besides," he continued, "she wouldn't want the people she's stalking trying to hump her all the time."

"Makes them vulnerable," said Farah, methodically.

Quinn laughed, and spoke to Kay. "Ha! She's right, you know. Maybe you should add a dress to go with that new cloak."

"You wish," she said, flatly. "Besides, this cloak isn't mine to give away."

"Whose is it?" asked Thea.

"A friend's."

Irulen looked at Kay with rekindled interest, a friend?

"A girl friend, or a boy friend?" Thea asked her.

"A man."

"What type of friend? Like a friend-friend, or a love-friend, or what?"

A look of grinding irritation spread through Kay's face like roots through soil. She took a breath and responded. "Love-friend, but not like man-woman, more like father-daughter. The one who saved me. The one who raised me."

"And where is he now?"

Kay's left eye twitched ever so slightly as she spoke. "Dead."

"I'm sorry," said Thea, and Kay looked like she thought the questions would stop.

But they didn't, they multiplied. "How long ago was

this?" Thea asked.

"Just about two years ago now," Kay said, with growing intensity.

"What happened?"

"We screwed up a job. He got killed."

"How?"

Kay startled the others as she spun on Thea. Her cloak whirled as it followed her movements. Kay stood in front of the smaller girl menacingly.

Thea cringed. "I'm sorry," she said. The girl looked ready to self-implode.

Kay was tense for another moment, and suddenly her shoulders went limp. She reached around her back and brought the cloak around to her front. She put a finger through a hole in its middle. "He was stabbed there, in the back." Kay rustled through her pockets and pulled out a worn piece of parchment. On it was a smudged drawing of a women's face. "This is the lady we were stalking—a serial killer. The sketch was composited by a group of young girls that had been orphaned by her. You see, she would kill full families save for the youngest of the girls."

The others closed around for a look at the picture. Fear gripped Irulen's heart as he shambled over. Kay looked at him, and he thought there was something wrong with the way she did it. She might have been searching his face for something. If she was, he was sure she would see what she was looking for; knowledge and guilt. He approached and looked over Farah's shoulder. The drawing was worn from two years of showing it to everyone she could, but it was Lynette's face that he saw— complete with the telltale facial drippings of an imp.

"That's..." He caught himself before he could say something he'd regret. "That's an imp."

Kay looked at him as she folded up the paper and pocketed it. "One that doesn't look familiar to you?"

"No, I haven't run into many until lately, and that wasn't one of them." In this sense he wasn't lying. He had never seen Lynette as an imp.

Still, something in Kay's look made him recoil. Does she

know? Has she known all this time? Had she planned this? Is that why she pulled the trigger on Comcka? Burning my bridges so she could go after Lynette with me in tow? But how would she know?

"Really gruesome, this one," said Kay. "By slaughtering the families of these girls, she thinks she's doing them a favor."

Irulen's eyes kept flicking up and down to find Kay still staring at him. He had never felt so exposed. The wizard's throat tightened as his heart beat loudly. Anger swelled within. Forcing a smile, he turned and took a few steps down the path while the others reacted to what Kay said.

"That's awful," said Thea.

"Why does she do that?" asked Farah, to no one in particular.

"It's a shame," said Quinn.

"A shame?" asked Kay.

"It's a shame—she looked like a pretty gal." Quinn's eyes darted from Kay to Irulen.

"Looks can veil even the most hideous of monsters," said Kay, matter-of-factly.

Quinn nodded. "Yes, well, imps were all people too, once, Irulen knows."

"I'm sure he does," Kay said, wryly.

* * *

The group made their way slowly as Thea surveyed the woods to their left. She bent down, looked across the forest floor, moved ten feet and did the same thing again. The girl's actions had a curious look as she bobbed her way along the path.

"It's quiet simple really," she was saying, "there's a sign I need to find."

"What is it?" Farah asked.

"Can't say."

"Maybe if you had said, we'd have found it by now," Kay accused.

Irulen continued. "And maybe if you will tell us now we can find it not long from now."

"Sorry," she said. "Can't say."

They continued on like that for the span of an hour that dragged on for an eternity. They would walk, stop, Thea would crouch, look around the brush, and then they would all carry on. The weather had refrozen, and short dollops of snow fell intermittently from above, further hindering their guide's progress. Thea had been complaining about the aches in her leg muscles for some time before one of her squats finally proved successful.

"Aha!" she exclaimed. "There it is, this way." She trumped into the forest triumphantly. They would learn later that Thea had never before navigated herself into Snowillow Pass— she always had one of her brothers or father to escort her. What the landmark was, however, is something she would never divulge. Secrecy was the one golden rule of the place, and everyone born in the village took it seriously.

Only a few outsiders ever knew the secrets of their location, Merlane was among them, Irulen was not. He had no doubt, however, that he could find the place with Max's help. Furthermore, he wouldn't be surprised if Max had stopped here during his quest for work. Irulen was becoming increasingly worried at the absence of his feathered friend and would welcome any news of the raven. Another worry bounced around the back of his brain. *Might Max miss this place? Nah, he's always been spot on finding me. But might he just fly right by and never see us? Damn.*

So it was that the wizard wore his face tightly as he followed Thea with the others. Beneath the layers of snow both powdered and packed, there was a slushy consistency underfoot. It was as if they moved through wetlands equal parts frozen and thawed. At times, it seemed as if the ground pulled at their feet, and their progress became slow and tedious.

"Couldn't you have just hidden a road leading to the village?" asked Irulen, annoyed.

"I guess the walk serves as an extra buffer against bandits," said Kay, matter-of-factly.

The brush had become thick, and Thea was a few feet

ahead of them, moving a branch out of her face. "You guessed right," she said. "Nothing is more sacred in Snowillow Pass than our security and solitude. There have even been times when we move the markers around, so that everyone who knew how to get to the village would cease having access to it. Then we visit them, or they will meet our envoy on the main road, to receive the proper code of access again."

"What's to keep them from carving out their own marks, leaving their own trail to follow again?" asked Irulen, a bit snobbishly.

"Well, nothing really. We do patrol for outsider marks being left on trees and stuff like that. If we find it, we'll leave a trap set near it, or we'll move it around if it's something like a rock or log. Nothing is perfect, but we haven't had a crime in our village since before I was born."

"For someone who values seclusion and security," said Irulen, as he stepped onto a rotten stump, "you sure have told us a lot about how you do things." He jumped down.

Thea's cheeks flushed at her own naiveté. She fell silent for a moment, paused where she stood, and then spoke again. "But…I trust you."

Irulen laughed as his sarcasm bounced off the trees. "You've known most of us for mere days. What has earned us the privilege of such a trust?"

"Well, you all helped me to safety. Quinn gave me a job. We've been through a lot together."

"What if we helped you because of a mutual benefit? Ever since we roamed the plains in small tribes, humans have a higher survival rate in numbers—a better chance of not being the one that gets eaten."

Farah, who had used the pause to catch up, spoke from behind. "You can trust me at least, Thea, if not this ruffian."

Irulen looked back with fake hurt in his features.

"Is trust such a thing to be earned and spent like silver?" asked Farah. "Trust is not so rational. I find myself still trusting you despite quite rational evidence to the contrary."

"Trust is a lot like love then," said Thea, innocently, as if to herself.

An awkward pause ensued, followed by Quinn's laughter. His jollity scraped clean where Irulen's sarcasm had been.

Quinn, not used to being the one that caught implications and context of what people said, had some more fun at Irulen and Farah's expense. The burly man spoke, pleased with himself. "I'd say they're related, don't you think so, Kay?"

"Certainly, they are," she said, dryly, raising one eyebrow at Irulen and Farah—both of whom shifted somewhat uneasily.

"Oh, shut up," said Irulen, evenly. "Lead on Thea, lead on."

"Very well," she said. She served Irulen a look of faux-suspicion, complete with squinty eyes, furrowed forehead wrinkles, and pursed lips, then carried on.

* * *

It was only a short while before the woods began to open up. The brush loosened its grip on the travelers and the trees became larger and more spread out. They moved with ease through the hard wood, and soon they were walking up to a small bridge standing over a small running creek. At the ends of the bridge were two arcs that still had bark on them. It looked as if two trees had been bent and made to stay. Quinn put his hand on the one in front and looked visibly impressed.

"Isn't this a beauty?" he asked, and spoke before anyone could respond. "I'd love to have something like this on my next tavern." He looked to Thea. "How'd they do it?"

"All I know is that trees were planted and trained from a very young age. You'd have to ask around, I never really thought twice about it."

"Maybe your old man will know something about it," he said.

The company moved beneath the tree-arcs, over the bridge, and into the village. The sun was in the later stages of setting, and dusk was settling in quickly. Not being used to strangers, the village folk were inside their dwellings eating supper.

To Irulen, there was a magical feeling to the place. The tops of the houses were rounded in a similar fashion to the bridge arcs. In the center of each dwelling there was a small chimney, and many of them lazily puffed smoked that carried a variety of appetizing smells into the air. Perhaps most impressive was that each dwelling had a window made of glass—something Irulen had only first seen in the object he had ended up purchasing from the merchant Merlane. The amount of glass present in this village surely amounted to a great expense. The houses were scattered among the trees and glowed like lanterns. There was no town square, no clearings at all from what she saw. The houses were scattered in between the trees.

Thea beamed as the company weaved its way among the cozy cottages and dusk-lit foliage. Irulen couldn't help but look for Max. It was time for the bird to check in, whether he had found work or not, and Irulen was finding it harder to push his friend's absence into the recesses of his mind. He kept expecting to see a dark silhouette at any moment, flapping its wings in an exuberant greeting. At one point, a bat fluttered overhead, and happiness rose, but quickly fell within him. The wizard was truly disappointed.

CHAPTER 15: FAMILY

The days after the murder of Lynette's father were a blur. Irulen had been honest about what happened, and the townspeople had turned on him for it. He was just as culpable for the murder as Lynette was, if not more so. The mob's anger grew over the next few days, culminating in his being literally run out of town.

Irulen found himself crashing through the woods as thorns pulled at his skin, stumps blocked his feet, and branches battered his body. It seemed as if the world was against him, pulling him down and demanding justice for his crime. He headed south, although he didn't know it at the time. He had little outside the clothes on his back.

A terror followed him. He had long ago ceased to hear the calls of the townspeople, but he was terrified of what had happened. He felt a great horror following on his heels. Behind every tree, under every bush, in every clearing—Irulen expected to find Lynette. Facing her was his worst fear. *A murderer, Lynette is a murderer. Through negligence I have become a murderer too. I own what she's become and everything she does.*

Over the past few days, Irulen had, of course, learned more about the effects that could accompany the bestowment of power. He had ensured the annihilation of Lynette's soul. Her humanity—her ethical makeup—was destroyed. She now walked the earth as an embodiment of spite. She was her shadow self— the ugliest bits without the empathy that kept them in check. Yes, he had killed Lynette much in the same way as he killed her father. She was no longer capable of free will, but Irulen was. He'd lent his magic to her freely.

He had heard, from the mob, that Lynette would be released if he died. No one knew what *released* meant, whether she'd die or go back to being the same Lynette Irulen had grown to love. As he ran, Irulen considered how easy it would be to commit suicide. He had decided that, if he was caught, killing himself would be better than a public execution. Once surrounded, he would put both of his hands to his head and cast one last spell. It might get messy on those nearby, but he would fall to the ground infallibly lifeless. Maybe if that happened then Lynette would be herself again.

Irulen ran face first into a tree.

The young man fell backward. Something dark came flapping from above. It fell down past him. His ears rang, his head throbbed, a stream of blood ran down his face. For a moment Irulen's vision blurred, but it slowly came back into focus. There was a black bird, a raven, struggling to get into the air. Irulen looked on dumbly. He recognized that the creature was a fledgling, newly brought into the world.

Irulen leaned against the very tree he had run into. He rested his elbows on his knees and rubbed at his temples. The dull pain of impact withdrew as the raven's nerves also settled down. The bird's feathers were fuzzy and ruffled. A stubby beak swung this way and that as the fledgling took in the surroundings. Its blue and black eyes stared Irulen in the face. The bird became suddenly very still, and the two beings sat quietly for a moment.

Irulen watched the raven's gaze as it lifted from his eyes up into the tree from which it fell. Straight above the young wizard's head there was a nest. He could hear the fallen raven's siblings calling for their parents, who—as far as Irulen could tell—were not present at the time.

"Shit," Irulen muttered, as he pushed himself to his feet. The raven followed his actions intently. The young man stumbled as he walked over to it. For a moment, he hovered over the animal. The wizard squatted and reached out. His hands wavered as he moved toward and then away from the fledgling a few times. Finally, satisfied that the bird was not old enough to tear into flesh, Irulen cupped his hands under the frail body and lifted it to his chest.

He walked his feathered friend over to the tree from whence it fell. The wizard's chest lifted and deflated with a deep breath. Then he placed the bird carefully into the hood of his cloak. Haphazardly, he navigated his way up the tree until he came to the nest. Awkwardly holding onto the tree with one hand, Irulen reached over his back with the other. He grabbed the fledgling and placed it back next to its siblings.

Irulen climbed down and turned his thoughts back to his own predicament. There was hardly a chance to ponder his problem when a ball of fluttering feathers came crashing down for a second time. The baby raven was again on the ground, and was again looking at him curiously. Irulen raised his eyes to the nest and was dismayed to see an adult bird staring down at him. The mother raven was perched on the edge of the nest and sounded off loudly at both Irulen and his new partner in misery. The bird's mother had rejected him, likely because of the newfound human smell she found when she had returned to her young.

Breathing a mixture of sympathy, for both himself and the young raven, the young wizard scooped the bird again into his hands. "Do you like *Max*?" He studied his newfound friend. The bird looked agreeable to the name.

"Well, Max." The young bird cocked its head at him. "It looks like you and I have found ourselves kicked from the nest." The fugitive wizard tucked Max into the back of his hood, and continued his escape. He found himself feeling less alone. The weight of his predicament had lightened just enough for Irulen to walk at a less desperate pace. He was no longer so much running from his past as moving toward the future—or so he thought at the time.

* * *

Thea walked up to the door and knocked gently. The light inside the house went out and for a moment things were still and tense. It wasn't so dark that they couldn't see inside, but the shapes moving about weren't very clear. Thea turned to the others and shrugged. Suddenly an angry voice burst forth from the other side of the door.

"WHO GOES THERE?"

"Papa! It's me," Thea exclaimed.

The door sounded of many latches being undone. It swung open, and a small man burst through it. His eyes squinted fiercely, pulling the skin taught around his bald head. Recognition helped lighten the wrinkles of his face as he pulled her into his arms. He squeezed her tight while regarding the others she had come with.

"Who is this you bring to our door? Quinn, is that you? And your wizard friend, *Rulian* was it? Something like that?"

"*Irulen*, at your service." The wizard bowed his head. "My friends call me *Ire*."

"But that makes no sense." The man squinted and tilted his head. "You pronounce the 'I's differently. A full name and a nickname must have some sense of conformity. Otherwise, what's the point? Consider William, and Will… Timothy, and Tim."

"What about James and Jim?" Iurlen lifted a brow. "Those don't sound the same."

"Fine, call yourself how you please." The man waved a hand, effectively dismissing the thought. "For my part, I am Terrowin, and my friends call me *Win*. You have, until just this moment, had my daughter, Thea, in your care."

"So I've heard," said Irulen, dryly. Quinn nudged Irulen on the back lightly. They hadn't discussed plans for food and bed, after all. The last thing anyone wanted was to annoy a potential host.

"And who are these other two mouths you'll be expecting me to feed?" Terrowin asked, bluntly.

Thea's cheeks reddened at her father's rashness, but she introduced Farah and Kay.

Terrowin regarded them through squinted eyes. "Pretty girls, I'll give them that. Though in need of some new clothes, they are. Perhaps in return for a night's lodgings, you will browse my wares?"

Farah nodded, smiled, and bowed in acquiescence. Kay stood rigid and proud. Terrowin stared at her, and the others used their eyes to plea for her cooperation. Finally, in a dramatic mockery of Farah, Kay used sweeping motions to indicate her willingness to peruse the man's clothing.

"Good, good. And perhaps the gentlemen will foot the bill." Irulen and Quinn stiffened at the thought.

Kay, sensing a reversal of fortune, spoke happily. "It would be an honor to browse your finest wares. I hear the looms of Snowillow Pass are legendary, and the craftsmen are foremost across the world."

Terrowin beamed happily. "Not as common as she looks, is she? A woman of articulate diction."

"Not always so articulate, I'm afraid." Kay's voice betrayed a hint of menace.

Terrowin regarded her calculatingly as he stepped aside and waved the travelers inside. He spoke as they passed by. "Well, the hot air of words alone shan't be enough to warm us all on this brisk night! Come in, you'll have to share the living space when you sleep tonight, but the fire will be sure to do the trick, especially with the added body warmth. We were just eating so the pans are hot. Eleanor relishes the opportunity to cook large meals."

"Speak fer yerself!" trumpeted a pleasantly plump, middle aged woman. She was already scavenging the food stocks to accommodate their guests.

Also inside Alice, Thea's older sister, and Bryce, Terrowin's apprentice whose age fell between those of the Thadmore sisters. Both Bryce and Alice were happy to see Thea return, for even though she had been gone but a short while, they had heard plenty of the strife at Northforge. For Thea, there were hugs a plenty.

After taking stock of her food stores, Eleanor offered the women a choice; they could eat first, or bathe. Behind the house was a torch-lit path, maintained by the town, which led to one of Snowillow's fabled hot pools. The volcanic nature of the north led to many such splendors of nature, though some were more sulfurous than others. The fresh springs beneath Snowillow Pass, however, were known for running mostly clear of sediment.

For the women, as much as they craved relaxation and cleanliness, the choice was simple, they'd eat first.

Irulen and Quinn gathered some bathing supplies, including two new towels they bought from Terrowin, and followed the torch-lit path as instructed. For less than five minutes they followed the dull flames until coming to their destination. The outlines of a natural hot spring flickered into sight. The pool was a sizable one. It was lined with large rocks, and stone steps had been added to the side closest to the path. The two men looked at each other for an excited moment and then stripped their clothes furiously. They were in the pool before the passing of another moment. For a while there was little in the way of words or actual cleaning. Both men stood toward the middle of the pool absorbing the heat and minerals into their skin. Steam rose into the cold night air. The two primates floated about lazily, occasionally filling the air with moans and grunts of relaxation.

Eventually they set about their business, exfoliating their skin with coarse sand from the pool's bottom. They took turns standing out of the water, soaping up quickly and jumping back in. The process was done in a timely fashion as to avoid the cold breeze.

Irulen washed his clothes while Quinn looked on thoughtfully. There was a look of hesitation on Quinn's face, as if he was debating whether to speak or not. Eventually he did. "You spent another night sharing a tent with Kay. What was that like?"

Irulen stopped scrubbing his shirt for a minute, looked at Quinn, and then resumed his work. "Well, we don't tell each other bedtime stories, if that's what you were wondering."

"Have you…you know…had any luck?"

Irulen laughed. "She's cold, man. She acts all hot like but no, when it comes down to it, I favor keeping my dick right where it is. I think if I so much as laid a finger on her you'd see a severed sausage go flying through the tent flap. I gotta say, it is a strange feeling to lie next to a woman who could kick my ass without breaking a sweat."

Another strange look crossed Quinn's face. Between his dark eyebrows and water-beard shone something between relief and hope. He pushed his luck a little further. "So you guys, you know…"

"No, we haven't. Not even close." Irulen paused then, reached down and grabbed a rock. He threw it at Quinn, "Why, are you interested in her?"

Quinn's eyebrows furrowed. "Is that bad? I haven't had a female touch me for weeks now."

Irulen laughed again. "No, if you want to show her the only part of you that fails to match your barbaric size, you go right ahead."

"You can be a real asshole, Ire."

"I know." He grinned.

* * *

Irulen and Quinn had dried off and were and heading back to the Thadmore house when the women crossed their path. Quinn was walking in front of Irulen and hailed them first. Farah and Thea giggled, each full of food and expectation. Kay walked behind them, her expression recoiled at the girls' immature antics.

There was a moment, a long moment, as Kay and Irulen passed each other. Quinn had just looked forward again and the two girls had rounded a bend. Kay stopped Irulen and put a finger over her mouth. She ran her hand under his shirt and over his abdominals, leaned in, and whispered, "Tonight, after."

His heart stuttered.

Quinn turned around, and Kay was gone.

* * *

"When I first found Irulen, he was quiet like this," said Quinn.

"I'm sorry, what?" asked the wizard, snapping out of his deep thought. He was sitting at the living room table with Bryce, Terrowin, Eleanor, and Quinn.

"And where in the minds were you just wandering?" asked Terrowin.

"Nowhere great, I'm just tired. No offense."

Terrowin shrugged his shoulders. "None taken."

"We were just speaking of Northforge," said Quinn.

Irulen's face stretched wide with interest. "Oh, what about?"

"The battle, of course." Eleanor stared at Irulen as if he had three heads.

"Right, right. What is the latest on that?"

"The city dwellers won the battle, but there's rumor of a coup. Supposedly their leadership was sold out, possibly executed or locked away somewhere. Some richies on the mountain used their money to buy a betrayal. An unknown amount of opportunistic rebels sold out their leadership for money and power. So it seems things may be close to square one, the new leaders the same as the old leaders."

Quinn lit a pipe and puffed at it, the smoke escaped as he spoke. "Such a shame, such a waste. The Roasted Duck, Anastas, so many others, all gone."

Terrowin ran his hands over his balding head and sighed loudly. "Aye, it's a sad truth that we small people often find ourselves rejected by the histories of the world. Our story, our legacy, burns like the herbs in your pipe. When all is said and done, the pipe is all that's left."

There was silence.

"That's deep," said Bryce. The others looked surprised to hear him, he was largely silent among his elders. The light-haired youth made to speak again, but he closed his mouth without passing words.

"Well, save for the bad news about Anastas and your tavern, these events don't concern us much out here. Business may be slow for a while, but our town is placed to withstand storms of both the natural and human variety."

Irulen tapped his fingers. "A deer might hide in the woods, but hiding does little good when the forest burns down."

Terrowin's face tightened in response. "Be that as it may, there's yet to be a fire large enough to eat us."

They soon moved on from politics and chatted about life's common things. The topics included the changing of the seasons, Alice's pending marriage, Bryce's last year of apprenticeship, Terrowin's famous crawfish boil, Eleanor's bad back, local economics, and even some myth and folklore. All the while they spoke, Irulen's mind kept wandering. Everything seemed trivial. He was thinking about his short history with Kay. Irulen suspected she had an angle to play, and kept thinking that he ought to stay away, but the memory of her lured him. He began to fantasize about the situations where they had been alone. They had shared a tent and an alley. You can lock it up tight as can be, but it's amazing how quickly an imagination can run wild. In just an instant, Irulen found himself going from trustworthy friend to fantasizing adolescent.

Eventually, Farah and Thea returned. Irulen's heart leapt. He stood as the door was still closing.

"I'm going to get some air and look for Max, he should be here."

"The bird won't find you in these parts," challenged Terrowin.

"That's the thing about ravens," said Irulen, as he walked through the door, "they'll surprise you."

"Where's Kay?" asked Quinn.

"Oh, it's been a long time since she's bathed. She— stayed behind a while longer."

"Hrrmph," Quinn grunted, and pulled out his flagon.

* * *

Irulen's head pivoted to and fro as he walked along the path. He felt stupid and sheepish, like he was in trouble and being summoned by a village elder. Still there was no stopping his feet from carrying him forward, no matter how hard he tried. One grueling pace at a time propelled him to where he needed to be.

A stick snapped nearby. The sound came from off the path. He squinted into the darkness and saw a lightness in the shadows. He went to it. Stepping past the glare of the path's torches, he saw her. Her exposed skin was accentuated by steam. There was a moment of tension between them. It snapped in an instant.

Kay pulled Irulen from the path and pinned him against a tree. He was stunned as her hand ran up the inside of his thigh. She cupped him gently. Breath blew hot against the cold air. There was no speaking, no thought, just a magnet to metal. Irulen pulled her face away from him and looked into her wanting eyes. He saw vulnerability. She was letting it all out. She smelt clean, the soapy fragrance driving him into a deeper frenzy. Irulen's hands worked to untie the front of her leather vest. The rope freed, exposing more of her tan body. Open air swirled around her erect nipples. Her skin was covered in goose bumps. Irulen felt swollen. He kissed her deeply as she pressed in close. Together they created heat against the cold night.

* * *

A flood of guilt surged through him. He didn't know how Quinn would react to finding out what had transpired. He also pictured the look in Farah's eyes. The wizard had no desire for anyone to know.

"Look, about Quinn…" Kay stopped putting her clothes back together and put a finger to his mouth. "Its fine, I understand. This can be our little secret." She ran a hand across his cheek as she walked away. He was left with baited breath and the fresh memory of her body moving against his. He sat on a nearby stump. His guilt gave way to a sudden feeling of fear, as if eyes lingered in the darkness. The sensation was inescapable. He stood and looked around. There was a slight giggling in the air, or perhaps just in his mind. His body froze between fight and flight. He stared into the darkness as the darkness seemed to draw closer.

Suddenly, something landed on his shoulder. Irulen

swatted at it and ducked. His open palm made contact, and he looked at what had assailed him. A raven stood on the snow looking discombobulated and confused. Max was perplexed that Irulen would smack him.

"Oh man, I'm sorry buddy." A new wave of guilt poured over him as he held out his right arm. Max flew onto it and offered his left leg into the air. There was a note in his container. A job, finally. Irulen removed his advertising sign from the raven's neck and tucked it away. Then he pulled out the note and unraveled it. It read:

Please come to Warwick as soon as possible.

Irulen hated this sort of correspondence. He expected a thoroughly detailed request of his services, complete with a distinct offer of money. Often, the wizard would not even consider such a proposition. There had been many times where he had passed on a case for such a reason. He learned the hard way after showing up to a town only to be sold short or misled. The worst thing, the absolute worst thing that could ever happen to Irulen was to travel for days only to find out there's no job, after all. There was even a time or two when Irulen arrived, only to find that pranksters had sent Max back with a fake note tucked away.

Figuring he had little choice in the matter—that the chance at work was better than no work at all—Irulen would go to Warwick. He'd just begun to roll the parchment when he noticed something on the back. There was a red blotch—it looked like blood. His interest grew tenfold. Man, bird, and note returned to the Thadmore house.

* * *

Quinn was waiting outside, and Irulen feared the worst. "Where'd you run off to?"

"To take a piss."

"They have an outhouse, you know."

"Yeah, well, you know I'm the feral type. Like to piss under the stars and all that."

"I'm sure you do many things under the stars."

"What are you getting at?"

"Have you seen Kay?

"No."

Quinn's eyes quested across Irulen's face. After a hot moment, they found what they were looking for, and relaxed.

"Max is back huh?"

"Yep, he is."

"With news of a job?"

"Yeah, if you're interested in making a few sheckles."

"Sounds good enough, things are too peaceful in this town. The quicker guys like us get out of Thea's hair, the better. Besides, her old man is being polite now, at least in his own way, but he isn't the welcoming type to willingly offer an extended stay. Where's the job?"

"Warwick. About a day south and a day east from here by way of road."

"Sounds as good as anywhere, I suppose."

CHAPTER 16: TRAIL OF TEARS

Tears fell onto the worn-wood floor as a little girl's chest heaved with sobs. She was surrounded by reddened splotches and lumps of dead meat, the remains of what had been her family. Not even an hour ago she had been running amok in the yard with her brother. Her mother looked on with pride as her father pushed a wheelbarrow of the night's firewood across the green.

Then she was called in for supper.

The potatoes were delicious, and they even had mutton courtesy of an old sheep that had seen the last of her days. The meat was tough but satisfying, especially since it was mixed with her mother's gravy—a recipe often sought after by the other village folk. The girl liked to cut her meat into small pieces, mash up her potatoes, mix it all together and dowse it in her favorite brown concoction.

Her plate, along with those belonging to the rest of her family, now sat half eaten on the table. The inside of their dwelling had the look of a dinner interrupted, and never resumed.

The little girl looked at the mouth of the thing that sent her family from this world. Her father, the closest to where the girl sat, lay on his stomach with a broken neck. His eyes were wide and his mouth was wide open—a scream frozen in time.

The creature smiled, revealing blackened, ill-spaced teeth. It opened its mouth to speak. "You may cry now, child, but you'll be thanking me soon enough. You are free...free to live your life however you want; to become your own person. There will be no more being yelled at, or being hit. There will be no more *shaping* of you anymore."

The girl shook her head as she cried.

"Oh, come now, why is it you girls never get it? You're being brainwashed. By your family. By society. Everyone wants to control you. They want you to become what they see you as being."

The girl blinked and snuffled. Her eyes stared blankly.

The monstrous mouth sighed, and spoke again. "You are better off, even if you don't know it. I was just like you, once. My parents were happy together, and I loved them very much. Only... I wish I had someone like me *now* to warn me *then*. It was all an illusion. Do you know what an illusion is?"

The girl didn't respond.

The mouth tightened until its light lips turned pale. "Answer me," it commanded, wispily.

The breath seemed to carry and collect around the girl's face. The girl grew quiet and raised her eyes. "I don't know what it is?"

"Can you pronounce it?"

"Eh-eh-ill-ew-shun."

The mouth smiled again. "Excellent! An illusion is when something is presented to you as a thing that it isn't."

"Like a magic trick?" The girl cocked her head.

"Something like that, but it can come in many forms. You see this man here, on the ground? Who is he?"

"My father."

"And what is he?"

"He's dead."

"Well I'm going to tell you something. He isn't your father, and you shouldn't be crying about him being dead. Let me explain. . ."

* * *

Farah felt fatigued. It took one day heading south and one day heading east before they arrived at Warwick. Late enough into the season and far enough south, the group finally felt the weather easing. The snow was less dense now, the chill less biting. As they neared Warwick, the weather was particularly warm.

"The town should be around any of these bends now." Irulen seemed to hope to inspire the others, give them reassurance to make it up the inclined path they currently walked.

Quinn responded between heavy breaths, "Aye, I believe ya…but you said that about twenty passes ago."

Breaking her silence, Farah chimed in. "I've never walked so much in my life as in these last few weeks."

"What's a matter, girl?" asked Kay, stoically. "Don't enjoy the exercise?"

Farah scoffed but found herself short on words. It had only been the better part of two days, and she already missed Thea fiercely. Before they left Snowillow Pass, Thea propositioned Farah to stay. She would seek permission from her father and she insisted he would be hard pressed to refuse his cherished daughter. Farah could have stayed in Snowillow Pass with them as a member of their household. Farah declined, and for reasons that were becoming less clear, decided to continue on the path she had been placed.

Still, she couldn't get away from the disenchantment of her savior. In her eyes, Irulen had become more human, resultantly, more flawed. She didn't hate him, far from it, but she couldn't help but question the logic behind the way he used his magic. Surely, someone who was gifted with his abilities need not hire out his services for money. He did not pay for the magic that was naturally bestowed upon him, and so he had little right to make people pay for his help.

Maybe it wasn't fair to blame Irulen for Jorin's death, or leaving the bloodshed of Northforge behind him. Farah was, after all, keenly aware of her own naiveté. It was this self-awareness that, perhaps, served as the engine that kept her going, the drive to learn more about the world and her place within its confines. As it was, she had decided to try her best to keep an open mind in regard to Irulen's dealings, all the while hoping that perhaps she could make a difference in the way he conducted himself as well.

In the background of these thoughts there was a primordial compulsion to help him in any way she could. Farah didn't doubt that her fate was intertwined with his. *I will see it through to the end*, she repeated for what must have been the hundredth time.

Max flew from up the road, where he'd been scouting on ahead. The raven landed on Irulen's arm and made a sound that Farah had never heard him make before. It was similar to a honk-two honks in tandem, one higher pitch than the other. Irulen came to attention and turned to the others. "There's someone in need of help up the road."

"Maybe it has something to do with why we were called here," Kay stated, rationally.

"Let's move faster and have a look." Irulen picked up his pace.

The group was unwilling to drop their things for fear of being robbed, and so they traveled as fast as they could with their gear in tow. It wasn't long before they came across what Max had found. A young girl was laid out off the side of the road. The child looked as if she was sleeping—her breaths were quick and silent. She looked peaceful. The group halted for a moment looking at her. Farah was the first to investigate. She called to the girl as she approached, but there was nothing in response. The girl's breathing grew louder as Farah edged closer, even though her eyes remained shut. Farah squatted over and reached out slowly to the girl's shoulder. Her hand hesitated for a moment, leaving two inches of air between her fingers and the child. The possibility of disease and pestilence invaded her mind. She turned from the girl to seek Irulen's advice.

She regretted her decision instantly, as the hair on her neck shot up and her back spasmed tensely. The girl sprung to life behind her, screaming and sobbing. Farah stumbled and lost her footing. Before she could do anything, she was on her back with the girl on top of her. Farah's eyes widened like a deer having its belly chewed. And then, silence. The girl passed out on top of her, once again sleeping as angelically as could be.

Farah didn't move as Irulen hovered over her. He lifted

the child up and handed her to Quinn who then hoisted the girl over his shoulder. Irulen offered his hand and helped Farah to her feet.

"We've been through quite a lot for you to be so frightened of a young one like this." Irulen dusted her off as he spoke.

"Yeah, well, with all the crazy shit I've seen recently... I guess I'm a little on edge."

"Careful." Irulen waved a finger at her. "Your level of profanity has risen, pretty soon you'll be sounding like Quinn or Kay."

"Hey what's that s'pose to mean?" Quinn did his best to appear indignant, but it was ruined by the sparkle in his eye.

"Nothing, my noble friend, we should get a move on."

"Yes," interjected Kay, "we have a lot of *shit* we need to do." She shot Irulen a quick glare before turning forward.

CHAPTER 17: A SMALL TOWN

The town itself was typical enough, it reminded Farah very much of Frostbridge minus the walls. The road also ran right through the middle of town instead of circumventing it. As they walked into the village, Irulen was greeted by a familiar sight. A mob of people holding an array of tools and makeshift weaponry were gathered. The people were so involved with each other that they failed to notice the group of strangers coming upon them.

The scene left Irulen and the others in an awkward position. For one, the people were obviously enraged. The very introduction of strangers to the scenario might ignite an already volatile situation. It would be bad business to get chased out of town before even learning of the job, let alone completing it. On the other hand, Irulen felt that the longer they waited the worse the situation would become.

The wizard raised his hand feebly. "Hello, does this girl belong to you?" He pointed to the defunct form Quinn was carrying.

The crowd fell silent. There was too much malevolence in the air for Irulen not to speak again. "I am Irulen, a traveling wizard often hired to solve crimes. One of you summoned me here, and we found this girl along the way."

"Which way was it that ye came?" asked a random voice.

"From the way it looks like we were walking from—from the north."

"We just went that way," said someone else.

"And there was no girl there," finished another.

"Well, there was one when we passed through." Irulen

signaled to Quinn, who brought the girl forward and laid her on the ground.

A lady quickly emerged from the crowd to join the child. The lady's middle-aged face was wrought with grief, and while some bit of relief came into her eyes there remained a deeper anguish. This girl, it seemed, was only the beginning of the story.

"This is Juliet," said the lady, "I am her aunt."

"And so you know where her parents are, then?" Irulen regretted his question instantly. The girl's aunt broke into sobs as other ladies from the mob emerged to console her.

"Aye, she knows where they are," said a man with long brown hair parted in the middle. His hair color matched his attire. "But the question, I suppose, is do *you* know where they are? Or maybe what happened to 'em?"

"Don't be absurd." Irulen bristled. What was this man accusing him of? "All I know is that there's been a crime and that someone summoned me by sending a note with my raven. Irulen reached under his cloak and fished out the letter. "Here." He offered the parchment to the man in brown.

"Well, I am one of two people in this town who can write this well, and it wasn't me. I saw your raven lurking about, but I didn't request your services."

"Perhaps you could point me in the direction of the fellow who did, then?" Irulen lifted a brow.

"I cannot, because he isn't to be found. He's been missing since last night. Apparently, he just walked out into the darkness and vanished."

"Why would he do that?"

"Because he's ashamed of his son."

"What about his son?"

"Look, mister, you aren't needed here, and I still find you suspicious. Maybe you should just go."

Just as Irulen turned to consult the others yet another voice cried out. "The man you are looking for is the father of a *boy* these people mean to kill."

The voice came from a young, pretty teenage girl with blonde hair and blue eyes. The man in brown spun on her. "He is *hardly* a boy. He's past eighteen years of age and ought to be held responsible…as an *adult*."

"He can't even put together the words to defend himself!" the girl protested.

While this conversation was happening, some of the townsfolk took away the young girl Max had found.

"Who?" asked Irulen.

The man in brown spun back toward Irulen. "Look, I said no one here hired you. This is no business of yours."

Irulen shrugged and turned to walk away.

Farah put her hand out to stop him.

"We *can't* leave." She met Irulen's eyes. She said nothing more and nothing less.

"I don't know, I've been from one mess to another," he offered, meekly.

"We don't know what they'll do to this person," she persisted.

"Do you know how many people have things done to them that we don't know about? All throughout the world?" he asked, fearing her answer.

"Many, I'm sure." The look she wore told him she wasn't going to drop this. "And I'm sure you are going to feed me a line about how this is the way the world works and you can't help everyone…" She paused for a moment to collect her thoughts. Irulen braced for impact.

"But," she continued, as she pointed a finger at him, "the hordes of faceless victims didn't have someone like you to help them. You're so busy saving your magic for the right moment that you don't realize the path that has already been set in front of you. Help who you can when they need you. You can't keep waiting for some world-saving event to spend your magic on. Maybe…you just aren't that special."

"Tell us how you really feel," said Kay, dryly.

Irulen shook his head and looked to Quinn, who shrugged his shoulders in return.

In an effort to avoid having to choose a firm course of action, Irulen turned back to the crowd. The interruption had left them less ravenous and, Irulen hoped, more agreeable. "Does anyone have a room we can rent for the night? The trail wears us thin."

Brown man looked appalled. "What's the matter with you? Can't you tell there's village business that needs to be handled?"

"There's always something going on somewhere—but everyone needs to make coin—and coin we have. Besides, there's a killing to be had, what better entertainment could we ask for?"

Irulen's words, along with the burning of time, caused the mob to become introspective. The frenzy they had been in was gone and, as if being snapped from a trance, they became individuals again.

An older lady stepped forward. She wore her white hair in a tight bun and walked with an air of authority. Judging from the looks of those around her, she was obviously well respected. Irulen bowed to her slightly, a gesture that was mimicked awkwardly by Farah and Quinn. Kay stood proud and defiant.

"I have accommodations for you, and perhaps we need someone from the outside to view our matter with fresh eyes. You see, there has been a terrible crime committed. One too gruesome to explain without tears. One you would have to see for yourself to admit. The boy of which Eleanor speaks," the lady indicated the girl with the blond hair and blue eyes, "was found at the scene of a murder. An entire family was killed…he had blood on him. His name is Merek, a troubled youth who struggles to communicate with the rest of us. He is always drawing, or *arranging* things, or just staring blankly. He is a daydreamer in the queerest sort of way. He isn't like the rest of us. The name of the man who wrote the letter to you—the boy's father—is Ayleth Builder."

"And he is the one who's missing," concluded Irulen. "For how long has he been missing?"

"A few days, at least." The lady paused and raised her right hand to her cheek in thought. "Which is odd because the Robin family murders only happened three days ago. I don't recall seeing him around."

"Since the murders, or before the murders?" asked
Irulen.

"Since before, for me at least." The lady enquired of the
other townsfolk whether they had spotted Ayleth. She asked
particularly whether anyone saw him deliver the note to Max, the
one that beckoned Irulen to come to Warwick. No one had.

"Perhaps the father had a hand in it all, and skipped
town," the man in brown suggested.

"Enough, Josef," said the lady with the white hair. "We
should allow these professionals to do their job, to find the
truth."

Josef spat on the ground, "I mean to give them a day or
two and nothing more, nothing less. Then I'll go shake that boys
head out of the clouds at the end of a rope." He stormed off and
the crowd slowly began to disperse. Many still lingered,
ghoulishly craving the unfolding of more dramatic details. The
crowd hovered, still, even as the lady in white introduced herself
as Ariana and led the strangers away to her tavern. Some kids
leaned in too close to Kay as she passed. She hissed at them and
they scurried away.

* * *

There were no other guests staying at Ariana's Inn that
night, and so the group found themselves spoiled. They each
were given a private room in which they dumped their supplies.
Rations of smoked rabbit and ale were doled out and devoured
greedily. Irulen asked Ariana to explain what had actually
happened. The foggy snippets he had gleaned from the mob
came more clearly into focus.

Ariana explained. "There was a triple homicide—a
family of farmers who lived on the far edge of town. We became
alerted when the boy Merek showed up with blood all about him.
His hands, his clothes, there was red everywhere. He could have
easily been mistaken for a ghoul or some other ghastly creature.
It was Josef and I who spotted him first, and perhaps that is why
he and I differ on our opinions so. He saw a dumb creature

guilty of murder, I saw a victim.

We asked Merek about what had happened but he stared blankly, he stares blankly still. Josef took custody of him and has him locked up at his house. What hasn't helped Merek's cause, is that he keeps drawing grotesque pictures of the crime scene. A more positive part of his…condition…is that he draws very well. The pictures he has drawn are so compelling and disgusting that Josef points to them as evidence of the boy's guilt."

"And you don't think it is?" Irulen's curiosity was peaked.

"No, I think the boy is coping in his own way. He might be aloof, but everyone has a soul, and his soul is hurting. He was known to show up randomly at people's houses and to get into trouble. Many people were creeped out by that. Imagine you are eating your dinner and then you notice a face watching you through the shutters. It doesn't serve him well at all—that people already found him suspicious and strange."

Irulen looked at the closed shutters of Ariana's tavern. He saw eyes peering through. He blinked, and they were gone…a simple trick of the mind.

When they were finished eating, Irulen thanked Ariana for filling them in. He then enquired about the location where the murders took place. Ariana gave him rough directions to the edge of town. She took it on herself to tell them that the bodies had already been removed and put to the fire. Many people in the north and beyond believed that after death the soul would be trapped in a body. The Great Conflict a long time ago had wiped the gods from the planet, but the people were still spiritual and believe in the *something after*.

Different towns had different customs of preparation, but for the most part, people believed in the cremation of the corpse and so the releasing of the spirit within. The ones who prepared the bodies and sent them to the beyond were called *releasers*. The spirit would return to the nature from whence it came, and the cycle of life would continue.

Be that as it may, these customs left Irulen with no

bodies to examine. The urgency to put the corpses to the fire also left Irulen with a crime scene that might not be as helpful as the wizard had hoped. Still, he was in the spirit of doing some mystery solving and so decided to check the scene before the end of a day that was already fading. With any luck he'd find a clue to Ayleth Builder's whereabouts. If the wizard located him, then maybe he could find someone to cover the costs of his services. Without such a patron, he would not use magic.

Kay and Quinn traveled with him, Farah stayed behind for a bath.

"You know, she's going to have to find a way to earn her keep," Kay said, about Farah.

"She will, of that I have no doubt," responded Irulen. In all truth, Irulen still felt responsible for Farah. "You could," he continued to Kay, "teach her to fight, for one thing."

Kay laughed. "Maybe, but I doubt it. I have been rather bored lately."

Quinn spoke up. "Quinn can't stand seeing a pretty lady bored. If it's boredom ye have then its time with Quinn ye need."

"Do you always advertise yourself in the third person?" asked Kay.

"Only sometimes, when there's something I really want to sell."

Kay met Irulen's eyes for the slightest of moments before she responded. "What are you suggesting? This isn't exactly the place for a night out on the town."

"Oh, well, we have a tavern to ourselves…a place to sit and ale to drink is all we need. A floor to dance and an instrument to play…even better."

Irulen could hardly hold back a mixture of feelings as Quinn showed more interest in Kay. He felt guilty knowing he had sampled the nectar Quinn was trying to harvest. Irulen was stuck between living a lie and watching irreparable harm cross his friend's face. Quinn had an honest heart that he wore on his sleeve. Quinn was a good man. Irulen felt despicable, even more so because he found Quinn's advances annoying. The wizard was feeling protective of his prize.

Still, even as Quinn looked to Irulen to put in the good word for him, Irulen felt it best to remain silent. Instead, his mind became focused on the memory of her; her smell, her touch, her sounds…her heat.

Irulen adjusted his clothes as they walked.

They carried on with the small talk for a while. They spoke of the warming weather, of the end of winter, and other such trivialities.

Quinn complained of his aching joints. "It has been a long while since Ole Quinn walked so much."

"You aren't even that *old*, you know."

"Maybe the aching is not in my body, but my soul. An ageless thing, that."

"Whatever you say."

As they walked, the men tried to identifying different birds flapping about in search of an afternoon meal…and they arrived at the house they were searching for.

To say the dwelling looked any different or more foreboding than the others would be a lie. To Irulen, though, the places that house death always radiate death. It was as if death clung to the wood and hung in the air. A place of death was the *unworld*, enshrouded by the veil between life and loss. No, it couldn't be described with any form of clarity, but Irulen believed in the visible identity of death. *He* could see it. *He* could *feel* it.

The front door hung open. The house appeared lonely against the open fields behind it. The fields were just beginning to thaw from the deep frost. Soon they would be ripe for tilling and planting, but there was no longer a family to do so. Irulen finished opening the creaky door with his left hand, and passed through.

The inside was dark and dank. Quinn coughed. They fumbled about and opened all the shutters they could find. Light poured in over the bloodstained timber of the floor. Near the kitchen area there was a table set with days old dinner. Insects crawled over the rotten food. Irulen surveyed the scene. The bodies had been removed, but the townsfolk had done little else to the inside of the house. Perhaps it was superstition that kept them at bay.

Quinn spoke, more to himself than the others. "You can almost see their ghosts, eating at the table."

"I don't see ghosts," Irulen answered, just as reverently, "but I see where the bodies were left. The mother was over there in the kitchen. She was likely retrieving forks for the kids, since their plates lack the proper utensils... Or at least something of the like. The father was the first to go down, here in the center of the room. The chair at the head of the table isn't knocked over like the others, it was slid. This tells me he likely answered the door. He was viciously attacked, surprised, and didn't realize what was happening. He stumbled backward, and so landed on his back. He was hacked brutally, but he was also finished quickly, so that the others didn't get away."

"Wait a second," Quinn interjected. "How do you know he landed on his back?"

Irulen pointed up at the ceiling. "You'd have to puncture someone's neck in the right place to get that sort of spray, and you can tell from how thin the line was that the man's neck spun rather fast."

"He could have spun and landed on his stomach, then," said Quinn, proud of his newfound skills of deduction.

"Yes, but look at the dried blood around his feet. There's an unbloodied patch and it fits the heel of the foot. If the heel of the foot was down then his feet were up. Maybe this person broke his feet and flipped them over. If you want you can ask the townspeople that. I think it's probable enough that he was on his back.

He was taken by force. He wasn't killed, he was destroyed. The pattern of blood spatter looks almost as if he was hacked and slashed by more than one person at the same time, but I can't say for sure. It just seems to me that the blood pressure of the wounds appear to be consistent with many wounds at once, or at least, very close together. The droplets of blood scattered about indicate a frenzy of stabs."

Irulen walked over near the table. "The son, who died

over here, came second. The mother, likely the one in the kitchen, was stunned. She went last, numb to her physical pain."

"What about the little girl we found?" asked Kay.

"Yeah, how'd she get away?" asked Quinn.

"The only thing I can think of is that she was in the outhouse at the time…which doesn't make a lot of sense." Irulen trailed off into a deep thought. Quinn waved for him to go on. "Because," Irulen continued, "if the killer was a local he'd know he missed one."

"You think it was a random killer then?" asked Quinn.

"Maybe." Irulen's brows drew together in a scowl. "We can start by finding out who had something to gain from all this. Perhaps someone needed land, or a house. Maybe someone owed money. Maybe someone *hired* a killer to come here, someone who didn't know the family."

"Or maybe the suspect they have really did the killing." When he looked up at her, Kay shrugged matter-of-factly. "Someone with a tainted mind wouldn't be diligently counting bodies."

"Very possible." He had to concede, though it still didn't feel right to him. "But we'll talk to him in the morning. I just wonder if this scene has anything else to offer…I wish we could see the bodies."

"A morbid employment you have chosen," said Quinn. "You revel in death and dismay. I on the other hand specialize in drunkenness and revelry."

"A perfect balance," Kay remarked, dryly.

"You're starting to sound like Merlane," Irulen pointed out.

"Oh, yes, I've been having quite the spiritual awakening."

Dusk was coming on and the light was fading. Still, Irulen combed over the scene as best he could. Much of the place had been disturbed from the dragging and moving of the bodies. That didn't keep the wizard from finding a couple more clues. He followed the blood spatter from the father's spot, and found that the ends of each spray were cut off short. It looked as if someone was sitting against the wall. Someone was sprayed by the man's blood, but seemed otherwise uninjured. There were only four family members, and he had identified three areas of murder.

"Someone was here." He pointed at the floor near the wall. "Someone was here whose body kept the blood from hitting the ground." Irulen stared intently at something on the floor near the area he was indicating. He took a large step and hunched over. There was a large metal nail sticking out of the floorboard. Attached to it was a ragged piece of cloth. It looked as if it had been torn from something. The wizard removed it carefully and held it up.

"With this, perhaps we can tie someone to the crime. Whether it be a victim or villain… Well, time will tell." Irulen wiped at his brow. He would often sweat during the heat of an investigation, even when the air was chill. The air suddenly seemed stagnant and dust-filled. *Air.*

Kay and Quinn joined Irulen to where he'd retreated outside of the house. The fresh air of dusk filled his lungs. He gagged on it, as if pouring water on a night of hard drinking.

"Are you alright?" asked Quinn.

"You seemed fine just a second ago," added Kay.

"Yeah, yeah. I feel fine. I'm not sure what that was about." Irulen rubbed his hands over his face and flexed the muscles in his cheeks. He worked his mouth around and jumped up and down twice. The wizard felt ready to get back into the game.

"Maybe your body is telling you something your mind doesn't know," Quinn suggested.

"Like what?"

"Like, get some rest."

"Yeah, let's do that. I'll speak to the kid in the morning."

"What makes you so sure he'll still be alive in the morning?" asked Kay. "That wimpy man in brown has him."

"A hanging tomorrow is as good as a hanging tonight," answered Irulen. "Besides, it might make *him* look guilty if he kills the kid during an active investigation."

"Do you think he had a hand in it?" Kay looked quizzically at him.

"Oh, I don't know, men like him often do. Many are just stuck in skewed ideals of justice. Perhaps a new day will tell."

CHAPTER 18: CLOUDWALKER

"I'm leaving."

Irulen's head snapped toward Kay in surprise. Sweat still sat upon her brow from their recent exertion. "What?"

She rolled toward him. "I'm going on ahead, to Riverfall."

Words eluded him. "Why?"

"Coin, of course. Riverfall is a hub for bounties. You don't need me here, not for your *work*, anyway." She smiled.

"But...I—"

"But nothing." She pulled at his chest hair.

"Ow."

Her hand flattened against his chest. "You all can join me after you've finished here, and we'll all be the richer for it." She sat up in the bed they shared, and looked around searchingly. Irulen found what she was looking for, and held her top in the air.

She snatched it from him and draped it loosely over her head. Irulen frowned as the fabric covered her breasts.

She stood. "You *are* still heading south, anyway, right?"

"Yes, I guess so."

Her undergarments in place, Kay pulled up her leggings. "Find me there then, after you find the killer." She moved back onto the bed and pressed against him. "Think of my absence as motivation." A smile of mischief crept across her face as she withdrew once more.

Irulen felt quite mixed over what was happening. Many stupid and crazy things crossed his mind to say: *Don't go. Wait. I need you here. I like you. Care for round two?* Only something trite passed through his lips. "Do you have everything?"

Kay laughed and tied her leather top. "Yes, I think I can manage."

Irulen sat up and moved backward until his back pressed against the wall. "I feel sorry for the people you hunt. I nearly soiled my trousers when you first crept into my room."

Kay shook her head. "I appreciate the visual."

"I felt like I was your prey."

"Well, I did devour you in a way."

"You know." He pointed at her and squinted an eye. "You have a way with words for someone who doesn't like talking."

"I like talking."

"Most people who meet you would beg to differ."

"It's not my fault if they don't interest me." She shrugged indifferently.

Irulen put his hands in the air, gesturing submission. "Fair enough, fair enough."

"I'm ready to go."

"Now, really?"

"Yes. Goodbye."

Kay cracked the door open, put an ear to it, and slipped out into the hall.

Irulen already wished he had urged her more to stay. There was no doubt in Irulen's head, however, that he would see Kay sooner than later. This was far from a permanent goodbye. In fact, he believed in her. She'd be waiting for him once business in Warwick was concluded.

Irulen figured Kay knew he was heading south to find Lynette. It was something they had never spoken about, but the wizard understood that Kay had a hand in leading him where he needed to be. She wasn't done with him quite yet.

So it was that he didn't miss her, per say, but a cloud had settled over his heart. Beneath it all was unsettled business between Farah and him. Things had looked so promising earlier, only to have soured over time. Still, with Kay gone maybe he would be able to have a look down that avenue once more.

At breakfast, Quinn had valiantly volunteered to accompany Kay to Riverfall. She politely declined, or at least as politely as Kay could, stating that Irulen was likely to need Quinn right where they were—especially if the investigation went sour and the mob rose again.

After Kay left, Irulen, and Quinn set out to the home of Josef, where the young boy Merek was being kept. Farah remained behind to offer her services to Ariana. The old woman agreed to pay a modest sum to Farah for her services. The girl would help clean and collect firewood while the wizard and barbarian were gone. It suited her just fine. Despite Irulen's failed appeals, she kept Max as company.

* * *

Josef was waiting outside his house when the group arrived. His wife lurked behind him like a beaten sheep. When they were close enough, he forced her inside. He then spat at the ground, signaled to them, and called for them to go around the back.

"The boy's in the barn with the other animals," he called out.

"Why's he have to bring animals into this?" Quinn asked Irulen.

"I've never understood why animals have such a negative connotation." Irulen shrugged.

"What's a *connotation*?" asked Quinn.

"'A meaning attributed to a word outside of its actual definition. He used *animals* as something detrimental, when in all reality animals have nothing to do with murder, spite, and the like."

"Hmmm…" Quinn mulled the thought over for a moment and seemed to come to an understanding with himself. He nodded and followed Irulen around the back of the house.

They came to a large, brown barn. Inside were two stabled horses, some chickens, and a prize sow gnawing at some feed. In the back of the place sat Merek, a relatively scrawny youth with pale yet comely features contrasted by curly black hair and deep, dark eyes. He sat with a chain running from his ankle to an eyebolt attached to the floor.

What was most striking about Merek was not that he was restrained or looked threatening or threatened in any way. He didn't look downtrodden, defeated, sad, or angry. No, what was fascinating about Merek was that he sat cross legged with a look of concentration on his face.

Seemingly impervious to the outside world, the young man was seated next to an unruly pile of hay. His left hand kept wandering over and sorting through the hay pieces. Once he found a piece the right size he brought it to where he was staring at a neatly stacked triangle of dried up grass. His left hand and brain seemed to be disconnected, as if they existed independently of each other. The boy stacked carefully with his right hand, seemingly content in his work.

"Doesn't look like he knows people are trying to kill him," Quinn blurted, loudly. Irulen winced at the insensitivity of the brute, but Merek seemed not to notice.

"You know what they say about these cloud walkers?" Quinn studied Merek. "It's said that these people are leftover fragments of the gods—all of the gods destroyed during The Great Conflict. They were shattered into many spirits, and some of these spirits inhabit the bodies of humans. They fear no human reality, and they often display miraculous talents."

"They say similar things about people like me, that we are leftovers from the same past. That, at least, seems untrue. Besides, if he has a talent, what is it? Stacking hay?" Irulen asked facetiously.

"No." The terse male voice came from behind them. They turned to find Josef standing in the entrance looking discontent. He glared past them and at Merek. "His talent, other than killing, is to draw." Josef thrust a pile of papers toward Irulen. The papers hit him in the gut before his hands could catch them.

Irulen took a few steps toward Merek and away from Josef. He had learned enough to be wary of Josef's type, to never show his back for too long. Instead of watching his back from the door, though, Quinn followed and peered over his shoulder. *At some point I really need to have a chat with the dolt.* Be that as it may, Irulen kept an ear listening for Josef to move while he flipped through the pages.

The drawings were immaculate in their detail, and they were mostly of the crime scene. The first was a drawing of the father, laid out on his back, his face frozen in an unfinished scream. The second was of a little boy, knocked off his chair, crumpled in a bloody mess. Somehow, the boy looked peaceful. The next image was of the mother, knife in hand, face-down on the floor of the kitchen. The final drawing froze Irulen in place.

"Hey." Quinn pointed to the drawing. "Isn't that the same lady in Kay's drawing?"

Josef spoke up. "You've seen that person before? I figured it was how the boy saw himself. He's a weird one, angry and vindictive. Watch."

Josef walked up to Merek and kicked his stack of hay. Merek paused for a moment and then lunged upward. The boy screamed incoherently at Josef as his length of chain ran out. Josef turned back to Irulen, looking pleased with himself.

"That mystery woman might have had something to do with the murders, but so did he," the man said.

"Do you have any paper?" Irulen didn't take his gaze from the boy.

"Sure do, Diane, his little darling, or whatever she is, brought some for him. I took it away from him when he started drawing this filth."

"Is Diane that young girl with the blond hair and blue eyes from yesterday?" asked Irulen.

"Yes," responded Josef. "She loves to come bat those pretty little eyeholes of hers at this monster."

"We need him to draw again," said Irulen, plainly.

"Why?" Josef protested.

"Look friend." Quinn placed his bear paw on Josef's shoulder. "Just fetch the paper, what harm would come of it?" Quinn's paw tightened menacingly around the man's shoulder. Quinn's face, however, was all smiles.

Josef stormed out of the place as quickly as he had come in.

There's a duality about Quinn. His smile told of a person who enjoyed life. He'd wear a smile whether sharing a drink or sharing his fist, it didn't matter. He was both a lover and a fighter, a warrior and an artist. His vice was that he felt guilty over how *much* he enjoyed it all. His friend Aldo could never do the same.

Merek had settled back down after Josef left. The boy was busily rebuilding his neat stack of hay. There seemed to be a newfound urgency in his movements.

Irulen tried to use the time Josef was gone to get something across to Quinn.

"You know, Quinn, you can't be so trusting."

"What do you mean?" The brute frowned at him, obviously oblivious.

"If we are dealing with someone like, say, Josef—who may be the *killer* we are after—try not to leave our backs to the man."

"Him? A killer? Nah, a man like that needs other men at his back to do such a deed."

"Maybe, but still, you're missing the point. I'm talking about now moving forward—he's coming."

Josef walked in and the men were silent. He eyeballed the other two suspiciously, as if he divined a glimpse of what they were saying. The farmer handed Irulen the papers, much more gently this time. Then Josef fished a chunk of graphite out of his pocket and tossed it in the air. Irulen grabbed it and brought the utilities to Merek. Once the paper and graphite was laid out next to the new stack of hay, Merek stopped everything. He looked from one project to another, and finally decided to grab the paper and start drawing.

"I hope you're happy," said Josef, "I hope he draws up a severed cow penis for your troubles." Josef left again, throwing his right hand up in a half-hearted attempt at saying goodbye.

Quinn laughed. "I like him!"

"You would, you like everyone." Irulen continued to

watch Merek.

"I don't like Lynette, and I like this situation even less," Quinn countered.

"What situation?"

"That's her, isn't it, in the picture?" He held Irulen's gaze.

"Yes." Irulen was unsure of how Quinn had connected the dots. His friend had the strength of a barbarian, but was still cunning all the same. The wizard reminded himself never to underestimate his friend—something he found himself doing fairly often.

"I don't like the way her name keeps popping up." Quinn scratched at his head. "It's like she's the one pulling our strings. She leaves bread crumbs and we're the pigeons."

The wizard let out a deep breath. "I don't deny it, but I need to fix this thing with her, and even though she may be leaving a trail for us to follow… I need to see it through."

Quinn laughed. "I guess you're right. She's out killing people and it's your fault, I guess."

"Thanks for the reminder, dick," Irulen retorted. "In all seriousness, though, I thought I could leave her be. Imps flame out quickly. They have a much lower threshold of magic than their masters. Then they are gone—at least from what I've gathered. But Lynette isn't going anywhere, and I'm not sure why. She's tied up with this mystery-man I'm hunting, a man who has the secret to unending magic. I'm guessing he has something to do all of this. Regardless, if Lynette isn't leaving this world through the natural order, I need to send her off myself."

Quinn let out a long whistle. "Well, that sounds grand. I can't wait 'til I'm whistling and walking away after you get yourself killed."

"Seriously, shut up."

The men's bickering was interrupted by the fury of Merek's drawing. The youth was so enamored, so busily scrawling on the paper that the sound of his labor dominated the silence. Irulen looked to Quinn, who raised his eyebrows and furrowed his lips in curiosity. All at once, they moved around the youth and peered over his shoulder. It was only an afterthought to Irulen that the young man might be dangerous.

Right at that moment, the only thing in danger was the parchment on which Merek perpetrated his work. He was working left to right from the bottom up. Irulen had expected the drawing to be another of the crime scene, but there were some obvious differences right away. The ground of the picture was a forest of blood. There were patches of melted snow littered with dead leaves. Irulen could barely make out the beginnings of what seemed to be a body laid out on the ground. A hand extended from the white part of the paper onto the drawn forest floor.

"Whose hand do you reckon that is?" Quinn leaned over.

"How should I know?" Irulen squinted at the page, as if bringing it into focus would give him the answers he sought.

Failing to come up with any other leads, they decided their time would best be spent waiting for Merek to finish. They went outside and found a comfortable tree to sit against, Quinn on one side and Irulen on the other. Quinn took out his flagon and pulled a healthy drought from it into his throat. Irulen at first declined, since it was still rather early for a drink. The cold air convinced him otherwise, and he took a drought to warm his insides.

He then pulled his hood over his head and closed his eyes. He had slept soundly after Kay had slipped out, so peacefully in fact that he had an inclination to sleep the day away. Sometime soon, when this case was wrapped up, Irulen would spend an entire day in bed—without a woman. He'd make sweet love to his mattress and whisper sweet nothings into his pillow. He'd float on a cloud and lock the door against intrusions.

Rest and relaxation, the pureness of remaining still, those things had eluded Irulen for far too long.

CHAPTER 19: A CLEARER PICTURE

Irulen was awoken by Quinn's mighty brick of a foot kicking at his. "Drawing's done."

"Really? How long?"

"The better part of two hours." Quinn laughed. "I didn't want to wake you, even though you snore an awful lot."

"No I don't."

"Well just now you did. You can sleep when you're dead, but the drawing is finished." Quinn handed the paper to Irulen.

"Now who is this, I wonder?" The wizard examined the new drawing.

A dead man lay across the ground. His sliced neck had bled out onto the forest floor. Behind him there was a large fractured tree, broken at the stump. It had the look of being blown over by high winds.

They brought the drawing to Josef who told them the man pictured was the same man who had sent Irulen the letter, Ayleth Builder, Merek's father. The farmer also thought he recognized the area in the forest. He had seen such a felled oak not too long ago. He walked them straight into the woods from his own back yard, something Irulen found suspicious. More suspicious still was the surety with which Josef navigated the forest. The man hardly ever hesitated, never questioned his path, just walked with a purpose. Before the passing of ten minutes he'd brought them to the spot, and there—at the base of a felled oak tree—was the corpse of Ayleth Builder.

The smell of the corpse was only faint in the air.

"Though it's hard to tell with the temperature

fluctuating below freezing, this corpse is relatively fresh. This man was likely killed shortly after the family murders." Irulen bent to get a closer look.

"There's something morbid about a man who calls a corpse *fresh*," snarled Josef. "This is the fourth of our people to be violently *murdered*, he isn't a *fresh corpse*. He was…is…an *old friend*."

Irulen was surprised to be caught out by a man like Josef. There wasn't much to be said, except "Sorry," which the wizard did utter, albeit unwillingly. "It's the nature of the profession," Irulen continued, "please, don't take it personally."

Josef nodded and took a step back as Irulen continued his investigation. Ayleth's tunic had been torn to shreds in the middle and his chest was exposed. Irulen reluctantly penetrated the wound with his hand, though he knew what he would find. A death diamond had been planted next to the man's heart. The blackness in the middle of it was larger and darker than ever before.

Merlane's old apprentice was growing in power. Since Lynette was involved with him, then she may be benefiting as well. Relying solely on his naturally endowed magic, Irulen had an uphill fight in front of him. His urgency to find the creatures doubled. He turned to Josef. "Did the other bodies have wounds like this, or were any gems like this one found?" The wizard lifted the diamond.

"No, you can double check with Erik, the releaser, if you want. He's two doors down from the inn you're staying at. Tall, gaunt fellow with long white hair. You can also sort through the releasing pyre."

Usually the way the imps worked was to get a human to do the killing for them, since human hands were needed to make the death diamonds work. Irulen had suspected that Ayleth might have been the killer. Had that been the case, though, the bodies at the house would have had diamonds, and Ayleth himself would have been left for dead and diamondless. *So the family was a cover, the cycle started after—Alyeth was the first to be harvested. If Lynette killed the family, she needed someone else to kill*

Ayleth. She's gone, but someone remained.

Irulen repeated his thoughts aloud. "The person who killed the family is gone from here. She is a repeat killer I've been tracking. But, there is likely still a killer at large, whoever killed this man."

"Are you saying the lady with the black streaks on her face is real?" Josef paled. "I thought she was nothing more than a sick kid's imagination. If it pleases you just the same, I'm still going to hold Merek until you find some proof of innocence."

Quinn took exception to what Josef said. "Where I come from people are innocent *until* proven guilty." The brute stiffened.

"Well, each town has a different code do they not? I need to keep this town safe."

"I won't find any more evidence of the first killer, she wouldn't leave any. But…" Irulen fished around in his pockets. The process took just long enough to make the silence awkward. He came out with a torn rag. "This may belong to the second killer, I found it at the scene. I'll ask the releaser about the clothing of the victims. This man here has no such tear. We can also test Merek."

"We already know Merek was there from his drawings," Josef pointed out.

"Yes, perhaps, but we don't know that he was alone."

Quinn had a thought. "Maybe we should get him to make another drawing," he suggested.

Irulen nodded his agreement. "Perhaps that well hasn't yet dried. Tell you what, let's go back to Merek and check his clothes. Then you stay with him while he draws, and I will go with Josef to question the undertaker and let him know about this bod—" Irulen caught himself, "Ayleth's whereabouts."

The men returned to find Merek, once again, building a pile of hay. Josef fed his livestock while Quinn and Irulen tried to carefully match the fabric to what Merek was wearing. His clothes had bloodstains on them, but the piece of fabric did not seem to apply to him. Merek, like Josef and many other members of the town, wore shades of brown. The cloth was a shade darker than Merek's attire, and he did not have any visible rips or holes. Irulen placed the parchment and graphite next to the hay stack and left the young man be. Quinn set himself back up at the same tree they'd been under before. Once Josef was ready, he accompanied Irulen back toward the town center.

Josef brought Irulen to where the bodies were put to flames. He sifted through an ash that had not been dispersed with the wind, but found no gems or anything else of use. They then went to Erik, the town releaser, and found him in his dwelling.

Everything about the man was long. Long fingers were attached to long arms. Long white hair fell alongside a long, aged face. His legs were long, his torso long. Even the way he spoke was drawn out and lengthy. "Gemss? Hmmm, nooo, noo gemss."

After another twenty minutes or so of drawn out responses from the releaser, Irulen thanked him kindly and stepped out into the chill air. It was a fairly cold day, and he could see through the canopy that heavy clouds gathered above. They were swollen with snow. Still, the weather wasn't close to as frigid as it was up in Frostbridge. A few days' south by foot and a generally lower elevation had taken the sharp bite out of the brisk air.

Irulen's gaze traveled to the nearby inn. Feeling like he had just dropped past the end of a rope, he decided to stop in and check on Farah. Perhaps even grab some lunch to bring to Quinn. Josef was no longer needed, and so left to go back to his day's duties.

Irulen passed through the stone archway and into the common room. A black fury of flapping wings bolted toward him, giving him a scare, and landed on his shoulder. Max's golden eyes met his, and Irulen could tell the raven was happy, not just to see him, but because Max had spent the day with Farah as well.

To the left of the room was a bar, a commodity that many ale houses did not have. Where most taverns, like *The Roasted Duck*, exclusively kept large vats of wine, ale, and mead in a back room or a cellar, Ariana also kept smaller kegs behind the bar. She had stools lined along the front of it, on which sat a few locals. Ariana herself was behind the bar, and she waved to Irulen as he walked in. Farah poked her head out of the storage room in the back, investigating the new commotion. Her head withdrew as soon as she spotted him.

Irulen walked to the bar and ordered two mugs of mead. He asked for, and received, Arian's permission for Farah to take a lunch break, and he ordered the lunch of the day. Soon he had claimed the table closest to the store room where Farah was working and set out the drinks and two bowls of rabbit stew. Max used one of the vacant chairs as a perch. With everything in order, Irulen went to claim his prize. He stepped in and found Farah busy dusting shelves.

"Enjoying yourself?" He leaned against the doorjamb, his arms crossed.

Farah smiled, but kept working as she spoke. "Yes, actually, I never realized how peaceful the simple things were."

"How's Ariana, good boss?"

"One of the best, I think I may walk away with a silver sheckle or two, on top of my room being paid for." She wiped at a shelf while Irulen stood silent. She stopped and looked at him. "Did you want something?"

"Oh…yes…I bought lunch for us, would you care to share it with me?"

"My, aren't we gentlemanly today," she quipped. She wore a headpiece, below which she ran the back of her arm. "Okay, sure," she agreed. After a series of quick refreshing splashes from a bucket of fresh water, she joined him at the table.

"My day has been rather normal." Farah took a large gulp of her mead. "I'm guessing you have something morbid to talk about?"

"You guessed right, we found another body, Merek's father."

"Oh?" She cast her gaze downward. "I'm sorry to hear that."

"Yeah, well, I think there's a killer still on the loose."

Farah stifled a laugh. "Isn't that obvious?"

Irulen was annoyed at the antagonistic tone of Farah's voice. "No, well yes, but not the person who killed the family. That person is gone. The person who killed Ayleth Builder—that's the person who's still here. I want you to be careful. Don't be alone with people."

"How do know the other person is gone?" asked Farah.

"Because the person pulling the strings is Lynette."

"That name is really starting to annoy me," said Farah. "So much fuss and fog about it."

Irulen reached over with his right hand and grabbed her arm. The movement caught her unaware, and Max flew into the air. The event drew unwanted attention from the bar. He loosened his grip and let go when he spoke.

"She was my best childhood friend. My first love even, if you want to call it that. She was... my betrothed..."

Farah, at first frozen by the sudden outpouring, coaxed him to go ahead.

He stared at her a moment before he continued. "But she had a bastard of a father. He abused her. I used to heal her wounds. We figured she would be free to marry me at her seventeenth birthday. So I kept her going best I could. We talked about our future as I helped remove the blemishes from her face."

Irulen took a tall draught from his mug and admired the metallic bands holding the wood of it together. Once his thoughts came back together he continued.

"He wouldn't give her up. The old creep wanted to make a maid of her. He wanted to keep her until he died. She made passing inferences that I should kill him, but I couldn't. She came to me one day and asked me to give her magical power. I lied to myself for a long time, but I'll admit now that I had heard rumors of the dreadful things that happened to people who were *unnaturally* bestowed with magic. I didn't want to risk it. I also feared what she would do with the magic even if the event was successful. I refused her. She went and jumped into a river, trying to drown herself. I went in after her. I used my magic to shield us from the water. It washed over us while we lay together on the damp river bottom."

Realizing he was rambling at an unnerving pace, Irulen paused and looked at Farah. The expression on her face held concern and interest, and she nodded for him to continue.

"I did it then… I had no idea how and had no time to think of the why, but I gave her magic. My shield collapsed and we were washed away. I woke up on an embankment and I couldn't find her, and I have never found her to this day. But something foul came out of that river on that day. A distortion of Lynette…all of her bad pieces were magnified by the corruption of power. She killed her father and disappeared. I was run out of town for my hand in what happened."

"She's the imp you made." Farah obviously remembered the short conversation they'd had under the stars, before bandits had attacked their camp.

"Yes." He leaned in. "And she's killed many, many people."

For a moment, Farah seemed uneasy and frightened, "What-What does she look like?"

"Do you remember the picture Kay had, of the imp that killed her mentor?"

Farah gasped. "You can't be serious!"

Irulen nodded, ashamed.

"Does she know?"

"Yes, I think she does. We've never spoken about it, but it's too much of a coincidence. I think Kay is the one leading me to where Lynette wants me to go. She helped make sure we left Northforge and headed south."

"You think she's been playing you for a fool?"

"*No!*" Irulen snapped a little angrily, but composed himself. "No, but I think Kay was directed to me somehow, and she sees my power as a way of helping her get revenge on Lynette. She couldn't defeat Lynette by herself. But with magic, especially the magic of Lynette's maker, it's a whole new game."

Farah leaned back in her chair. "A *game*," she said. "One

I surely wouldn't want to lose. When I was taken, I was so scared. I never knew that sort of fear, I felt like a deer being eaten alive."

"I'm sorry you had to go through that," said the wizard.

Farah leaned forward on her chair again and ate some more of her soup. She stared into her bowl pensively. Then, without looking up, she asked, "Did you have anything to do with *that* imp?"

Irulen reacted instantly and vigorously. "No, no, no," he said, "but that imp's master also has a hand in what Lynette is doing. He's the one these imps are working for. They are using death diamonds to collect the souls of the dying. The resulting power is being siphoned into this man. He's hoping to keep his magic permanently. To what other use he may put his magic beyond that, I don't know. I'm hunting him, though, the same way I'm hunting Lynette. If I find her, then I can get him next."

Farah fished a piece of potato out of her stew while she spoke. "Get? You mean kill?" She held the potato out for Max to eat. The raven remained perched on his left claw, and grabbed the treat with his right. He brought the food to his mouth hungrily and pleasantly.

Irulen sighed. "Yes, it will probably come to that."

"How?"

"With a sword, hopefully. It is said that using your magic to kill invites darkness into the heart. That's the road to becoming a dark wizard, like the one I'm hunting. It is also the reason I try to fight physically whenever I *have* to kill. I fear myself. I fear the darkness in me."

"Don't we all," said Farah, more to herself than to Irulen.

He continued unfazed. "If I kill the man with my power, I might absorb his, or something else crazy. To be honest I have no idea what would happen. But as they say, power corrupts, and absolute power corrupts absolutely."

"*Who* said that?"

"I'm not sure, I think some Lord coined the phrase."

* * *

Irulen had just finished his lunch with Farah when Diane burst through the front door. Her blonde hair was tousled and a look of desperation wrought her face. "Help, come quick, she's dying!" Irulen, Farah, Ariana, and the stragglers at the bar all cleared out to follow the hysterical girl. As she ran, she yammered incoherently about blood and somebody missing.

CHAPTER 20: A COUNTRY HOUSE

The house wasn't far away, and they came upon it before a minute's time. The door was swung open in a mocking gesture of invitation. Irulen gestured for everyone to wait outside then pushed his way past the house's stone foundation. Like most of the dwellings in Warwick, the interior was a wide open space. This house, though, was also a place of work. Beds were scattered among tools of the weaving trade. It was at the base of a weaving machine that Irulen saw the body. She wasn't dying, like Diane had said, she was already well past dead.

The wizard made sure to hold up his cloak as he crouched over the fresh pool of blood. The body was face up. He checked for knife marks in her clothes. *Nothing on the front.* Pinching his cloak where his legs met his torso, he placed one of his hands on each of the lady's shoulders. He flipped her over and quickly located the fatal wound. She had been stabbed in the back. The location of the wound indicated a puncture to the lung. *A terrible way to go.* The lady had drowned internally. All at once, her lungs would have collapsed while filling up with fluid. She didn't have long, but long enough to see her killer and to contemplate whatever people think on as death approaches. *Or maybe she was just numb with fear and shock, and left the world like mute prey.* He felt thoroughly disgusted with himself, the human race, and the entirety of the world.

Right then, a startling revelation took hold of him. *The girl! Where is the Girl?* Irulen stood up and looked around frantically. The house was obviously vacant, but it was as if she might manifest out of thin air if he willed it hard enough. *Shit.* It was all Irulen could do not to throw up his hands and plop down on the floor in despair. He did find himself squatting again, his arms resting on his knees as he looked at the ground.

It took him more than a moment to notice the shirt that was dangling in front of him. His eyes raised, and he quickly realized that next to the weaving machine hung a brownish shirt. The fabric had signs of mending on it. Irulen snatched up the item and brought it outside the door. A group of people had started gathering around the woman who had accompanied him. Diane was sobbing as Ariana consoled her. Farah looked on blankly. The crowd shifted uneasily, the murmuring of their voices gave way to a single droning noise. Irulen's voice sounded as if it were not his own. "The lady is dead, the child is missing."

"Mira?" asked a voice from the crowd.

Irulen didn't know the lady's name, and so Diane spoke up between sobs. "Yes, it is…was…Mira." She buried her head into Ariana's open arms.

"Was Mira a weaver?" asked Irulen. Several members of the crowd nodded that she was.

Irulen held the shirt up for them all to see. "Who was she mending this for?"

Diane lifted her head to look at the thing. She spoke in between sobs. "That…that's Josef's. He paid her to fix it for him."

"When?"

"Just yesterday or the day before, I think."

Irulen beckoned for Ariana to come to him. The older lady paused for a moment, unsure of what to do with Diane, but Farah went over to comfort the girl for her. Once Ariana was close enough, Irulen asked what was on his mind. "This is the second killing in this family, I need to know… Who stands to gain from it? Who absorbs the property and business?"

Irulen could see in Ariana's face that he wouldn't be surprised. "Josef, until the girl, Juliet, comes of age. Mira's husband has long been deceased, and she has no children of her own. Josef is a distant cousin, but the only relation left in town."

Irulen put his right hand to her left shoulder.

"Look," he said, "keep this between us right now. I

don't want these people getting in my way. I'll go take care of this."

Ariana nodded her agreement, but it was too little, too late. The mob had already begun the first stages of a frenzy. Josef's name was bouncing around the pile. Irulen tried to disperse them. He asked them to form search parties for the girl, but they were persistent and insisted that Josef's would be the first place they checked. Reluctantly, Irulen found himself at the head of a lynch mob. The farther they walked, the more unruly people became. What were hushed comments of speculation before, had become promises of proper punishment. Irulen, sobered by their growing rage, urged calm.

"We have yet to know that he is responsible for these deaths," he said, as they walked. His declaration fell on deaf ears. He declined to try quelling the mob's growing anger any further. It seemed only to piss oil onto the fire. It's an amazing thing, the mob. One day, Josef was their leader, the next, their target.

Still, as they lacked a leader with a true thirst for blood, they weren't so enraged that Irulen couldn't control them. They fell in line behind the wizard as they arrived at Josef's house. They were frightened by the prospect of confronting an old acquaintance and possible murderer. Irulen had seen the reaction often, the looks on people's faces when friends become criminals. Much of his work was in small villages, and so many of his investigations turned up skeletons in the most ironic of places. Irulen had seen bonds of friendship, of family, and of order fractured in a split second.

Although the evidence was strong, Irulen couldn't stave off a gut feeling that Josef wasn't the man he was looking for. Josef had an opportunity to be that person, surely—the last murder happened after he left Irulen's sight. Irulen wasn't able to compare the torn fabric to the mended shirt, but it looked close enough a match to the naked eye. He had kept the two pieces at hand nevertheless, just in case an impromptu trial needed to be performed. In towns like this, justice was often swift and decisive. There were no jails in the way of the larger cities, so sentences rarely ranged far from monetary compensation, exile, or some form of capital punishment.

Irulen had, on occasion, found himself feeling very sorry for even the most wretched of criminals. For reasons he only partially understood, he saw himself in them. He was, after all, responsible for as much murder as any of them were. He may not have plunged his sword into the heart of an innocent, but Lynette surely had…and her hands were as good as his.

Irulen was about to enter the house when a high pitched scream erupted from inside, followed by the sound of a struggle and the pounding of running feet. Whatever it was, it was running right toward Irulen. He steeled himself as the others cowered behind him. It was a familiar position for him. Having power always placed him in front of others, but truth be told, he wasn't an overly brave man.

A small girl came crashing out of the house and into his arms. It was Juliet. Her clothes were tattered and she had bruising about the face. She was crying hysterically. Irulen pushed her as gently as he could to Ariana's open arms and asked her and Farah to bring the child back to the Inn and lock the doors.

"I'll knock four times," he said.

Farah acknowledged with a nod. Ariana picked the child up, and they headed off with due haste. Irulen turned back to the house, took a breath, and stepped in. Josef's house was different than the others. It had two stories and multiple rooms, a rarity in this region, and Irulen cursed the amount of nooks and crannies it hid.

"Josef?" he called. "Quinn?"

He moved slowly through the lower portions of the house. The main living room was full of deer skulls mounted on the walls. An uncanny feeling overtook him in that place, as if the antlers were pointing at him. He felt either mocked or accused, and with neither option did he feel comfortable. Rousing himself from his sheepish state, Irulen marched suddenly with purpose toward the storage under the stairs. It was more of a crawl space than anything, and the door hung slightly open. His right hand grew hot as he approached it. He ripped the door open and flared light into the darkness. There was nothing beyond some old chairs collecting dust. The kitchen also had no story to tell.

The wood above Irulen's head creaked.

"Josef?" he called again, as he stepped back toward the stairs.

The stairs groaned with melancholy as Irulen scaled them. There was a hallway at the top. As it came into view, Irulen could make out a crumpled figure on the floor. It was a lady, likely Josef's wife. Freshly pooled blood encompassed her. All of the upstairs rooms were to the right. The first room was furnished with a crib and toys. *Does Josef have a child? No, I would have seen. She...was pregnant?* She hadn't been dead for long.

"Hey!" he yelled, without turning his head. "I need people up here! A healer! Bring a knife!" He turned the lady over while his eyes frantically switched between her and the room down the hallway. Every second could count. Perhaps Josef would hold his ground while Irulen saved his child. Still, Irulen felt as if the hallway grew smaller every time he looked up, the last door on the right was coming closer. Claustrophobia threatened to suffocate him. He tore his gaze from the door and looked back at the woman, whose belly was fully swollen. The baby was likely developed enough...

Irulen was joined by two middle aged men and a woman. The woman identified herself as the town healer.

"Please, she hasn't been dead long, but she's gone. Try to save the baby."

"I will," said the lady. "She was a good woman." The healer pulled apart the clothes of her old friend. Her hand shook as she brought the knife against the skin. Before she cut, Irulen grabbed her hand.

"It's all right," he said. "It's going to be all right."

When he let go of it, her hand was steady. The two men helped as she set to work. Irulen stood and moved toward the last room. He didn't bother calling names anymore. He turned at the end of the hallway, and the room swung into view. Josef was there, lying on his bed, staring at Irulen. His head was propped up on pillows. He had a smile on his face. But behind the eyes that accompanied the smile there was nothing except death. Josef had also been killed. Irulen felt as he had in Frostbridge, when he missed what was truly happening. His head spun. Tears welled in his eyes.

Then he heard the sound of a baby crying. His brain cleared. He walked past his smiling helpers and out into the sunlight. The wizard grabbed the shirt he'd dropped near the entrance. He pulled out the rag and laid them side by side out on the frozen front grass. Reaching under his cloak and into a satchel, he pulled out the enhancing glass Merlane had given him. He held each fabric up to it in turn. The fabric had different striations. The rag had not come from Josef, after all.

Quinn came running around the back of the house. One of Merek's drawings was clutched in the brute's paws. Merek followed behind him, angry that Quinn had taken the drawing. "IRE! IRE!" Quinn screamed. Irulen had never seen him so animated outside of a fight.

Irulen stood up and ran toward his friend. Quinn shoved the drawing into Irulen's hands and then turned to hold Merek back as the boy grabbed for his work. Irulen looked at the paper, dropped it on the floor, and started to run back toward town. He summoned Max with all his strength, hopefully he was close enough to heed his master's call. Quinn ran after Irulen.

Merek kneeled down on the ground and collected his drawing into his hands. On the paper, drawn in vivid detail, was Juliet. She was standing over the corpse of Merek's father, Ayleth. In one hand was a large knife. In the other, she held a diamond. There was a face in the background of the drawing, further into the woods. The face was Lynette's. It looked satisfied.

* * *

Ariana carried Juliet as they walked silently through the woods. Farah walked ahead of them, scouting for potential dangers. The trip was a short one, and they had left the likelihood of peril behind them at Josef's. Farah felt important for the first time in a long time. She had been tasked to protect someone, an assignment that held her responsible for someone else. Truth be told, Farah had begun to feel like dead weight, worth nothing else to anyone outside of playing the victim. Working at Ariana's Inn had infused in her a sense of worth and purpose, but nothing that came close to wiping away the haunting pain of recent memories.

Farah peered past the wispy strands of red hair that were dancing in her vision. It was unlikely that any threat would make it past Irulen and the mob, but she still saw phantoms lurking behind every rock and tree. She had a knife in her waistband. It was in her possession from her lunch with Irulen. Since they ate soup there had been no use for it at lunch. Farah was going to put it away when they were called away. At the moment, having a weapon felt good. Violent thoughts ran through her mind. She saw the skin shifting imp that had abducted her jump out in front of their path. Each time she stabbed him in the heart. In her own way, Farah fantasized about killing someone. Someone evil.

There was a commotion from behind her. Farah turned, thinking that Ariana had tripped and fallen to the ground. The lady was lying down, her face toward the ground as if she were rising to her feet. Juliet was standing, and at first Farah thought the girl was helping the old lady to stand.

But then she saw the stabbing. The girl's right arm rose and lowered furiously, a previously hidden blade repeatedly puncturing Ariana's back. It was over before Farah realized what was happening. Ariana was on the ground choking on her own blood. Juliet turned toward Farah and laughed.

"Are you Farah?" the girl asked innocently.

Farah didn't answer. She was frozen.

Juliet licked the knife and laughed again.

"Farah, do you want to play a game?" the girl asked. "Do you want to play hide and stab?"

"N-No." It was the only thing Farah could muster. She was rejecting the situation more than what the child had said. *This can't be happening.*

"It would make me happy to stab you, Farah. I did old lady Ariana fast so we could have some fun together! Please, can we play?"

The girl started walking toward Farah in short steps. "Please?"

Farah backed away, tripped, and fell on the ground. Juliet giggled. The girl looked like she could hardly contain herself. It was as if she were full of giddy energy just waiting to be realized through an orgy of chaos, blood, and violence.

Juliet stood over Farah and looked disappointed.

"This stinks!" she huffed, stomping the ground with her feet. "I thought we'd have fun! Lynette promised."

"What did she do to you?" Farah's voice was sad and sympathetic. The sound of it must have irritated Juliet. She screamed and raised her knife, ready to plunge it deep into Farah's face.

A loud raven's call caused the little girl to hesitate. Farah sprang to her feet and leapt forward in a desperate grab for the blade. The girl was uncommonly quick and squirmed out of Farah's grasp. She giggled uncontrollably as she raised her arm and rushed Farah again. Max swooped down and smacked Juliet in the face. Farah lunged again and pinned the girl on her back. She held the creature's arms as strong as she could, but Farah felt her strength fading. There was a crazy look in the child's eyes that she could not hope to match. It was easy to hate someone who looked the part, but a cherubic face proved a different story.

Farah's arms burned. The unexpected struggle left her body ready to give up. Even the rush of adrenaline flowing through her blood could do little against the supernatural strength Juliet was showing. In a flash, Farah somehow found herself on the ground with the little girl straddling her and laughing mercilessly. Max was doing his best to distract the girl. He kept swooping down at her, but the maneuver worked to a lesser effect each time.

Farah saw the blow that would kill her. She watched the dagger go up, and she saw the look of a true killer.

Then, just as quickly, she saw Juliet get pulled away.

Farah's vision blurred and went blank.

* * *

Irulen had the girl in hand. He was trying to remove the spell from her. But what life would she have if he did? There was no one to take her in, no one who could get over their superstitions of lost souls and true evil. She certainly wouldn't have been able to travel with them, knowing that Lynette had been the one to arrange the situation. There was nowhere left in the world for the girl. Irulen would always claim later that he failed to save her, that he couldn't exorcise the magic that clutched the girl's heart. It wouldn't be fair to call him a liar, but the girl fell silently asleep in his arms and passed into the afterlife just the same.

CHAPTER 21: KEEPING COMPANY

At first, there was darkness.

Her eyes fluttered open. The ceiling was plain and wooden. Max peered down at her. He was perched on the headboard above. Past Farah's feet and beyond the edge of the bed sat Quinn. There was a melancholic smile on his face, and she found herself looking at the wrinkles around his eyes.

"Good morning," Quinn said. She hadn't yet found her voice. While Farah yawned and gained her bearings, Quinn beckoned Max over to him. The bird obliged and Quinn took him outside the door. It was a long twenty seconds or so before Quinn walked back into the room.

"Irulen asked to have Max join him when you woke up."

"Is Irulen that worried about me?" she asked.

"Oh, I think so. But, he also wanted to let Max watch over you. The raven hasn't left your side. To be honest, now that I think about it... I doubt Max would have gone with Irulen had he been asked. Perhaps Irulen was just trying to save a little face."

Quinn was talking too much for Farah's headache. She winced at the pain of it all, slowly realizing that this was no typical morning. He kept yammering. The sound of his voice dampened while her mind set sail through a sea of thoughts. She became deaf to whatever he was saying.

There was a flash of Juliet standing over her. The girl's smile. Ariana... As if expelling these thoughts, Farah blew air through her lips. The hot air carried her thoughts away.

She was more detached than sad. The dull throbbing in her chest would have to be addressed at a later time. Right now, hollowness is what she needed. She leaned back and closed her eyes. Nothing invaded the solitude there, and in the darkness she slept peacefully.

* * *

Irulen sat alone atop a waterfall. The river, if you could call it that, was a mere ten to fifteen strides across. His feet hung over a ledge that was sturdy and dry. The water rushed by and fell into an old sinkhole. The plunge wasn't overly far, but he guessed that it was easily far enough to bash his brains out, if he felt the urge to do so.

The bottom of the hole was illuminated just enough to make out its distinct features. The waterfall poured over a rocky outcrop from which stuck many stalagmites. These pointy rock formations were long ago abandoned by their comrades that had hung from the ceiling when, of course, the ceiling collapsed. The thought of being impaled repulsed him. Ushering a preemptive return to the inorganic might have been more than a passing fancy, but to be *penetrated* was not desirable. No, he'd rather splat like a grape and turn his brain into mush than to catch a stalagmite.

The wizard had just finished, for an uncountable number of times, rethinking and regretting his life's path. There was, without a doubt, something that could have been done at some time that would have left things better off than what they were. He had made terrible decisions. His father had told him once that a man's character wasn't in the decisions he made.

That's because, son, every man makes mistakes. A man's true character is in the way he reacts to them. Be responsible for your actions. Apologize and make amends for the things you do. Make the things that are wrong because of you right again.

Irulen leaned over the hole and spat. The wizard wished he'd asked his father a simple question. *What if there's no fixing it?*

Killing Lynette would, of course, save an untold number of lives from being torn asunder in her wake. However, the thought still lingered in his mind that killing her would leave his original transgression unresolved. Killing Lynette was not going to fix what happened to Lynette. Conceivably, deep inside her being her innocent self was trapped behind bars. Or, maybe, her soul was just as empty as the sinkhole before him. Either way, redemption would never be something Irulen could own. It simply wasn't possible to dispel an imp's magic without removing the creature's life as well. Just maybe, though, if the good Lynette was still trapped in there, she would want to be free in one way or another. Just like he wanted to be free now. Maybe sometimes death was a better means of happiness than life. Maybe he could make her happy one last time.

Maybe Irulen wouldn't leave the world a better place than he had found it, but he could minimalize the damage done. Before he left Warwick, he had asked Quinn to take Farah back to Snowillow Pass. Perhaps there she could find a semblance of peace and belonging. The wizard couldn't stand the thought of looking at Farah anymore. She may not have been the cherubic virgin he had originally thought, but she was innocent and unassuming in her own way—she was normal.

He had exposed her, through his selfish attraction toward her, to terrible things. The pain of what happened to Juliet still hung heavy in his heart, and he was accustomed to death and murder. Hopefully with time her wounds would heal.

Truth be told, cleaning up a mess could never be near as gratifying as preventing it in the first place. Before recently, Irulen had been a good solver of mysteries. He had, without fail, pointed to the perpetrators of various crimes, collected his money, and gone on his way. Only recently was it that people began to die on his watch, deaths that could have been prevented if he was better at what he did.

Irulen was more convinced than ever that—other than his magic— he had no talent what-so-ever. There was no true skill under his command. He was a failure as an investigator. Besides that, he couldn't sew a stitch, or draw, or build. Heck, he couldn't even snap his fingers or whistle. His magic defined him. One day it would leave him, and he would be left utterly worthless.

He felt worthless enough as it was.

The wizard was startled by the snapping of a branch. He tensed and listened intently to the ensuing silence. The woods, of course, were made of such sounds, but he had been made more wary as of late. Since he left Warwick he couldn't fight the feeling that he was being watched. He wished Max would hurry up and meet him. Irulen felt exposed without Max's eyes in the sky. He shook the paranoia away with a fierce nod of his head and snapped to.

The wizard slid himself back from the pit, pushed himself up, dusted his clothes off, and followed the river back to the road.

* * *

"So King Irulen wants to send me away?" Farah asked Quinn obstinately.

"Well, we can't stay here." Quinn indicated the activity around them. They were in the tavern, and the townspeople were coming to and fro. The place had become a center for the community as it began the long process of healing. Meanwhile, the releaser was preparing the bodies of Josef, his wife Ariel, Ariana, and Juliet for the night's ritual. Some people had protested that Juliet was a demon that shouldn't be given the same rights as the others, but the majority believed Irulen when he had told them about the magic that was the child's undoing.

Some of Ariana's relatives had started convening at the inn to mourn and settle her estate. Farah feared that she and Quinn would soon find themselves looking even more out of place than she felt now. Redeeming the somber mood was the occasional glimpse of the newborn baby. It was a girl, and had been named Ariel by the town healer, after her mother.

"So Kay runs off, and then Irulen, and you are left as my babysitter?"

"I prefer the term bodyguard, or escort," Quinn said, resolutely.

"The only place you are going to *escort* me is to wherever that scoundrel is heading."

Quinn sighed. He looked dejected. "I can cleave a man's

head in two, but I'll never know a woman's mind," he said, more to himself than to her. She took exception just the same.

"Maybe it's because you and Irulen think that one needs a penis to make bad choices. You run around *cleaving* people and sticking your noses into the business of others. You drink and make questionable decisions on a nightly basis. Death follows Irulen like a wet fart because of choices he has made. I have every *right* to make my choice, you have the right to offer your opinion, but my fate is what I will make of it…not something forced by you or anyone else!"

Quinn wore a look between apprehension and intimidation. Then, he smiled and laughed. The laugh was uproarious, and Farah felt instantly ashamed by the inappropriateness of it all. People were grieving. She had to keep Quinn on a leash.

"Look," he said, with an amused look on his face, "Irulen just doesn't want this for you, whatever *this* may be, neither of us do. Lad or lass, he wants you to go because he cares. If you want to go after him, we can. But don't let your dreaming get in the way of what is really going on, and don't disregard our suggestions so easily. You're right, we made our choices, and we regret a great deal of them. However, you have nothing to regret, except not going back to Frostbridge." He laughed. "But you haven't done anything *regrettable*. And if you stay with us, rest assured, you will. And when *that* time comes, I'll look you square in the face." Quinn squared up on Farah as he spoke.

His face was set in stone. He continued all serious like. "And I'll say… I told you so." Quinn's face slowly melted into a smile.

Farah had picked up on something unmistakably dark and painful in Quinn's words. It was a quality she found herself being attracted to. It was something Quinn, Kay, and Irulen all shared. It was an odd ponderance, but she seemed to envy their misery. It could have been because they had seen the bottom, and only from the bottom could one climb again. In a way, she'd rather find the nethermost level of sadness than to sink further into uncharted depths.

"You would be happy in Snowillow Pass, and we can eventually get you back to Frostbridge should you wish to return," Quinn said.

"And tell Mayor Frostbridge all about his son's valiant death? That Jorin died because I kept him too long at Northforge? No. Cheers for the concern, but no. I want to go on. We should go while there's still a good amount of daylight to be had."

Quinn shrugged and proclaimed, "So be it. Make ready."

* * *

Being so deep in thought had left Irulen unsure of how much daylight he had left. He looked upward. The sun was still high in the sky poking bright holes through the forest canopy. He wouldn't make it to Riverfall today, nor did he really want to. There was a desire, of course, to see Kay again in the larger town. Being alone for a night, however, would undoubtedly do him some good.

Just then he heard a familiar call. *Max.* Irulen turned around and looked back from where he came. The path turned from the left about fifty strides away. After a few seconds of looking, Max darted around the bend. The bird's wings flapped at full speed. Irulen thought Max might just gore through him if the raven didn't slow down. As it was, Irulen braced as Max hit him in the chest and hopped up on the nearest shoulder.

"Ow. Dammit," Irulen rubbed his right pectoral. Max fluffed his wings out, an action that always caused the raven to look two times as fat.

The happy reunification was short lived, however. Max indicated to Irulen that someone was farther back on the trail. Someone was following in his footsteps.

Irulen had three choices in front of him; turn back, confront and chase down his stalker, or play the situation in a calmer manner. Being in no mood to run, and in less of a mood to fight, he chose the latter. Instead of wasting the energy, he scratched Max under the chin and continued on at an inconspicuous pace. The trail continued to veer to the right slightly for a long while, at such an angle that vision of the trail disappeared about fifty feet back. Eventually there was a sharp left turn to counter the gradual, right-leaning bend. It was here that the wizard found a large oak tree worth hiding behind.

It might be that hiding was out of character for Irulen, or that recent events had paranoia getting the best of him, but he was rather awkward behind that tree. His right shoulder was square against the bark. His head bobbed erratically as he kept peeking out onto the trail. The wizard felt his nerves like little spiders crawling under his skin. Feeling a little angry with himself, Irulen kept still and waited.

There was silence, and more silence.

Still more silence filled the air, and Irulen's body began to relax in spite of his mind's racing. Max never failed him. Someone would come, and soon.

After a long three seconds, footsteps sounded. There was only the slightest layering of snow on the ground, but just enough to hear against the silence of the forest. *Crunch, crunch, crunch.* The footsteps halted at the bend. Irulen could make out where the person was, but there were thickets of defoliated brush to look through. The detail of the person simply wasn't there. Irulen waited with baited breath while the walker contemplated the situation. Was it possible that Irulen had made it to the next bend down the path so quickly? The footsteps commenced and the stalker came into clear view.

"Oh, what in the world?" Irulen left his cover for the path. A young man fell backward from fright, and crab walked farther back still. The darks of his eyes were choked by the whites of fright.

"Merek! Merek! Calm down!" Irulen yelled, as he thrust his hands forward in a calming fashion. It took a moment for the wizard to realize that his own excitement was doing little to quell the situation. He backed up a few steps, took a deep breath, and tried again.

"Merek, everything is fine. Everything is going to be just fine…" Irulen fought the impulse to try to reach out and comfort the youth. He knew the boy was capable of lashing out. The wizard held his ground instead. Moving animalistically, Merek rose to his feet. The boy looked stuck between fight and flight. Being controlled himself, Irulen put his hands up again in a calming motion. This time Merek seemed to loosen a bit. The tension left his shoulders and arms. Still, he seemed far from comfortable.

Not knowing what else to do, Irulen found himself shrugging and clearing a space among the snow and leaf litter. Once there was a relatively dry patch of fresh ground, he sat. Merek, in turn, duplicated what Irulen did the best he could. He used his right foot to scrape away the top layers of snow and soil. Since he seemed intent on making his work into a perfect circle, the process took unnecessarily long.

Irulen thought hard the entire time Merek nested. *What am I supposed to do now? If I bring him back I'll have to deal with Farah. If I bring him on…then what? Man, I can't bring him with me. It's already been determined that I'm a terrible babysitter. Farah is proof enough of that. And I wanted to look after her…*

While Merek's work was tedious, he finished soon enough and sat cross-legged opposite Irulen. Satisfaction poured from his face and features.

"What do I do with you?" asked Irulen. "What do you want?"

Merek smiled and spoke for the first time. "I'm coming."

Irulen shook his head and pointed back the way they'd come. "No. No, *you* are *going*. That way. Back home."

"Home?" Merek laughed.

Irulen waited for Merek to add context to the remark, but it didn't happen. *Like pulling the meat out of a catfish.*

The wizard tried communicating again. "Yes, don't you want to go home?"

"Yes…No."

"What does that mean?!?" Irulen's hands were outstretched in befuddlement.

"My home now." The youth indicated the direction they

were heading. "Is that way." Merek stretched and nodded his head. It took a while for Irulen to understand, but this gesture was effectively the end of the conversation.

Irulen spoke while Merek kept shaking his head no. "You don't even know what's over there. There are people back that way who would look after you. You can't survive out by yourself. Look at you, you aren't even clothed properly, just wearing a light, white shirt and shit-colored trousers. You look bad. You are going to freeze. You are going to freeze while looking bad!"

These things and more Irulen used to dissuade Merek from venturing out. Merek shook his head with increasing intensity at each point. At the last point the boy popped. His neck cracked from the fury of his head shake. "NO!" he screamed.

Max flew upward onto a high branch. Irulen fell silent again. *I don't understand, I've been doing this sort of thing for years now, and it has never been so...sticky. First Farah, now this guy. Quinn, Kay...so much baggage. How'd this happen?*

Irulen felt more weighed down than ever, a trait that he felt physically as he pushed up with his thighs. Merek mimicked him as he stood and dusted off his rear. Irulen opened his mouth to protest the copying, but decided there was little to be gained. He sighed audibly, gathered his things, and started walking again. Merek sighed and followed.

CHAPTER 22: THE FAIRE

Irulen heard it before anything—the whispering sounds of flutes and fiddles chiming along the forest path. Traffic on the trail began to pick up as other paths from other towns converged. Mules and other beasts pulled carts of goods and supplies. The smoky smell of meat and merrymaking was in the air. Irulen had pushed on to the town, since Merek's company had disenchanted him of the idea to sleep outdoors. The sun was still high in the sky, although it was clearly declining. Festivities were beginning as the day came to an end. There was a faire happening in the town of Riverfall.

Irulen kicked himself for forgetting. He knew about the annual Spirit Faire of Riverfall. In fact, the wizard had attended it more than once himself. It was a great place to blow off steam and lose himself in drink and women. Indeed, the festivities had been more than friendly to him. He remembered three warm, welcoming female bodies. The ratio of which they were divided over his visits remained a mystery. Irulen thought he'd visited the place two or three times before, but he couldn't remember whether fortune smiled on him once each time, or three times during one trip. Whatever the reality of the faire was, it was covered by a mask, a mask of smoke, alcohol, drugs, and lustful bodies. Most of the participants wore masks themselves, styled after the wild inhabitants of the forest and mythological creatures.

There were many purposes to the faire, among the least of which was procreation and the celebration of our sexual nature. By donning masks, the people returned to their baser selves. As an avatar, they were able to enjoy nature's bounty without the pain of guilt or recognition.

However, do not be so naive as to think the night simply dissolved into a haze of drugs and sex. It should be said that there were many activities for the young ones, and many other forms of entertainment for the family.

The town gates were flung open in welcoming gesture. The gate's arch was decorated with paper lanterns each imprinted with images of differing animals. As Irulen and Merek crossed town lines, they were greeted by a man dancing with fire. He was using two sticks to control a baton with flaming ends. His mastery of the skill resulted in a spinning circle of flare and flame. Merek flinched at the spectacle and turned to Irulen for guidance. The wizard took out a coin, gave it to the man's assistant, and signaled for the boy to follow him.

The faire was lit and warmed by a series of staggered bonfires. People danced around these pits, and their shadows danced with them. Merek was obviously taken aback by the vast variety of street vendors, jugglers, jesters, dancers, performers, practitioners. Pretty girls with fair complexion moved about in giddy flocks, giggling at loitering groups of boys swollen with mischievous thoughts. Traditionally, the girls wore mostly masks of prey, and the boys wore those of predators. Two large-busted women in rabbit-like masks approached Irulen and asked to pet Max. The raven accepted their advances happily, and the two went snickering on their way.

It had occurred to Irulen that it might be hard finding accommodations on such a prolific night. He hoped to find Kay before the night was through and perhaps impose on her. Or perhaps one of his acquaintances might be able to scratch up some space. Had Irulen not been weighed down with Merek, his options, which kept walking past, rubbing on and winking at him, might have been more tempting. He was sure some of these ladies would have happily put him up somewhere for the night.

As it was, they wandered aimlessly as Irulen's hopes of finding Kay that night began to fade. The street they walked opened up into the town square. The place was chock full of tents and tables. Long tables had been brought outside, and people feasted merrily. Games were played for prizes. Parents won prizes for their little ones. The music kept changing as roaming fiddlers and other musicians rotated in the streets.

Through the middle of it all ran a river, and over that river stood a stone bridge. In many of the more superstitious parts of the north, a stone bridge was bad luck. Trolls saw them as habitable dwellings and fought tooth and nail to claim them. Of course, we all know the mischief a troll makes once it's settled. The people of Riverfall had no fear of such a thing, however. They were quick to point out that trolls can't swim, and so the bridge, over water, posed no threat at all. Irulen often wondered how the locals would respond if the river ever dried out.

"Are you hungry?" Irulen turned to Merek. The youth didn't signal yes or no but his eyes betrayed him. "Okay, then," said Irulen, "let's find some grub."

Merek stayed on the wizard's heals as they meandered through various stations of food. Irulen stopped in front of one with a small line and Merek ran into him. He reminded himself to be patient with the overwhelmed boy, stepped back, turned to Merek, and asked, "Do you like rabbit?" Without waiting for an answer, Irulen said, "Sure you do," and stepped up into a spot as it was vacated. He waited a moment as a large, fat old man with a rag tied around his head sauntered over to him. The man's nose wart moved as he spoke.

"We ha' rabbit on eh stick. Ha many you wan'?" the man asked. *He looks Trollish*, Irulen thought. "Well?" asked an impatient troll-man.

"Four, please."

"Ver' Well." The man sauntered to the back of his canopied kitchen. There he had his rabbit sticks slowly roasting over a metal trough filled with smoldering charcoal. He came back with four sticks of charred rabbit meat. Irulen handed two of them to Merek and paid the man. Then the unlikely pair found a space at a nearby table to eat.

Merek tore at his meat voraciously. The boy ate so fast Irulen thought he might throw up. Irulen tried cautioning the youth against such a vigorous pace of mastication, but his pleas fell on deaf ears. Merek had finished his second stick of rabbit meat before the wizard had completed his first.

Irulen shrugged and went back to eating. As he munched, Merek took up one of the empty rabbit skewers. He raised it before his eyes and brought it to bear on the table. He started scraping at the wooden top.

"Hey, don't do that!" Irulen leaned over and snatched the skewer from Merek, who scowled in return. Merek picked up the second skewer and continued what he was doing. Irulen leaned forward again, and this time Merek tensed up with violence. Noticing how upset Merek was, Irulen decided to back off. Afterall, there were festivities aplenty, no one would notice any harm done. The boy turned back to scratching at the wood.

Irulen was just about to take a bite out of his second rabbit skewer when it disappeared from his hand. He turned frantically, ready to defend his meal and himself. Max flew in fright. His surprise was doubled when he found Kay sitting next to him, nibbling gently at his once cherished prize. Max landed again on his shoulder.

She wore a mask flipped up on her head. Her features were accentuated by the shifting colors of sundown. She was beautiful, and he wanted her. She knew it, and he knew she enjoyed exploiting his primordial self. He didn't mind being her toy.

"Hello to you too," he said, cooly.

"Yeah, yeah," she replied between bites. "It isn't polite to stare at someone while they're eating."

"Oh, right." Irulen turned away, uneasily tapping his fingers on the table. Merek was still busy working on his project. Irulen turned more. There was a pair of dueling flutists nearby. Irulen had more affinity for stringed instruments, but since his eyes had little elsewhere to take solace, he enjoyed the performance. His fingers tapped against the tabletop as he waited. His foot bounced with the tunes.

Eventually, he felt Kay's eyes on him. He faced her again and found her smiling.

"Who is this handsome guy?" she asked.

Irulen felt only the tiniest pinch of jealousy as he responded. "This is Merek, the person people suspected of killing the family in Warwick."

This piqued Kay's interest. "Oh, really? And I'm guessing he wasn't the killer, or are you aiding and abetting his escape?"

"No, he wasn't responsible for anything that happened there." Irulen studied Merek as the boy continued to work intently.

"Should I ask?" Her gaze flickered to Merek as well, before she turned it back to Irulen.

"No. Maybe later."

She cocked her head at him. "Where's the drunk and lil' miss dainty?"

"Behind, at Warwick, or maybe heading back to Snowillow Pass. Quinn said he'd take her back there and catch me up later. What happened just wasn't good for her, for Farah. People like us ruin people like her."

Kay laughed. "How so? By showing them there's a big bad world out there? We do people like her a service."

He shrugged, in no mood to argue the point. "If that's how you feel."

"It is," she confirmed.

"Let's just forget it. The case was closed. Didn't make any money though." Irulen added the last bit as he divined her next question. "How about you?"

"Tracking a drug dealer. There was an overdose last night, bad dose of mushrooms. Bounty out for the guy they think is responsible."

"Wouldn't he have left town then? Or does he know?"

"He most likely knows, but with all the masks and what not…" She paused a moment while pulling her mask down over her face, it was of a fox. It covered the top half of her face, leaving her lips on full display.

She continued. "He can easily hide. Besides, I think he's hiding out in one of the tents here. I'm keeping tabs on one of his minions. The guy with the bear mask over there." She indicated the next table to her right. Irulen leaned around her and looked. The man undoubtedly looked like he was performing a shady transaction. His clients were the bunny-masked, big busted girls from earlier.

"I know them," he said, before thinking. He regretted it.

"You do?" Kay regarding him suspiciously through her cat eyes.

"Well, not really, they just wanted to give Ol' Max here a scratch."

Max puffed up and readjusted his feathers.

"Like you could handle those two anyway," she said, matter-of-factly.

"Ha! You don't know who you're talking to…" *Stupid! Again!* Irulen opened his mouth to backtrack, but Kay interrupted him.

"Don't bother," she said. "Look, you and Merek enjoy the heaving bosoms and music. I need to go collar this guy. His minion is moving. I'm following him back to the tent. After I bring him in, we'll celebrate."

"I'll help." Irulen rose to his feet.

"It isn't necessary, this guy's an amateur, besides…" Kay gestured to Merek. "You need to look after him, seems like something is wrong with that boy."

"He's a cloudwalker."

"Ah, one of those, well, I'll be right back." She ran her hand up his side as she left. He didn't like not going, it seemed stupid of her, but it was what it was. He walked around to where Merek was scratching at the wood. He had etched a finely detailed rabbit.

"Very nice," he complimented.

Merek smiled without looking up from his work. The worn skewer twisted about in his restless fingers.

An idea popped up to Irulen as he surveyed the artwork. *Of course! Maybe I can profit from Warwick, after all.* He set off to collect some supplies. Merek, momentarily reluctant to leave his work, followed.

CHAPTER 23: WHEELING AND DEALING

Before long, Irulen's savviness at bartering had landed them a deal with an arms merchant. An unremarkable, skinny man, the merchant cleared some of his swords and flails from the corner of his vendor's table. He provided Merek with an extra stool, and Irulen purchased parchment and graphite from a nearby seller. The wizard provided his own cup he carried in the satchel and placed it in front of the young artist. He scribbled a price on a piece of parchment that read, *One coin, any kind!* and placed it at the front of the table.

Swallowing a pang of anxiety, Irulen forced a smile and went to work recruiting customers. He didn't have much luck at first, but an idea came to mind. A model was needed. Since Kay wasn't around, Irulen decided to pick his way through the crowd. It took all his skills of deduction to decide which female to demask, for only the fairest of faces would sell Merek's work.

He did his best, reading mannerisms and bodies, but had a hard time deciding. The last thing the wizard wanted was for Merek to draw, in great detail, a face that was snarl-toothed, wart infested, and generally unkempt. Granted, people with one gangly feature or another were in the majority, but these were also the people most attracted to beauty. At last, Irulen found a woman too young to have developed unsightly features, negotiated a price, and paid her to come sit at Merek's table.

To Irulen's surprise, the youth drew her without qualms or hesitation. The wizard half expected the artist to impose random unicorns, or horns, or who knows what to the paper. Instead, he depicted her face to the most accurate detail. The finished product looked well enough, but Irulen tried explaining to Merek that perhaps he should cut back on the detail for less comely people. This, Merek did not seem to comprehend. Irulen began to suspect that, at certain times, Merek was more cognizant than he put on. Cognizant or not, the young artist clearly had a strong will.

So it was that Merek worked remarkably quick, and the demonstration of his art worked its function. By the time the girl walked away pleased with her newfound fame, others had lined up to have themselves or their loved ones drawn.

The illustrator worked quickly, his graphite scratching furiously at the parchment. The movements were so fast and furious that Irulen believed the papers would tear in pieces. But they never did. Soon the wizard found his initial investment had been compensated, and they began turning a profit. They did so well, in fact, that Irulen bought himself a new pipe along with a local blend of herb-weave, a mix of dried herbs meant for smoking.

The wizard offered Merek a puff of his bounty, but the artist was too infatuated with his work. His eyes darted to and fro, and his hands worked as if he were a machine powered by magic. Irulen smoked his pipe and smiled. His brain tingled as he listened to the intermittent clinking of coins hitting the cup. Some people were so pleased they gave extra, even after Merek had finished. For a handful of hours, Irulen enjoyed a new life with a fresh profession.

The wizard was not completely without worry, however. Kay had been gone for quite a while, and Irulen began to doubt her job had gone so smoothly. Convinced that Merek would be fine doing what he was doing, the wizard emptied the cup of coins into his satchel and went looking for his bounty hunting beaux. He had barely walked a foot when she passed him. She pushed her quarry in front of her. The man looked enraged and ragged, but moved along at each prod of Kay's crossbow. She wasn't in the clear quite yet, though, as Irulen spotted two of the man's henchmen shadowing them. Irulen stepped in between her and them, and blocked them with outstretched hands.

"You lookin' to geh hurt?" asked one. This was the man

Kay had been following earlier. He had led her to the right tent, after all.

"Get out of our way," said the other. This man Irulen had not yet seen.

"I want to show you a trick of magic." Irulen stepped in front of them as they tried to go around him.

"You wan' to see my foot disappear in yer ass?" said the first man.

The other man chortled. "Rather disappear his teeth! Or shu' we send his balls to a far off place?"

Irulen kept his hands between the thugs and himself. "Look, I meant nothing—"

"I guess thaz wut we call, what is it? Lahst in trans-lay-shun?" First man looked pleased with his knowledge.

Second man had to think on what was said for a long moment. Once he was convinced he understood what first man had said, he added his touch to the mix. "Ye-uh, cuz we taught you wur' askin' fer a beatin'."

"Not quite," said Irulen.

He had back-peddled to where he wanted to be. As he lifted his hand, he hoped it would land where he wanted it to. He brought his hand on a swift, downward motion. It passed by his body and slapped the person behind him, right on the rear end. The contact was loud and the lady's scream reverberated. Irulen spun out of the way, and an angry husband was revealed. He was large, well over six foot, and well close to the size of a bear. He even made Quinn look smallish.

Other locals began swarming to the bear-man's side. One of the henchman tried pushing through the crowd and was repelled. The other tried a more polite way through, begging his pardon and apologizing for the inconvenience. His advance was also summarily rejected. The do-gooders were bent on defending the woman's honor.

The thugs tried pointing after Irulen, but the wizard blended with the growing mob. Lest they lose the initiative, the crowd surged forth. A struggle ensued. The brazen thug swung wildly to no avail, and the other thug cringed passively. They both received their fair share of a drubbing and soon found themselves being dragged toward the icy river. They squirmed like worms nailed to wood and pleaded for mercy like pillaged villagers. The mob did not heed their cries, and the men were limp and quiet by the time the bridge was reached.

They were forced to stand on the edge, facing the crowd that had brought them there. They shrunk as the bear man came forward.

He stood in front of the men and bellowed with a thick country accent. "It's with hot hands ye' touched my wife, and it be my hands that cool yours off!" With that he used one arm each to push the men over. They fell into the icy river, and the frigid water shocked them into heightened awareness. The crowd laughed and dispersed as they slowly pulled themselves to a set of stone stairs leading from the water. Beaten, bloodied, and embarrassed, the thugs soon crept out of public sight and back to whence they came.

CHAPTER 24: RENDEZVOUS

Meanwhile, Irulen, quite pleased with himself, looked for Kay at the local dungeon. He had been surprised to find such an establishment the first time he'd visited Riverfall. The town wasn't small by any means, but the presence of a full-fledged dungeon was often limited to cities such as Northforge.

Irulen was walking across a variety of inns and taverns when he felt a great weight fall against his back. He was shoved into an alley.

"Sheesh, talk about familiar territory," he said to Kay. She pinned him against the wall and kissed him.

"We love our alleys, don't we?" She smirked and pulled something from behind her. "I got you a mask."

She gave him space as he took the thing into his hands. "A beaver, really?"

"I like beavers, they're the engineers of nature." She grinned.

"Wouldn't it be nature's engineers?" Irulen asked, facetiously.

"Shut up, and put it on," she ordered.

He obliged. "So what'll it take to paddle your ass with my beaver tail?"

Kay rolled her eyes and started walking away. Irulen grabbed her arm. "How about we start with a drink?"

"Sure, you're buying," she responded.

"No problem at all, I'm drowning in coin tonight."

"So you were compensated for your work at Warwick, afterall?"

"No, not by the people anyway, but I have Merek now.

The kid's talented. He draws. I have him draw people, they drop coin. It's great."

Kay laughed. "You know, this inn here that you're leaning on...that's where the room is I rented. I was going to take you there."

Irulen opened his mouth to speak, but she put a finger up to his lips. "But this I have to see, and you offered me a drink I have to have!"

She almost skipped as she walked away. Irulen had never seen her so carefree. It warmed his heart. Needless to say, he had to drag his caveman's lust with him like a giant ball on a chain. This was, of course, well worth it all. Besides, the herb-weave had him feeling good, the night was young, and he had little interest in expending all his energy in bed. There was a faire to enjoy. *At least for a little while.*

* * *

"You were damn right he could draw." Kay leaned over Merek's shoulder. She held Irulen's pipe in her hands. She lifted it to her mouth and inhaled. The herb-weave fired and a release of fragrant smoke filled the air. "It almost smells and tastes like honey."

"Now that you mention it." Irulen accepted the pipe as she gave it to him. "You're right." He took a long drag, held it, and let the smoke seep out his nose.

"You look like a drugged dragon!" Kay said, laughing. She refused the next puff in favor of her ale sitting idly by on the table.

"Careful, I don't know what Merek'll do if you spill on his drawings," Irulen cautioned.

"Sounds to me like Merek is a little tight, isn't he?" Kay put her hands on the artist's shoulders. He tensed for a long moment, and then went back to drawing. "You see," she said, "he likes it."

"He may be a cloudwalker, but he's a man first," said Irulen, defensively.

"Jealous?" Kay asked.

"Maybe, he is pretty dashing."

"We should find him someone for tonight," she said. "With the way he works those fingers, some girl might find herself feeling lucky."

"Maybe instead of sexual conquests we should start with helping him cut loose—"

"What better way is there of cutting loose?"

"Well, maybe sex would be cutting too much loose too fast. How about we grab him some liquid nourishment?"

"Sounds good."

Kay stayed with Merek as Irulen fetched another round.

Irulen returned with two full mugs in his right hand and one in his left. As he reached the table, a young couple was standing there. The man had paid to have the girl drawn, but Kay was antagonizing him. "I suspect, you know, that this is a ploy for him to see under that little mask of yours," she said to the girl. The girl giggled awkwardly.

"More like he's so convinced of her *inner* beauty that he wants her *outer* beauty to be documented and cherished for years to come," Irulen interrupted. The eyes in the man's mask looked relieved as the girl removed her mask and posed in front of Merek. She was pretty young, innocent in her looks. Irulen wondered whether she'd regret or cherish this night tomorrow.

Irulen was unable to get Merek to drink his beer, but Kay proved herself to be more persuasive.

* * *

"Do you hear that?" asked Farah.

Quinn stopped in his tracks. The moon was high, but they were pressing hard to reach town.

"Yeah, music. Sounds like a nice party. God knows Oll' Quinn could use a drink or ten." As if his hands were reading his mind, they worked the hanging flagon up to his mouth. He drank of it and offered it to Farah, who surprised him by accepting it eagerly. It had been a long day and a longer journey.

"Might be hard finding a good place to stay." Farah drank.

"P'raps your right, but I've spent many a cold night with naught but whiskey to warm my veins. B'sides if we find Irulen or Kay, maybe they'll have a place we can sleep for the night."

"Then the sooner we find them, the better." She handed the flagon back to him.

"Aye, looks like the town is right on ahead now."

* * *

"Merek's drawings aren't looking so good," Kay remarked dryly.

"That's because of all the crap you've convinced him to have." Irulen rose from his seat. He placed his pipe down and looked over Merek's shoulder.

"Yeah, sorry honey, but this looks nothing like you."

The girl sitting across from Merek frowned. When Irulen turned the paper toward her, a smile again found her face. "I like it anyway!" she exclaimed, with girlish delight. The picture was of a flying unicorn. There were waterfalls and rainbows in the background.

Irulen laughed. "Well, Merek, it seems you can do no wrong. Needless to say, I'd better make a new sign here saying, *Coin for a random drawing! See what comes out!* or something like that."

In fact, Irulen drew it up there on the spot and slapped it down on the table before the next patrons came about. He also unloaded the cup of coins one more time. The wizard was just about to sit again when his squatting motion was interrupted by Kay's outreached hand. "Wait," she said. "Let's go."

"What about Merek?"

"He'll be just fine, look at him. He'll draw until his fingers fall off. We'll get back before then, maybe."

* * *

"What is all this?" Farah asked, as she looked around. "What are the masks for?"

"Oh, I doubt the townsfolk even know. They've been putting on faires like this one for a long, long time. I reckon the basic jist is to celebrate nature and the coming of spring. And procreation. This definitely smells of procreation."

Farah didn't know what to say. Sometimes she wondered whether Quinn's words came out the way he planned them. Or whether he planned his words at all. Despite his hopefully figurative claim, the air did not smell of sex. There was no reek of genitalia emitting from the fires of the cooking tents. On the contrary, every ounce of faire-space seemed clad with appetizing scents from sweetness to savory. Farah's belly growled in response.

"I need food." She held a hand over her stomach.

"As I require drink, p'raps we can find a place with both."

Farah took the lead. She followed her nose as they meandered through the crowd. This was one of those occasions where she cursed her shortness. Not that she was *that* short, but her vision was always met with shoulders when in a crowd. Luckily, there weren't many crowds that she'd been a part of. In Frostbridge, such a faire was a rarity. Frostbridge did enjoy a farmer's market during the summer and a celebration at summer's height, but nothing of this scale. She felt herself being pulled into something larger than herself. The music, the food, the drink, and happy people all contributed to the feeling her journey was on an upswing.

Soon she and Quinn were sitting at a table, enjoying freshly cooked catfish, potatoes, and sweet honey mead. "Do you see this here?" Quinn indicated the table surface. "Look at this rabbit."

Farah leaned over and looked, but the picture was upside down. She stood and walked quickly around. There, over Quinn's shoulder, a finely detailed rabbit had been etched into the table

"Very nice." She returned to her seat.

Quinn's forehead furrowed in deep concentration. "It looks familiar somehow."

"You had a rabbit once? Or maybe you cooked one like that at *The Roasted Duck*?"

"No… Ah, forget it."

Farah turned her attention to the charred catfish. She brushed aside the crisp skin and separated the flaky white meat from the bones. A wooden fork brought the first mouthful of tenderness to her lips.

Quinn ate more hastily, taking large bites and not bothering to separate the smaller bones. Farah was amazed at his ability to fit everything—fish, potato, mead, and all—into his mouth before he swallowed. The man was truly a champion consumer.

"You have some bits in your beard," Farah pointed out.

"Savin' em for later, lass," he responded.

They ate in relative silence while the faire carried on around them. There was little sign of the party slowing down, and it would likely carry well into the night. Fewer people were about, but only because couples were slipping mischievously into the woods. Groups of single men hazed each other, more than one found themselves pushed into the river.

"I'm surprised we haven't spotted Irulen yet," Farah remarked.

"Oh well, you know Ire by now. He's either in the spotlight or the shadows, but very rarely caught in between."

"I guess you're right." She shifted uneasily in her seat and looked around. Even if Irulen was around, there were many men with similar enough attire. Add masks to the mix, and there was little to do except wait for him to notice her. Lifting the mug to her mouth, she finished her drink. "Time for another," she said as she stood. "Can I get you one?"

"Such a good friend you are. Yes, please."

As Farah walked to where they had bought the mead, a handsome young man caught her eye. He was sitting at the edge of an arms vendor table, scribbling hastily at a piece of parchment. There was a familiarity about him, but she couldn't place it. She paid for their refills and brought the booze back to the table. Quinn drank his greedily as she sat across from him.

"Quinn, do you know that person?"

Quinn spun on his chair and had a look. "Indeed I do!

Ha! That there is Merek, from Warwick, the cloudwalker everyone thought killed everyone! You saw him I'm sure. What's he doing here?" Quinn pushed his chair back and stood.

"Perhaps we have a lead, then." Farah stood again from her chair. Quinn walked over to Merek and Farah followed. The previous customer was just leaving her seat across from the illustrator, and Quinn beckoned for Farah to take her spot.

"Look at this!" Quinn exclaimed, while dropping a coin in the mug. "This little operation is Irulen's handiwork. Merek, do you know where Irulen is?" Merek had already started drawing. He stared at Farah's face for an intense moment, and she found her cheeks run hot.

Quinn signaled for the booth owner to come over.

The small man came to him with a look of suspicion dotting his eyes. "Yeah?"

"I'm looking for a friend of mine, he was likely with this fellow here. Do you know where I can find him?"

"That man paid me well. I don't think he'd want me to give away his whereabouts so freely."

"Well." Quinn reached into his pocket. "I'm a friend of his." He dropped coin into the man's hand. "Don't worry about it," the burly man reassured the merchant.

"Old Miller's Inn, the one with the gable, straight over there."

Quinn gave the man a pat on the back. "No worries."

Turning toward Farah and Merek, he said, "You two look fine enough where you are. I'll go fetch our wily wizard."

* * *

"Don't stop." Kay pleaded softly as she wriggled beneath him.

Irulen never knew she had such softness inside. *Vulnerability. Trust.* These were things he never imagined applying to the fierce woman. He had suspected more and more that her overtly sexual innuendos hid a more complex girl full of, not only wants and desires, but hopes and dreams. Irulen grew more hungry, but she calmed him down.

"Don't rush," she breathed. "Stay with me."

He ran his right hand up her side and rested it against her face. He caressed her cheek softly and looked into her eyes longer than he ever had. She flushed under his scrutiny.

Who is this I've found? With her, happiness seeped back into his soul. Such feelings had been long dormant. Thus regressed the supreme weight of guilt and regret. Tears welled behind his eyes, but she didn't appear to notice. He leant down to her level. Their skin pressed tightly together.

"I will," he found himself saying. "I'll stay with you."

* * *

"I'm looking for a man with a raven, or a tan-skinned woman with leather trappings."

"Can't say I've seen either," said the wooden-faced innkeeper.

"C'mon lady, I know he's here at least. I'm a friend of his."

"Lots of people don't always want to see their friends," she said, plainly.

Quinn reached into his pocket once again. "Damn town," he mumbled under his breath.

"What's that?" the lady asked.

"Oh, I said I'd put money down." And he did. The lady snatched up the two coins faster than they hit the table. "First room on the right up the stairs," she said, pointing.

"Which one?" he asked.

"Both," the lady answered.

"Oh? Well, I guess you don't have any vacancy do you?"

"No."

"That 'splains it."

"Explains what?"

"Nothing," Quinn responded, as he scaled the stairs. "Thanks for your help."

Quinn found the door and raised his hand to knock. Something interrupted the knocking motion, something he heard, and felt. He put an ear to the door and listened.

* * *

Irulen was lying in bed. Kay's head rested on his chest, her fingers played across his skin.

He stared at the ceiling blankly. "Why did you go on ahead, really?"

"What do you mean?" Kay propped her chin up on her hand, and regarded him closely.

"I know why you've strung me along,"

"I know you do."

"You want me to kill Lynette."

Kay laughed and rolled to him. "It isn't that simple?"

Kay rolled onto her back and joined him in contemplating the ceiling. "I know. That's why I went ahead. I wanted to try it myself."

Irulen broke his stare and regarded her. "That's suicide." Fright wavered in his gut. "She'd killed you".

"Maybe. Probably. But I didn't, I don't, want to use you anymore."

"It's my fault your teacher died."

"I know, and for a while it was good enough for me, to justify what I've been doing." They both stared upward in silence. Kay turned toward him once more. "But I've forgiven you. I overheard a nightmare of yours, recently. You were rambling in your sleep. I realized how much you were hurting over what you've done. I felt sorry for leading you back to her."

There was a knock at the door.

"Not now!" yelled Irulen.

A loud voice boomed from the other side. "When then?"

Irulen rolled off the bed. "Shit, Quinn."

"So what?" asked Kay.

"You know…"

"Oh please, he needs to know sometime…or just don't let him in."

Irulen pulled his trousers up as Quinn's bear fist nearly ruptured the door.

"Okay, okay, just wait a second," Irulen pleaded. He

looked around at the situation for which there was no answer. *Ah, screw it.*

Kay pulled a sheet over her as Irulen opened the door. He tried leaving it half-cocked, but Quinn pushed it the rest of the way. There was shock in the beast's eyes like an arrow-pierced bear. Shock, and pain.

"Look…" Irulen started.

Quinn raised his fist and punched Irulen in the jaw. Detached from the pain, the wizard felt something crack at the moment of impact. He never thought Quinn would hurt him so badly. Irulen's head burst into ringing stars as it hit the ground. Kay was up in an instant, standing naked, ready to fight. Quinn looked at her hard, spat on the floor, and stormed out of the room. She hovered over Irulen. He was dazed and gagging on his own blood. She helped him turn over and the red poured out of his mouth. One of his back molars fell onto the floor. The metallic taste of his blood continued to ooze from his teeth and gums. It washed over his tongue.

He staggered to his feet and followed Quinn as best he could.

"Wait!" urged Kay, but her plea was too late.

* * *

Irulen caught up to Quinn outside the inn.

Red fluid spat from his mouth as he yelled. "Wait! Quinn, hold on!"

Quinn didn't turn back. Instead, he raised his hand and flung it down in Irulen's direction. It was a gesture of disgust, and of lost hope.

"Please!"

Quinn showed no indication of slowing down.

Irulen's mind spun. At that moment, he used the only crutch he knew, his magic. Quinn stopped in his tracks. Unable to move on, the bear turned toward Irulen with renewed ferocity.

"Let me GO, Ire!" he bellowed.

"No, yes, just let me explai—"

"No! Let *me* explain! *You* know how I feel! *You* are a

selfish *twat*. You always have been. You are only a good friend when it *suits you*. But it's Irulen first. It always has been, and it always will be. Now, Let. Me. Go!"

Irulen relinquished, and the faire soon absorbed Quinn into the night.

* * *

Irulen stared after Quinn for a hard moment. He spat at the ground, equally disgusted with himself and everything else in the world. The wizard soon felt the claws of his familiar friend digging into the skin of his bare shoulder.

"Ow," he said, impulsively. "Where have you been, anyway?"

Max looked unusually happy. "Probably with those two girls," Irulen said, as he turned and stormed back to the inn. Max flew into the air after the sudden movement, and followed Irulen back inside. The wizard trounced up the stairs and opened the door to the room. Max flew onto the bed post as a makeshift perch.

Kay, still nude, was lying on the bed. Her head rested on her right hand, propped up by her elbow. Her legs were laid out straight and long. Irulen sat on the floor, using the bed as back support.

She ran her fingers through his hair. "Poor baby."

Irulen removed her hand with his and pulled away. "We didn't finish," she went on.

"We have, we're done."

"What are you saying?"

"If Quinn's here, Farah may be here too." Irulen gathered the rest of his clothes as he spoke. "We need to make sure she and Merek are alright."

"Suit yourself." Kay spoke as she laid flat on her back, baiting Irulen into looking. He did, his eyes ran along her tan skin. She smiled, sat up, and slowly slipped on her clothes.

He wasn't sure why, but Irulen was annoyed with her. His mind felt clouded, and a buzzing noise tickled deep in his ear. Refraining from saying anything he might regret, the wizard walked out the door. Max flew through the crack as it closed and onto his shoulder.

CHAPTER 25: THE RAVEN'S CALL

Farah sat comfortably on her stool. She usually wasn't keen on being drawn or admired in any way, but she found Merek quite unthreatening. His dark eyes glanced up and down frequently as his hands worked at the paper. Merek was working so hard that a bead of sweat appeared on his forehead.

Suddenly, he stopped. The teen looked down at his work and smiled. Farah found it odd that he didn't give it to her. Her curiosity swelled as he made no move to do so. Finally, she reached slowly across the table and took it between her fingers. Merek tensed up for a moment, loathe to surrender his work. Farah froze in response, and continued only when he relaxed. The drawing pierced her deeply. The picture had her sitting underneath an apple tree on a summery day. There were animals about her and a bright sun in a cloudless sky. A river ran through the background, extending into a distant ocean.

"It's...beautiful," she told him.

"Yes," he responded.

Silence.

"Wow, if I didn't know better, I'd say he has a crush on you."

Farah turned to find Irulen lingering over her. "What happened to your face?" she asked.

"Quinn and I had a, uh, disagreement."

"What about?"

"Well..."

"Quinn is angry Irulen is having sex with me," said Kay, as she caught up.

Farah was taken aback. "What?"

"Now isn't really the time," Irulen began to say.

"You two…really?" Farah pressed.

"Yes, no, I don't know."

Kay frowned with concern. "What are you saying?"

"Nothing, I'm not saying anything. I just want to make sure Quinn is safe. He's likely to drink himself to death."

"Can you two just find him? Keep him from doing something stupid?"

Kay shrugged, Farah nodded vacantly.

"You check the taverns, I'll keep Merek close by out here."

"Sure thing, *boss*," Kay remarked, sarcastically. Nevertheless, she signaled to Farah who instinctively followed her.

* * *

Irulen looked after them for a suspended moment. In that time, it was Farah who looked back. Her eyes beheld his, and slowly lowered to the ground. She didn't turn again. The buzzing grew louder.

Irulen's chest was suddenly empty. He knew disappointment when he saw it, and it was written all over Farah's face.

His eyes winced tightly. *Who is she to judge me? She's been showing me nothing but disinterest and malice.* He forced his head side to side. His neck stretched and cracked.

Merek's voice sounded off next to him. "Why anger?"

Irulen clenched a fist and turned toward the boy. He wanted to punch Merek in the face. *Accusing little son of a bitch.*

It was Merek's expression that helped Irulen to calm down. His face was soft and innocent. There was nothing personal in the words he spoke. It was as if the words fell from his mouth without any greater understanding. Irulen thought to what Quinn had said about cloudwalkers. They were conduits, vessels to be filled with the messages of gods. *But Quinn was wrong, the gods aren't just dormant, they are dead. The Great Conflict killed them. The world burned and the gods with it.*

The buzzing was suddenly no longer ignorable. It stood front and center in his mind, and Irulen realized its source was not outside. It had grown inside him. He slowly realized what it was. He had learned what it was when confronted by the goblin-man. *Magic. Magic's here.* Irulen turned and scanned the fairgoers. He was taller than most, but many of the masks extended upward, forever poking into his vision. Irulen hadn't perfected the art - the strains of magic were drawn out like a complex emotion. But he knew *she* was near. It felt like a shade of himself.

Just like that the faire turned. Laughter seemed maniacal and menacing. The dancers and performers were threatening. The bonfires raged like angry beasts.

Irulen was obviously alone in his perception, but he remained undeterred. The wizard pushed forward through the crowd, moving in erratic patterns. The buzzing grew louder and more quiet, like the crashing and resciding of a wave. His eyes took lead of his other senses. All the while he searched out the magic's source, Irulen kept an eye out for Quinn's massive effigy. He hoped to glimpse his friend in the silhouette of a bonfire or among the ocean of revelers. Perhaps Quinn's face would surface among the endless sea of masks. Irulen moved like a disgruntled shark through happy waters.

A female voice slithered behind him. "What's wrong?"

Irulen spun, but he was too slow. The voice had slipped back into the crowd. Max held on tight as his master weaved through the throng, shrugging off invitations to dance and drink.

For the splittest of seconds, the crowd opened naturally. Everyone had moved in a way that opened a line of sight before him. At the end of the vision tunnel was a slender figure dressed in black. The mask over her face was different from the rest. It looked like an undecipherable mix of animals. Her mouth was the only part of her face exposed. It was smiling. The crowd closed over her.

Irulen stopped where he stood, stunned by a piercing lack of control. His teeth and fists clenched in unison. That smile, as distorted as it may have been, was familiar to him. *Lynette. Why now?*

The buzzing, the feeling he had, it was all her. *After all the evasion, the leading, she comes to me. Now. Why not any time but now? Quinn…Kay…Farah…*Merek…*. Where was Merek, now, anyway?*

Suddenly, none of it mattered. Irulen remembered his inquisition at the hands of the Brotherhood. The time had come to do what he was tasked to do. *Time to wake up.*

There was a tug at Irulen's leg. "Mister, are you alright?" Irulen looked down to find a little squirrel-masked girl looking up at him. He squatted to be at her level, Max flew into the air.

"Yes, thank you." He put a hand on her shoulder. "Run along, now."

"Good! Because mommy wants you." The body of the girl was still, and the eyes behind the mask were dead. Irulen slowly withdrew his hand.

"Do you want to see her?" asked the girl. Irulen stood and stepped back from the child. She laughed and ran away. Irulen watched the ripple she caused through the adults as she moved beneath them. Her path was soon swallowed by a swell of the masses.

Loathe to follow the girl, Irulen felt utterly directionless.

It was then that Max called him to action. The wizard's finely tuned ear disentangled the raven's squawk from the crowd noise. Max was perched on top of a vendor's stand near the top of the festivities. Irulen made his way toward him. The feeling of Lynette's magic increased as Irulen approached Max's location. It withdrew as he arrived, as if she had just given him the slip. Max moved again, this time hovering over a section of the crowd. The raven evaded a piece of fruit that was thrown at it, and returned to the hunt. *She's getting angry.* Max indicated that she had fled the main crowd. Irulen jogged out to where Max was perched at the edge of the festivities, and the raven joined him at the shoulder.

Soon man and raven stood at the outer edge of town, peering into the dark wilderness.

Lynette's voice called from beyond the veil of darkness. "Well, are you coming?" The giggles of her child-followers filled the air.

Irulen's foot moved across the wild divide. With no clear

path visible, he ventured haphazardly into the darkness. Many other sets of feet joined his as they stamped through woodland fodder. Irulen felt like a part of a twisted game of hide and seek. One set of little feet ran toward him, stopped, and ran away again. Then another. Some came closer than others. The girls were enjoying a game, seeing who could get closest to him.

Lynette's voice came from beyond the blackness. "Why have you never summoned me?"

"Not worth the magic," he replied, cooly.

"Oh? And here I thought the master was afraid of the slave."

He tried to pinpoint the direction the sound came from, but it surrounded him. "I'm no master, Lynette. Only you are responsible for what you've done."

"But you don't believe that."

There. "No, I guess I don't. At least, not completely."

Irulen could almost make out the sounds of her back-peddling as he walked toward her deeper into the shadows. He lifted his hands in the air, one slightly below each side of his head. "I can't let you go this time."

A fire was lit in the darkness.

"I beg to differ," she said, her outline barely visible at the edge of the light. "I think you can't let me go, period."

She came more into focus as he approached.

"And since you could never let me go, you would never hurt me."

"Is that what you think?" He stopped and stood at the opposite edge of the fire's light. "Do you think I'd watch the world burn if it meant keeping you alive?"

"Isn't that what love is?" she asked.

"What do you know of it?" he shot back.

"It's why I'm here." She stepped into the light. Her face was a wretched reflection of what it once was. Her facial skin caved along the edges of her imp-sign. Her eyes were apathetic.

Irulen also stepped forward. "Yeah? Me too. I poisoned you once, Lyn. I'm here to make that right."

"Ha! You know there's no way for that to happen."

"No, I know there's only one way for it to happen."

Lynette drew backward into the wall of shadows. For the first time, Irulen summoned her back to him. There was a look of terror on her face as she again met the light.

She spoke frantically.

"You know what's funny, Irulen? Even after all I've been through—and all I've done—I still find myself missing you. There's some strange attraction, or connection, or whatever you want to call it. I wanted to *kill* you. But I couldn't. I can't. I just can't. What happened to me screws a lot of things up, of course. But not certain feelings, or certain memories. There are many of those I still have. I'm now a *little* more temperamental than you are, mind you. I do what I want, when I think about wanting it. If I need money, I take it. If I'm angry, I'll hurt somebody. If I'm lonely, I'll free another girl."

"Free?"

"Yes."

"I don't understand."

"And you wouldn't, even if I tried explaining."

"You can't free a person through slavery."

"Oh?" She cocked an eyebrow. "What about me? You freed me through slavery. You freed me from *that man* by enslaving me to you. Everything I've done has been done under *your* control."

Lynette waved her hand, gesturing to her girls. "Enslave? No, I am not like you. They are not enslaved, nor could I enslave them. My ability may increase a person's...receptiveness, but only for a little while. I can't persuade the same person twice. They have free will after my breath wears."

"Bullshit, you're lying to yourself. Even if there's no magic involved, the damage is already done. And even if they have free will, they wouldn't know how to use it."

Lynette cast her eyes over the girls. "Leave us," she said. "Go wait by the river."

Irulen laughed as they withdrew.

"You don't want them to listen anymore?" he asked.

"I don't require them to be here, anymore."

"Afraid of what they might *think?*"

"Are you kidding?" she scoffed. "Do you think these girls are capable of redemption? I suppose you think I am as well?"

"No, I don't think you are, though I do hope."

Something in Lynette's eyes darkened. "Wait!" She called out into the woods. "Come back."

Irulen readied himself for a fight. The girls' faces emerged from the moonlight. "Everyone take their knives out and grab a partner."

"Wait—" Something pressed outward from Irulen's chest.

"Now when I say go, you all stab the friend across from you as deeply as you can."

"Wait!" His ribs ached as if they were being pried open. "GO!"

Something broke forth from him.

* * *

Lynette danced happily around the bonfire. The town was celebrating an unusually rich harvest. She hopped away from the flame and grabbed Irulen by the arm. They rotated clockwise and counter, lifting their legs in gleeful stomps. *Today*, thought Irulen, *Today for sure.*

It was as they finished their dance that Irulen performed a minor trick of magic. A red rose appeared in his hand, and she smiled delightedly. Truth is, Irulen had no idea how to materialize things, or whether such magic was possible. He had slid the rose out from his shirt as he twirled her. The motion proved hazardous, and a thorn had ripped along his arm as he removed it.

Be that as it may, he winced away the pain and tried his best to match Lynette's smile. It was futile, for she was smarter than he was, and far more observant.

"Are you in pain?" she asked, looking him over.

"No, well, yeah…"

"Let me see," she said. Irulen hesitated. She insisted

again.

He held his arm out and indicated that she should have a look. She rolled the sleeve up, revealing some bright red scrapes running along his pale skin. One in particular looked nastier than the others. Expecting sympathy, Irulen was surprised when the girl laughed at him.

She talked in between the comical heaving of her chest. "You…was this from…from the rose?"

Irulen protested through silence.

"Oh, you are just adorable," she said. "You make me happy."

She stood, grabbed his hand, and started to pull him away.

He questioned her while rising to his feet. "Where are we going? What about your father?"

"He's passed out in an alley, more like. He's not gonna ruin this, c'mon!" She pulled him harder and ran fast through the merriment. It was all Irulen could do to keep sight of her weaving through the crowd. He followed her to the edge of the crowd, to the edge of the town, and beyond. She ran happily through the fields and into the woods, through the woods and to the river. To the spot they had always shared. She sat on their rock and hung her legs and waited. Irulen plodded along shortly thereafter. He was breathing heavy, and wore an expression somewhere between pleasure and pain.

"You really should run more, you know," she said, poignantly. "Fourteen years old and breathing like that. Tssk tssk."

"I have magic, what running will I need to do?"

"Well you have to chase me, don't you?"

"Do I?"

"Yes, and you have to be healthy if we're getting married someday."

"Will we? Be getting married?"

"Yes."

"Wow," he said, as he sat next to her.

She laughed and hit him on the leg, "Wow, nothing!"

"Ow!"

"Ow! Wow! What's next, are you going to bowwow like a dog?"

"Would it make you laugh?"

"Ha ha, maybe if you surprised me with it sometime, but there will be no barking necessary. There's only one thing I want."

"What might that be?"

Lynette leaned over and kissed him on the lips. It was hastily done, and he wasn't expecting it. Overall, it was pretty lousy.

"Hey! I wasn't expecting that, could I have another go?"

She nodded her head happily. He leaned over slowly as her smile grew in size. They each closed their eyes, and in that darkness they found each other.

Today, thought Irulen, *I knew it would be today.*

* * *

The fire was out, and everything was dark.

"Irulen... Irulen..."

Irulen pushed himself up on all fours and shook his head. All the while, a faint voice floated around in his head. He looked around him, uncomprehendingly. He was deaf to the world, like he had been standing in front of a mine shaft when it exploded.

"Irulen..."

"What?"

"Sorry... I'm sorry."

"Lynette? What?"

"Not the first time we've escaped a party..."

"Hold on, I'll get some light." Irulen pictured his hands illuminating. They didn't. Confusion set in. He felt as if the world spun in the darkness. Disoriented, he crawled toward the voice which was now hardly louder than a whisper.

"Irulen... please...it's alright..."

Irulen's hands ripped as he crawled faster. Jagged ice, roots, and tree litter covered the forest floor. His fingers were numb with pain. "Lynette?" he called.

"Here…"

"I'm close."

"Here…"

Irulen came across her in the darkness. His eyes had adjusted somewhat to the lunar glow, but her features were still difficult to make out. He grabbed her up in his arms and held her tightly.

"I'm sorry," he said.

"I'm sorry, too. It's alright, Irulen, I feel better now. This…going to be alright…"

Irulen felt her open his right hand and place something into it. It fit in palm of his hand, bulbous and dried out.

He heard Lynette's mouth open again, her breath hot against the air. "The rose you gave me, our first kiss, that day…"

"I don't understand," he lamented, clutching the defiled rosebud in his hand. "What happened?"

"I'm in that day now, Irulen. It's all clear. Clear." She became still in his arms.

Irulen felt wetness welling in his eyes, but his insides were dead. He had held the head of the innocent girl he had known in a different life.

He thrust the dead rose into his pocket.

It was a long time before he let her go, and even as his magical ability returned to him, he refused to illuminate her face. The way he saw her in the darkness was how she'd be remembered, and he soon left her without ceremony or further comment.

As he walked, sounds filled the air of Lynette's girls beginning to stir, but he had no stomach to deal with them. He was apathetic to their being alive, not knowing what would become of them, but he wished them the best. Maybe there would be healing down the road for them, maybe he'd end up investigating one in the future. Regardless of what road they traveled, it would be theirs to choose alone. Lynette would no longer lead them, and Irulen would not take their lives.

CHAPTER 26: THE RAVEN'S BANE

Farah and Kay were having a tough time searching the inns and taverns. They were forced to cut swaths through hordes of horny and drunk revelers. Farah had never been petitionedso much in her life, and the atmosphere made her uneasy. She followed Kay's lead, kept her head down, and stayed on her heels. Various men, some masked, some not, assailed them with advances ranging from poetic to perverted.

There were fist fights, and drinking games, and fist fights over drinking games. Farah followed Kay as they focused on taverns with older folk, people who were dedicated to their frothy liquids. They checked the alleys in between, the latrines behind, and inquired into rooms all around. Many of the places had seen such a man, draining wide draughts of one drink or another, murmuring to himself, and stewing in a pool of discontent. Quinn's depression left him memorable with the locals, since he was the only man of the bunch so miserable.

Still, even as Quinn's trail grew hot, the ladies kept running into cold ends. Kay's stoicism bothered Farah. She stared at the back of the bounty hunter's head. *So casual, and yet Quinn could be in serious danger.* The main drag of inns and taverns had been thoroughly vetted, and still their hands were empty. For their last lead they were told of a tavern set apart from the others, on the far edge of town. For all their luck it sounded right that Quinn would be holed up in the last place they'd check, and the farthest away.

They navigated the outskirts of the town square, avoiding the masses of revelers as best they could. Once on the other side there was a road outlined by lit paper lanterns. There were family dwellings on either side, and each one had been decorated—some more extravagantly than others. The women passed through an open gate manned by a lone, drunken sentry. The man tipped his cap to the ladies as they passed by, and Farah thought she heard a whistle. In this area, the town spread beyond the security of the walls. Homes were spread more haphazardly, and were generally of a lesser quality.

At the end of this sprawl stood a lonely building, and beyond it nothing but darkness. In the slight wind creaked a hanging sign. It read, *The Drunken Dragon*.

Kay turned to Farah. "Not the most original of names, but this should be it—the last tavern."

"I didn't think a town this size would have so many," remarked Farah. "By my count, we've checked at least ten."

"Eleven, including this one." Kay pulled the door open and walked in. Farah caught the door before it closed and followed her inside.

Once inside, Kay let out defeated sigh. There were only two men in the whole of the place; one tending a bar, and the other sitting across from him. They were both going about their business quietly. Kay sat at the bar and signaled to the keeper, who came over to her and asked, "Hard'r soft?"

"Hard," she said. Farah stood next to her as the man fixed the drink. The alcohol was so potent she could smell the bottle from where she stood. Kay indicated for her to take a seat.

Farah looked concerned. "Aren't you gonna ask them?"

Kay shrugged as a shot was placed in front of her. She threw the drink back, placed coin on the table, and signaled for another. Not that they had to try, but the women had grabbed the lone patron's attention.

He swiveled on his stool. "Come here often?"

Kay scoffed and rolled her eyes.

He flashed a smile that she ignored. "Sorry," he said, "I must've left my lines a town or two over."

Kay drank in silence, a silence that was too awkward for Farah.

"We're looking for a friend," she said.

"Oh?"

"He's real big, and has a rugged, black beard. Carries a flagon slung across his chest…"

"I've seen him."

Kay turned toward the man.

"So it is possible to get your attention," he quipped, in between smiling.

She turned back to her new drink and attacked it.

"Now to keep it…" he was saying. "The guy you're talking about, he was here maybe an hour ago. Can I get your next round?"

Kay shrugged.

"And you, my dear?" he asked Farah.

"Yes, please," she answered. Something about the man interested her. He had a plain face, but there was confidence behind his eyes, in his movement, and about his presence. It was a feeling similar to when she first met Irulen.

"Forgive my assumption, but would you enjoy something sweeter than she has?" he asked. Farah nodded.

He signaled to the barkeep. "A round, please."

"Sure thing." The barkeep seemed to be relishing his good luck. It was obvious that he didn't do much business, even with the faire happening in the center of town. His stone-demeanor began to melt in the face of prosperity. He even hummed as he poured.

The patron raised his cup to the women. "Cheers," he said, and they drank. Kay finished her drink, but Farah's was larger and not meant for fast consumption. The brew tasted of honey and fruitful flavors. Truth be told, it was one of the best drinks Farah remembered ever having.

"My name is Halfur," said the patron.

"I'm Farah, and this is Kay."

"Pretty names for pretty girls."

Kay turned to him again. "You said you saw our guy. What happened to him?"

"Oh he mumbled something about heading back to the party and left."

Kay stood up abruptly and headed to the door.

Halfur protested. "What, that's it?"

For a moment Farah was frozen between the two. Her drink was still half full, and to depart so suddenly would be extremely rude. She saw two nights in front of her eyes; one with him, and one with the same people she had been spending every night. Even against her own will she found herself standing and following Kay out the door.

"Sorry," she said, "but we really must find our friend and keep him out of trouble."

Halfur waved good bye. "Maybe we'll cross paths again."

"I'd like that," she said, as she passed through the door.

* * *

By the time Irulen made his way back to town, the festivities were dying down. He didn't want to see Kay, Farah or Merek. Quinn was probably a half-town away by now, navigating a moonlit passage. Irulen wanted to feel alone, but he also wanted to be near people. In need of a stiff drink, he walked into a tavern on the fringe of town. There was a bar to the left, much like the other taverns in the region. There didn't seem to be a kitchen, simply a stone wall and a fireplace in the back. To the right, stools surrounded old wooden kegs which had been stood upright for the purpose of holding drinks.

The place was empty save for a man sitting at the bar. A bottle of liquor and a mug sat in front of him. The man greeted Irulen as he walked through the door. Since the man looked fairly insignificant and unassuming, Irulen took the seat next to him. Max hissed at the man, and flew atop the fireplace.

Irulen felt the need to apologize to the man. "Sorry 'bout that, he's had a long day."

"It's not a problem. He's a beautiful animal. I bet he makes great company."

"He's the only thing I can count on," said Irulen. The man seemed to detect a tone of melancholy.

"Why's that? You have that face on, my friend," said the man, as the wizard sat nearby.

"What face?"

"Let me guess, a woman? Friends? Life?"

"I'd say a mixture of all those. One big, poisonous cocktail of it."

The man laughed and raised his mug. "Here's to the shitty taste of life!" With that said, he slammed back all the liquid in his cup. "Oh, I'm sorry, you don't have a drink—it's been a long night."

"Tell me about it," Irulen responded.

"My name is Halfur."

"Irulen."

"Well, Irulen, can I pour you a drink?"

"Is this your place?"

"Ha, no," said Halfur, as he reached over and under the bar. He came up with a mug that he placed in front of Irulen. "Truth be told, I haven't seen the barkeep for a good hour or so. I bought this bottle from him and haven't seen him since. But they say misery loves company, and to share a drink of loneliness is better than drinking alone. So since we're both miserable and alone, how about I fill your cup instead?" Halfur took hold of his bottle and leaned over to pour.

Irulen held the handle of his mug as it filled. It was an overabundant amount for straight liquor. Irulen couldn't be happier with it. After lifting the mug to his drinking partner, the wizard brought it to his lips. His mouth opened and accepted an avalanche of alcohol. The stuff poured down his esophagus and slowly burnt the bottom of his stomach. The wound in his mouth burnt wild with pain.

Irulen held it in, breathed heavy and hit his fist against his chest. "Whew," he exclaimed. "Rough stuff, but tell me, why are you so lonely and miserable on such a festive night?"

"I lost a friend of mine," answered Halfur, without looking.

"Well, that makes a pair of us yet again," said Irulen. "I lost my best friend tonight, and the love of my life. I doubt I'll be seeing either again."

The corner of Halfur's mouth rose slightly.

"Cuckolded?" he asked.

"No, no."

Seeing Irulen's unwillingness to elaborate, Halfur offered a piece of his mind, "I lost someone dear to me recently, too, and I *know* I won't be seeing her again."

"Oh, Sorry."

"We had a disagreement. She had this…addiction. She just couldn't leave it alone."

"So that's it, you went your separate ways?"

Halfur opened his hands as they rest on the bar. "Her addiction got her killed."

"I'm sorry to hear that, truly. Truth be told, I worry about my friend too—he drinks like a fish."

"Does he now?" asked Halfur. "We could use a man like him here now."

"Right now, I'd rather he weren't. I'm swallowing enough blood with my drink already."

"Oh?" asked Halfur. "So you got into a fight?"

"Yeah, the asshole knocked my tooth out."

"I was gonna say, your face looked a little beat, but I didn't want to offend…"

"No offense taken."

"We all take our lumps at some time."

"Not all of us," replied Irulen. "Some of us skirt through life easy-like. Not many of us, but some do."

"I haven't known such a person," Halfur remarked, blankly.

"My brother," said Irulen. "He's…special. The fellow isn't altogether in his head. He doesn't see the world in our light. But he's happy, even though he doesn't understand much. Sometimes I wish I had that…the ability to just not care. Or sometimes I wish I didn't have the knowledge of how to care. Sometimes I wish I were nothing. Just blackness suspended in blackness."

"Man, that's heavy. Are you alright? Are you going to be?"

"Yeah, I'll be fine. I guess it's weird to fantasize about

things like death, huh?"

Halfur nodded. "Yes, and no, we can't help but think about the end of things, but it isn't good to look forward to it at such a young age."

"I don't know if I look forward to it so much as wear it, like a cloak. The thought of death is a comfort to me. No matter how bad things get—how painful they can be—there is always the blackness waiting to take us. The end of it all."

Halfur drank and slammed his mug down. "That's worrisome—worries me about you."

"Why's that?"

"It's not natural. You're supposed to fear death. I fear it. I'd do anything to avoid the blackness you mentioned. It's *terrifying.*"

Irulen shifted on his stool to better face the man. "So you want to live forever?"

Halfur shrugged. "It'd be nice, one way or the other."

"What ways?"

"Well, there's the literal sense, to live as we are for as long as we want."

"And is there a realistic sense?"

"Legacy. To leave a legacy that speaks for you for years and ages to come."

"Are you an artist, then?"

"Ha! Yes, well, I script things."

Irulen rolled his eyes back and finished his liquor. "You're starting to sound too much like a politician."

Halfur put his arms up in the air. "Guilty as charged," he said, emphatically.

"Really, a politician?"

"Yep."

"Where?"

"Well, nowhere yet, but I'm working on it."

Irulen was amused. "A politician without power."

Halfur held his mug up again. "Yet another reason for my miserable state."

Irulen toasted with the man, and they both threw their

drinks back.

The wizard looked around the empty place. "So, this person really just left the bar to you?"

"It's the charm of the northern territories, the trust of some of these towns."

"Maybe so, but things have been changing."

"Oh, why's that?"

"People are scared."

"Are they?"

"I'd say so, traveling where I've traveled."

"What do you do?"

"I solve crimes, mysteries, some odd jobs here and there."

"Sounds like quite the interesting lifestyle."

"Yeah, it is. I actually feel I'm getting close to cracking a really big case, too."

"You don't say?"

"The largest I've ever worked on."

Halfur's smile widened, he leaned toward Irulen. "You have me intrigued."

"There's this one coward, and he has caused a lot of people to suffer. He's a magician who wants his magic to last forever. Heck, he probably wants to use his everlasting magic to *live* forever as well. It wouldn't surprise me."

"Simply unbelievable. Sounds almost like a myth! Tell me though, what has he done bad?"

"Well, I'm assuming you are familiar with certain things regarding magic, specifically that each person is born with an expendable amount of it. Most people are born with mere specks that they'll never even know they had. But some people, and I'll concede that I'm one of them, are born with something more— something *tangible*."

Halfur, thoroughly engrossed by now, signaled for his drinking partner to go on.

Irulen continued. "Some can use it in different ways than others, but most of us can use or move energy, even mold it. There may be some of those who have gained other abilities through the dark arts, things such as shifting shapes and faces—I suspect this man is such an example—but regardless of how the magical power is honed, it'll run out eventually. Every magic born will end up like anyone else, and die a very similar death."

Halfur protested Irulen's pause. "Don't stop now!"

"But this man found a way—well, he *stole* a way—to replenish his magic. A type of gem that harvests the power of souls. The only kicker is that a non-magical human must perform a ritual, and this ritual involves the killing of innocents."

Halfur's bottle was empty. He hopped over the bar and searched for another. He clinked and clanked himself through an arrangement of things, found what he was looking for, and returned to his seat.

"You should be a traveling bard," he said to Irulen.

"If only I had a better tale to tell."

"This one seems right enough."

Irulen met Halfur's eyes with an even stare. "I don't think Merlane would agree, and neither do I."

Ithial laughed. "How long have you known?"

"Not long, really...before I drank."

"If you knew who I was, then why'd you accept my liquor?"

"Because I really didn't care at the moment. And I figure you had something to say. I figured wrong, I think."

"Lynette is gone, though, right?"

"Yes, but you don't really care."

"To the contrary, I cared for her very much. She is, was, the only imp I worked with who wasn't of my own making. Let me say, Ire. May I call you that? She was one heck of a creation. She was a finer imp than anything I've made."

Irulen stood menacingly.

Ithial put his arms out and backed away. "Which is why, of course, I wouldn't meet you without insurance."

Irulen stood his ground.

"But I'll get to that soon enough. Just know that you can't hurt me. Okay? You know I wouldn't be so stup—"

Irulen's fist smashed the man's nose. He fell over

backward, knocking over a keg and some stools.

Ithial laughed as blood poured from his nose. "Maybe you're right," he said, as he scrambled to his feet. "Maybe I'm not as smart as I think I am. But I have a question for you."

Irulen took a step toward his adversary.

"Will you hear it?" Ithial asked. Irulen stood over the man. He grabbed a stool and smashed it downward. Ithial's fingers were crushed as he tried absorbing the blow. "Ow, ow." He scurried backward along the floor. Specks of blood followed after him.

"Why'd you kill Lynette?"

Irulen stopped where he stood.

"Why'd you kill Lynette when you could have saved her? Didn't you know there's a cure?"

"You're lying, there is no cure. I would have found it."

"Would you have? No, I don't think so. Not where you were looking. But where *I* looked, well, that's a different story." As Ithial talked, his hands began to glow. He worked at rearranging the bones to where they needed to be. Within seconds he was flexing his fingers again. The wounds were sealed, and the broken bones even seemed to fuse. Irulen had never seen healing at such a technical level. He was able to put his energy into people, to speed their natural process, but he had never been able to mend broken bones himself. There was no sort of healing he could do so fast.

"That's right. You could have had your old Lynette back. The one you drooled over for all those years. She was still in there. You saw it too, didn't you? At the end? It's amazing how the human part of the imp emerges when one dies, isn't it?"

Irulen thought about the blackened rose petals now lining his pocket.

"Tell me," Ithial continued. "What did she say? Did she have a chance to speak? Or was it too fast? Just how quickly did you snuff her out, anyway? You have a bit of a temper..."

"You haven't seen anything yet," Irulen growled.

"And here we come to the insurance bit of our conversation. I fear you enough, now. You see, Irulen, I'm not simply a wizard as you are. I think of myself as a fisherman. I used to fish all the time with Merlane. He can attest to that. Of course, the most important part of a successful fishing venture is the baiting of the hook. You simply need the right bait for the right fish. Not all fish prefer worms, or bugs, or bread. So you need an understanding of what your quarry truly *wants* more than anything."

At that point someone came through the front door. Irulen realized straightaway that it was an imp. Clad in a typical black cloak, this imp was uncannily short. It would be generous to say he was half Irulen's height. Needless to say, an Imp, no matter its size or appearance, was always dangerous. Irulen tensed up as he faced the creature.

"Relax, relax." Ithial gained his composure as he walked to the bar. He sat and indicated for Irulen to again join him. "Gonkle here is simply our new bartender, since he just finished getting rid of the old one."

The halfing-imp chortled as he disappeared behind the bar. The drinks, both having barely a splash left in them, were soon snatched and disappeared behind the bar, only to be returned shortly thereafter, refilled.

"So there's this question of the fish and the bait," Ithial said, getting back to the point. "Let me tell you that you are, indeed, the fish. And I, being the angler I am, need to reel you somewhere. That place is the Canyon of Crystal Caves, many days journey south of here. The problem is you've already swallowed the bait, and I'm not keen on pulling you out of the water yet. I need you to swim still."

"Get on with it," said Irulen. "Before I take Gonkle here and choke you with him."

Ithial responded. "It'll go faster if you don't interrupt, so if you don't mind, I'll continue."

Irulen made a winding motion with his right hand in an attempt to speed things up.

"Since you've so callously removed Lynette from the equation, I've had to rebait my hook. Now, to do that I had to ask myself what would best *motivate* you enough to follow my instruction: Guilt? Revenge? Duty? I decided to diversify. I reckon just showing myself might be enough. Professionally, of course, you would set upon hunting me, but then I'd have to leave a trail of breadcrumbs for you to follow. I am, by a rule of thumb, invisible. This is not even my true face. Revenge, yes, I've considered killing your friends, and I reserve that right if you seem to falter in any way, but no, revenge alone isn't reliable enough. Besides, you are goin' to need help getting to where you've got to go. So I thought up a way to invoke guilt, duty, and revenge. A person to skewer on the end of my hook. "

Irulen felt his anger swelling just below his surface. His poker face slowly twisted into pain and rage. "Who?" he asked.

"Quinn."

"Bullshit."

"I must admit, he was my last choice. I've heard he's a pretty brutal warrior, but what is a warrior without his spirit? And spirit is something I found him lacking. Do you know why that would be?"

Irulen grabbed his drink and gripped it tightly. He drank it down. The alcohol burnt, and his body did its best to reject it, but the wizard needed the pain, it grounded him.

Stools hit the floor. Irulen stood facing Ithial. His eyes welled with menace. Ithial put his hands in the air between them. "Whoa, whoa. Look, he's all right. He's going to be fine. We're fine."

Hotness filled the hollow of Irulen's hands. Streams of fire ran along his palm lines.

Ithial clapped his hands together. "So *this* is *Ire*. I've been waiting *so* long to see this!"

"If you know so much about me, you'd never see it willingly." The room darkened, the midget-imp looked to his master for reassurance. Ithial raised a clenched fist that shook with power. Irulen stepped toward him and paused.

Ithial's fist opened, and it was empty.

There was a sudden loss of senses, and Irulen fell to the ground. The fire had left his hands. A drug had crept from Irulen's drink, and had grabbed ahold of his soul.

"Don't fight it," said Ithial.

"Ithial…"

"Yes?"

"Eat… Shit…"

Ithial laughed and went on. "I found him in an alley. He had lost his weapons. He was drooling. He followed me like an obedient zombie. Now, I think just having Quinn around may be enough to ensure your servility. But just to make sure, I want to let you know that I plan on making Quinn an imp. I plan on giving him some of my magical power, and I plan on watching everything good in his soul wash away. There's the guilt for you, Irulen. You killed Lynette when you could have saved her. You betrayed a friend and you *can't* save *him*. Relax and rest, now, but don't take too long. We'll be waiting."

Irulen's eyes closed and Ithial put his hand on the man's head. "Ssshhh," he said.

* * *

"You know, you've been my best customer, but you don't talk much."

Irulen looked up to find the grinning face of a bear looking down at him.

"Name's Quinn," he said, through his scraggly beard.

"Irulen. What's it matter if I speak or not?"

"Bad for business. Don't worry, I'm in the business of jollity. A professional, in fact."

* * *

Fight!

Get up!

For Quinn!

Irulen fought himself awake.

Ithial stood with his minion. He raised an eyebrow. "Oh?"

The fire returned, and this time it was let loose.

ABOUT THE AUTHOR

Will is a library manager and an adjunct instructor of English. He graduated from the University of Auckland, New Zealand with an M.A. in English writing a 40,000 word thesis entitled The Magic of Humour: Comic Effects in J.R.R. Tolkien's The Hobbit and The Lord of the Rings. He is a world traveler and freelance copywriter. He lives with his wife, dog and Quaker parrot on Long Island, New York.

Proof

Made in the USA
Charleston, SC
09 May 2015